THE BLOOD DECANTER

THE TALES OF TARTARUS

COPYRIGHT DISCLAIMER

THE BLOOD DECANTER

A Novel by

A.L. MENGEL

A.L. MENGEL'S BOOKSHELF

From The Tales of Tartarus —

Ashes (The Complete Novel)

The Transformation

Dirty Little Secrets

The Coming of the Green Mist

Nesmaron's Egg

The Quest for Immortality (The Complete Novel)

The Mortician's Mortician

A City Full of Bodies

Attack of the White Worms

My Lipstick Leper

The Story of George Stanley

Other Works —

Curtains and Fan Blades

The Other Side of the Door

The Ashes Special Hardcover Edition

Writestorm

Join the discussion in "The Writing Studio" on his Facebook page. Follow him on Twitter, Google+ and Goodreads. Discover A.L. Mengel's storytelling at www.almengel.com

A NOTE FROM THE AUTHOR

To my "Beloved Readers from *'The Writing Studio'* –

I must discuss this with you before you read this novel.

There are elements to this story that suggest that the Catholic Church may be involved with underground organizations of enlightenment (similar to the *Illuminati*). This is merely for story and entertainment value.

I want to make it clear that this story is fiction, and while this story has many elements and traditions of the Catholic Church realistically portrayed in several scenes, which have been researched and are accurately presented, as far as I am aware, the Catholic Church has no ties to any underground organizations whatsoever, and any references in the story you are about to read are pure fiction and should be regarded as such. I'm Catholic myself, so I wanted to make sure to say that. Felt it was necessary.

That said, I highly recommend starting "The Tales of Tartarus" series with this novel. It's a fascinating character study of the Blood Ancestry of the series thus far. Aside from the plot, it's also a dive into the deep cosmology that we all share: blood relation. Our family trees are diverse, branching out in several different directions, and spanning centuries. We all have our 'Blood Lineage'.

Why I recommend starting with this novel (as opposed to *Ashes*) is for that reason – it gives you the option to explore the characters' origins before starting the story (which really starts in *Ashes*). If you so choose. It depends on what type of reader you are. When I wrote *Ashes*, these characters were not fully revealed to me. Now, Antoine, Darius, Claret and Delia have spoken much more to me – telling me their stories in far greater detail, which I am sharing with you in the upcoming pages of this novel.

Ashes is a novel that sets the stage for "The Tales of Tartarus", and is a must read to fully experience the series, and it is the true genesis of the story. However, starting with *The Blood Decanter* will give you a much more enriched read of *Ashes*. So the choice is yours.

The Blood Decanter was one of the most challenging novels that I have ever written. It was not only a story that has deepened and expanded so much since *Ashes,* but also a story that has required a tremendous amount of research on my part. This novel will take you to Piazza di San Pietro in Rome, Paris, Lyon and Cairo, as well as Badulla, Sri Lanka – all sequences that have required quite a bit of exploration on my part.

My personal life also had its challenges while writing this novel. I remember calls to my Editor, on several different occasions, questioning if I should even write this novel at all. I was concerned about its content, wondering if the message would be misunderstood, or maybe even, as the author, that I might have been misguided myself.

But I continued on, I managed the fierce inspiration, and finished the story.

What I have done – challenged my abilities, developed my talent and my writing skills, with a clear mission: to take you on a fascinating story with compelling characters, with an important message that hopefully will endure for years to come. My writing goal was to place you right in the locales, standing next to Maderno's Fountain in Piazza di San Pietro, right across from the Sistine Chapel in Rome; to the streets of Paris, the dusty markets of ancient Jerusalem and bustling Miami. You, the reader, are left to judge my efforts and measure my success.

So I invite you to experience *The Blood Decanter*. And let's let the horror continue…

Always,

FOR TY

For coming into my life and showing me that I am not alone;

FOR MY MOTHER

For showing me at the start of my life and continuously that none of us are ever alone.

There are many others who were involved in the creation of this novel.

For all those of you who have encouraged me and my writing career, whether it be a supportive father who has fielded countless phone calls discussing business, marketing and promotion related matters; a brother who supported my first rough copy of *Ashes* by reading it and analyzing it using his Princeton PhD skills to identify the themes of the story – which helped me, as the author, better understand *what* exactly I was writing *about*, and also helped me tell potential readers what the books *really* were about. Or a sister who helms a photography firm who snapped some of the first A.L. Mengel photos and has become the official photographer of the brand.

Or a beloved writing instructor who provided much inspiration needed to write a novel of this magnitude. Many days I had difficulty getting the words out, and my talks with her have been irreplaceable. I learned from all these wonderful people that these books in the Tales of Tartarus are so much more, so much deeper, than typical 'horror' stories. I learned that these books have meaning and purpose, and the messages they deliver between the lines are for far more than just me.

THANK YOU ALL.

ORIGINS

THE VISITOR

ACTUS CONTRITIONIS

THE HOODED MAN

BLOOD LINEAGE:

ANTOINE NAGEVESH

DARIUS SAUVAGE

DELIA ARNETTE

CLARET ATARAH

LIBERA ME

TOWER OF BABYLON: BLOOD RAIN

THE CRUCIFIXION

AGNUS DEI

No matter how the clouds part,

Nor the skies clear,

I open my eyes to blood rain;

Wash the tears away,

And weep again for a different purpose.

ORIGINS

THE ORIGINS OF THE TALES OF TARTARUS

You can absolutely start reading "The Tales of Tartarus" with this novel. The series was designed for the reader to start with any story they choose. You can start the series with this book and you won't be lost.

But if you have already read *Ashes* and *The Quest for Immortality*, you can opt to skip this section, and skip forward to "The Visitor". This section may appear redundant, or unnecessary to those readers.

I have placed this short reference section in an unorthodox location – at the front of the novel, rather than at the ending, where many authors will place a section for the reader to refer to. The purpose of this is for the reader to better enjoy the story – by skimming the items, or referring back to them, the reader can educate themselves and gain a sense of familiarity with the world before they read the story, or even as they read the story. Or the reader can choose to skip past these few pages and dive into *The Blood Decanter* right away – but these pages will remain here, for easy reference, if there is something (or a someplace) in the story that might have been explained in the earlier novels.

"The Tales of Tartarus" has been an interesting series thus far. It has intrigued me to look back on each novel after it's published and I move on to the next, and notice how my writing and research has matured and grown from one book to the next. It all started with *Ashes*.

But now, in *The Blood Decanter*, the story has matured. It has entered adolescence; the characters have changed and become more complex and multi-layered, just as we do as human beings when we grow, mature, educate ourselves, and essentially become more complex individuals.

I have chosen to include this first section, to serve as a reference for the reader – whether it be a seasoned reader who has embraced this series of novels from the point when *Ashes* was published, to the reader who is just discovering Antoine, Darius, Claret, and others with this particular book.

When compiling this, I worked painstakingly hard to ensure that there would be no spoilers – especially for those readers who have chosen to read the novels out of order (which is absolutely perfectly fine) – and I am interested in feedback from those readers on how different the series may present itself when being read in a different order from whence I wrote the books. Please note that *The Quest for Immortality*, due to the length of its title, will be abbreviated, in this section only, as "*TQFI*".

Always, A.L.

ASMODAI – The Demon Asmodeus, for the Cardinal Sins of the Flesh.

ASTRAL, THE – A paranormal research society.

INSPIRITI, THE – An underground society (some immortals; some who have lost "The Gift" and seek renewed eternal life). They are in place to assist former immortals regain "The Gift". Delia Arnette is their current leader.

BADULLA – City in Sri Lanka. Antoine's hometown. He worked in the coffee fields before being discovered by Darius.

CATHEDRALE DE NOTRE DAME – Notre Dame Cathedral in Paris, France. Darius meets Madame here when he is searching for a son.

JERUSALEM (ANCIENT) – The city of Claret's origin.

SACRAFICE – Nightclub on Miami Beach which Darius and Antoine own together.

OCEAN AVENUE – A fictitious street in Miami Beach based on Ocean Drive.

LES LIVRE DES VAMPIRES – "The Book of The Vampires" (French derivation) Published by Parchman's Press (*Ashes*)

DAS BUCH DES TARTAROS – "The Book of Hades" "The Book of Tartarus" (German derivation) Published by Parchman's Press (*TQFI*)

CATHEDRAL OF THE GARDENS – Fictitious Cathedral in Coral Gables, Florida.

PLYMOUTH CONGREGATIONAL CHURCH – The church which the Cathedral of the Gardens is based upon, located in the Coconut Grove neighborhood of Miami.

ASCENSION CEMETERY – Fictitious Cemetery which appears in several scenes in *Ashes* and *The Quest for Immortality*, located in Miami, USA.

NEW'S CAFÉ – A Café and restaurant in Miami Beach, Florida which appears in several scenes.

PARCHMAN'S PRESS – A mysterious publisher in the story that published both *Les Livre des Vampires* and *Das Buch des Tartaros*.

ABSINTHE – A high-proof liqueur distilled from wormwood. It is generally green in color, drank from a small, stemmed glass, and poured over a sugar cube on a slotted spoon, which is placed on top of the glass.

HELL HOUND – A supernatural dog, known to carry souls to Hell.

THE GIFT – All immortals have the gift. It is a gift given from one immortal to another, a maker to a child/son/daughter, and it grants immortality. The gift can be given in different forms – some makers will choose to bite the neck of their human selection for the gift, others simply bond intimately with them. Once the gift has been received, there is a similar process where the new immortal needs to adjust to their new powers, such as the adjustment period of a newly created vampire. Typically, the new immortal "sheds their skin" and no longer is mortal.

HIGHNESS – A term of respect used among the eldest immortals.

BAAL – The order of the demons to which Antoine and Darius belong. As not every newly created immortal is of the Baal, some are more like the lower rung of "vampires". Many newly created adopt ways of vampires, but evolve to Baal over time.

PIAZZA DE SAN PIETRO – The outdoor Piazza in Citta del Vaticano (Vatican City) in Rome, Italy. The Piazza is surrounded by soaring columns, four deep.

MADERNO'S FOUNTAIN – The infamous fountain and obelisk in the center of Piazza de San Pietro.

SISTENE CHAPEL – The Chapel in Vatican City on which Michelangelo painted the masterpiece ceiling. In the novel, it is frequently shortened to "Sistene".

NETHERWORLD – A term used to describe other dimensions. Most often evil in derivation, it can also describe areas of enlightenment which are believed to be located on a different plane from physical reality.

SEA OF SOULS – A sea filled with tormented, writhing bodies at the gates of Hell. Demons guard these gates, and this sea figures in to several of the novels.

THE VISITOR

Miami.

The Devil's city.

The land where the sun sets later, and the days are hotter, brighter, sweatier, and filled with more caffeine. Where the tall royal palms line the sidewalks; where the manicured lawns are a deep, forested green all twelve months of the year; where the water remains blue and bright and brilliant.

But the darkness of the Devil –

Miami.

It's the crystalline jewel on the tip of the Atlantic coast – hugging the Caribbean, surrounded by tropical waters and majestic million dollar mansions that line the docks and the inter-coastal waters which were usually scarcely used, except by Hollywood elite and celebrities. Most of the time, the waterfront palaces remained empty. And not far from the mansions and high-rises one finds the tiny, shoebox single level cement homes, dirty, bars covering the windows, litter on the lawns and too many cars parked along the streets.

Ah, Miami.

The brightest city with the darkest shadows. Yes, the city has a dark side. But it's the place that I call home. The place where I work; where I follow my calling. The city I love, and have come to love. And it's the city where I truly feel that I came face to face with the Devil himself...

Do you remember me?

Have you possibly seen me before? I always wear my black suit and tie. My hair is gelled, slicked back, cut tight and cropped to the sides. I most likely tower over you. I am quite tall. I am also somewhat quiet and reserved. Most of my chatter takes place inside my head. But I still can exude charisma. Can't I?

But if you have seen me before, you probably won't ever remember meeting me. Especially if you are wheeled in to my preparation room, just waiting for my trocar. Some of you may recall when I first met you when I was embalming in the preparation room.

Preparing a body. It's what I do.

The whole process relaxes me.

The cleaning and sterilizing, and then the actual procedure where I plunge the trocar – that long, reflective needle – with its wide mouth, into the neck, pumping the pink fluid into the corpse.

But my descriptions aren't always so clinical. For when that body arrived, there were always relatives waiting – those who were devastated, awash in loss and despair.

But that is when and where the art really begins.

For then, when a body arrives in my preparation room, that is when I can allow my creativity to run wild. I have a kit – a small, plastic box filled with makeup. Creams and foundations, even lipstick and nail-polish. I apply the foundation to both men and women, bringing life back to the skin, making it appear as if blood still flows through the empty veins, as if the person lying in the casket is not really dead; but just merely asleep.

For that is my calling.

But there was a time, not long ago, when I had a visitor. I only remember it because it was the same day that the man I described above moved through my chambers –

There was a day when I was not in Miami, but across the ocean, thousands of miles away, in a small preparation room in a similar chamber, for the body that I was called to prepare was a close friend. And I was asked to fly to Frankfurt – and so I called upon my fellow Mortician; the one family member who understood me so well. And I was able to use his quarters.

The sun shined through the small, square window in the little preparation room. It was small and boxy, the walls a stark and pale green, the overhead florescent light was harsh that morning as it had been every other morning. I would pick at the grit in my eyes that was usually there every morning. But that particular morning, there was a knocking on the door, it broke the silence.

It wasn't the door to the long, barren hallway covered in the noxious green tiles.

It was on the door to the outside.

And the only one who would come knocking on that door was either the coroner – or better have a pretty damn good reason. I set my coffee on the table.

I lay my clipboard down on the black body bag before me, and looked towards the door. I didn't see anyone in the small, square window. But then, I usually don't. There aren't too many people who will peek inside the lower levels of a funeral home.

I placed my hands on the cold, steel handle, looked out the window, and saw a small man standing in the frigid air; his clothing devoid of color and dressed in black and grey, with a black hat, and dark sunglasses. He looked up towards the window, and smiled. "Can you open for me?" His voice sounded muffled through the glass, like he was speaking into a pillow.

"We do not accept outside solicitations, sir."

The man took a few steps back.

He didn't seem very tall or imposing in the slightest, standing there in his black coat and grey pants. He shoved his hands in his pockets, then looked down at the pavement, and then back up. "You will want to let me in, Mr. McCracken. I have spoken intimately with Monsignor Harrison. I just returned from Rome."

I stepped back and swung the door open. The cold air was striking. The man took a step towards the threshold and looked up at me. He had wisps of grey hair under his hat. But I could not see his eyes through his dark lenses. "Are you going to let me in?"

I stepped aside and he entered the preparation room. He stopped just short of the stainless steel table in the center of the room, and looked around. His mouth dropped open slightly, but he did not make a sound. I closed the door and moved towards him, and he spoke. "I have never been inside a room like this before."

"Understandable. Most haven't, until the one time at the end of their lives when they come into this room."

The small man stopped and looked directly towards me. He removed his dark glasses, and his eyes pierced me. Dark brown, against an olive complexion. Much more noticeable under the florescent lighting, without the sun shining in my eyes. "Oh, Mr. McCracken, I have heard many things about you."

"What kind of things? And from whom?"

The man folded his sunglasses and placed them in his coat pocket. "Rome sent me. Antoine sent me. Because I have a warning. A warning of the greatest importance for the immortal kind."

I grabbed the clipboard from on top of the body bag and flung it on the counter. "Do you have identification?"

The visitor looked at the clipboard as he fished through his pockets. "Who is in that body bag?"

"That isn't any of your business until you have shown me identification that proves that it is."

I waited. And watched for him to fish his ID out. And then I remembered. It was such a distant memory, but it stuck out in my mind nonetheless. It was of Stephen. My, brother, who died on the side of Telegraph in Michigan. "I have had a lot of experience with Funeral Homes," I said, accepting his ID. "And it says here you are a Mortician as well?"

The man nodded and removed his coat and placed it on the counter. "Yes, Ned. Yes I am."

I nodded and handed him back his ID.

"I'm Hector Tabares." He started walking around the preparation table as he talked to me. "Rome sent me, as I said, with a warning." He looked down at the body bag on the table. "You see, this man here, I know who is in there. That is why Rome sent me."

I took a step back. "Okay. So Rome sent you. The Monsignor? Can you tell me a little more about the purpose of your visit here today?"

"I come with a warning."

I nodded. "Okay…would you care to elaborate?"

But I didn't mind the silence that followed. For I already knew the answer. He stood next to the preparation table, and reached towards the counter for the clipboard and death certificate. He picked it up and looked down, examining the document, as he adjusted his glasses. "Darius Sauvage," he said, studying the paperwork. And then he looked over at me, removing his glasses. "Why am I not surprised?"

"What is your warning?"

The man set the clipboard down, sighed, and walked closer towards me. He walked right up towards me, and I looked down at him. I noticed his snow white hair. He looked up at me. "My warning concerns Darius here. For he was an immortal. And he was attacked – and there is someone out there who is set to end the reign of the immortals."

It took me a few moments. I had to process what he was telling me. Somehow, this tiny little man knew who was in the body bag (aside from his reading the death certificate on the clipboard). And it seemed he really knew who was in the body bag and how he got there.

And the little man stepped forward. "Do you know who I am? What purpose I serve?"

I shrugged my shoulders. "I know you are here about the body on the table. I had a pretty good inkling that you knew who was here when you came inside."

The man closed his eyes and nodded. "And do you know why I am here? Why I am visiting you?"

I shook my head.

"Yes, I know who you are. And I know that you don't usually operate out of *this* funeral home. One in Miami, right?"

I nodded. "You knew him?"

The man looked down at the black plastic body bag, and his eyes fell. "Yes. Yes I did." And then he looked up and over at me. "There is something you are keeping from me."

"Absolutely not," I said.

He took a few steps closer towards me. "Yes. Yes there is. You are somehow connected to this body. Am I right?" He looked downwards and removed his jacket, and then back up to me. "Are you going to tell me the truth?"

I paused.

Was there something going on here that I was not aware of? There was only one more individual who was aware of this body. I was certain of that. I checked, and rechecked countless times before accepting it here, in my brother's establishment. Oh, dear.

"As I said, I come with a warning."

I ushered him past the body and towards the door. "Come with me," I said. I led him down the hallway towards a set of stairs that rose upstairs. I shuddered at the mosquito carcasses on the pale green paint over cinder blocks – but that was a common occurrence. The heels of his shoes clicked on the cement floor. As we reached the stairs, he turned around and looked me in the eyes. "I don't need to go upstairs to give you a warning,"

"So why don't you just tell me?"

He took a step closer towards me. "I know who you are preparing that body for."

I took a step back, looked down at the man as he looked back up towards me, smiling.

"I had a feeling."

And then I could feel the dread filling the room. Hector looked at me directly. "A man did this, Nathan. There is a legend of sorts. Of a man in a hood. Who appears on a cloud of white mist. They say he carries a crystal decanter. Convinces immortals to drink from it. Says it's their salvation."

I looked down at the body bag. And then I focused on the zipper. There goes that damn zipper again. "So…what are you saying, Hector?" But I had a feeling. I had spoken with Antoine at great length about the body in that body bag. Hector really didn't need to answer the question – but he came close to my side anyway. "My warning is this. You must warn Antoine. And Delia. The entire 'Inspiriti' group. Their days are numbered. But the man who visits them – the immortals, the victims – is a man of evil. He is not bringing salvation."

"How do you know all of this, Hector?" I looked up at him. His eyes were still wide and mysterious. Like white orbs when I shut the lights out, and started to climb the stairs. I felt that I could still see his eyes. And then he followed me, upwards towards the light and a small, wooden door. I fished the key from my pocket.

"I know because this man in the hood pursued me as well."

I looked down at him. He stood a few steps below me, and looked up towards me with raised eyebrows. His skin looked a bit orange in the dim light. "Yet you stand here before me."

Hector looked down and nodded. "Yes, yes. I stand here before you." He spoke quickly, high pitched. "I cannot tell you the entire story here, Nathan." I fumbled with the lock and the door swung open. The smell of incense wafted down the stairs. Cool air. Hector followed me into the West Viewing Room. The one in the horrid pink pastel with the flower print curtains. I turned to face him as he stepped aside so I could close the door. "Okay, so you still didn't answer my question. How are you standing here before me? Giving me a warning? How is that possible if this man visited you? Didn't you explain to me that it was certain death?"

Hector grabbed a small, white folding chair and sat down as I arranged some programs on the lectern at the front of the room. He sat, legs spread wide, and rested his elbows on his knees. He looked up at me. "I am here because this is *my* calling. Just as this is what you are called to do. I am called to protect."

I looked up and down at Hector. His face was solemn. "So I can sit here and try to explain to you *how* I am sitting here. Or you can listen to me. It's your choice, Nathan." He sat back in the chair and crossed his arms.

I stopped arranging the programs and shrugged my shoulders, walked over to the casket and adjusted some of the flowers. I turned back around to see Hector following my every move. "So this warning you are giving me…"

"Yes?"

I stopped busying myself and walked over to where Hector was sitting. I sat down next to him and looked him in the eyes. "Why are you giving it to me?"

"Because you have the connections to make a difference."

"I see."

Hector sighed and shook his head. "So have I done my duty? Are you going to take my warning seriously? Or do I need to show you first hand?"

"How could you show me first hand?"

Hector did not answer, but merely looked up towards the ceiling, towards a hanging cross across the room. "There are ways. And there are gifts, Ned. There is so much to be explained. But for now, just heed my warning. Please."

I paused for a moment, looked down, and then back up and over at Hector. He looked pained. Worried. His eyes were wide and he kept smoothing his hair. "Who shall I tell about this?" I asked.

"You must tell Antoine, first and foremost. And he will take it from there."

The meeting did not last much longer.

We exited the viewing room, and he walked out the front door of the Funeral Parlor, into the cold, wintry mist. As I watched him navigate the icy, wet stairs, I thought, again, of Antoine. And then of Darius. And then I thought of the body lying downstairs on the preparation table. And I thought of how Darius might have died, and I made a mental note to call Antoine, and shut the door.

I walked back to the door at the other end of the foyer and grabbed the handle. I stopped for a moment, and closed my eyes. I saw the street, the dark street lined with trees, just south of Telegraph, where I had left my bike. Such a far cry from Frankfurt.

I remembered the night in Southern Michigan, when Stephen was transformed, and later when he died, and then, I shuddered. Had this Hooded Man visited Stephen? Had he come to him on that cool night when I watched him through the trees? Could my brother be suffering an eternal damnation?

Of course, I didn't think those thoughts back on the street south of Telegraph. When I was just a child. But that was then, this is now, and that was another story...

But then, do you remember me now?

I am the one mortician who enamored you once before, am I not? I was in a similar room with another body – across the ocean and in a different time – but the situation was the same. Then it was a macerated drag queen. Now it's Darius. And it just feels so much more personal.

I was also the one who ushered Sheldon's body into the afterlife. I was the one who boxed him up, slid him into the crematorium, and turned the bitch on. I am the one who walks the hallways, day and night, with a clipboard in my hand, ignoring the insect carcasses on the pale green tiles. And the flickering florescent light above my head doesn't phase me. I am the one who bared his soul to you, and told the story of how my brother was selected for this seemingly dark "gift".

And there are others, perhaps many of you, who do not know my story. Who do not know about what I do, or what I have done. There will be those of you who are reading this, and which are the first words of mine that are read. Those who do not know the entire story.

For those people, I have probably not appeared to them. But rather, they appeared to me. Rolling in on gurneys, loaded out of hearses or coroners vans; all with different origins – but all with the same destination.

My preparation room.

And in that room, that single little, solitary room, I would work my magic...

If you've read to this point, you probably might have thought you had gotten rid of me. But honestly, have you really? You may find ways to elude me throughout your life.

But in the end, I always win.

Did you read the last story?

The story that told the tale of how Darius got on my preparation table in the first place? Did you see how I demystified death? If you haven't, I urge you to. There was a certain point, in that story at least, that I really wondered why – if anything – that we were there.

Any reason.

But my purpose is to demystify death. Or at least make it somewhat tolerable. And that is really, my friend, why I exist.

Now at last, permit me to introduce myself to you.

I am Ned McCracken.

Truly and formally.

As I mentioned earlier, I stand about six feet tall. I'm a Mortician. Some of you may know me as a Funeral Director. But I like Mortician. Seems more I typically always wear a black suit. Although sometimes blue. And if I feel daring – I might put on a light grey. Always with a conservative tie. And a button down shirt with a traditionally cut collar.

My hair is dark brown, and always slicked back (I like the wet look). A little wavy on the sides, near where it curls up around my ears.

But enough about me.

I decided to pop in and let you in on a little secret. Now look around your shoulder. Anyone standing behind you? If so, tell them to go get their own copy of this book. And if you are on a Kindle, you can always darken your screen for a moment.

Great.

Now lean in forward. Closer.

Closer!

So here's the deal.

This story is quite different from all the rest. So different. But it's still related. You'll see your beloved Antoine, and Darius, and all the rest.

And you might even see me here and there.

I can't tell you where I might poke in and show my face, but be assured that I won't interrupt. I never interrupt. I am standing off to the side, my hands clasped at my waist, my head bowed down, and eyes closed as I listen.

I would listen to sliding doors opening, to people arriving, with light chatter, and then silence. The silence usually befalls the room when the family members have seen the display. The casket. Their loved one, who I always would care for so tenderly.

I would hear the tears falling, the whispers, the stories and the remembering.

So I'm used to standing off to the side.

And here, I will do the same for you. Experience the Blood Ancestry. Take the journey through the eyes of someone new, but don't forget, I never miss the opportunity to pop in and say hello to an old friend.

The Morticians Mortician

ACTUS CONTRITIONIS

Oh my God,

I am sorry for having offended you.

I detest all my sins because of your just punishment, but most of all because they offend you;

For I fear the loss of Heaven,

And I dread the pains of hell...

ONE

There was a certain time, and in a certain place, that they knew when they were being hunted. The rumors had, in fact, been true. They had been circulating for decades, but were never taken seriously.

Until the one precise moment when the revelation came.

But the knowledge of their potential demise did not come so easily; for it was months, if not years, of research, relationship building, and foraging trust missions where the truth had been revealed: the immortals were, undoubtedly, being extinguished.

And a small, bulbous crystal decanter was the culprit.

The decanter was thought, for a great while, to be the key to eternal salvation. There were many who had talked about it, and about the mysterious one who carried the decanter, who would visit the immortals in time of need; and the one who carried the decanter visited those immortals who were stripped of their gift, who lay dying and aging, heading towards a quick and final death. The decanter was viewed as the ultimate salvation; a catalyst to continue the gift, to add to the dark destiny for which they had been chosen.

But that was a fallacy.

Those who drank from the decanter did *not* find the solace that they desired; they did not receive the expected gift. They did not regain their immortality or strengthen or increase their intelligence. There was an utter agony which propelled itself on them. An infection filled with anxiety, torment, and a slow and painful death.

There were no gifts. There was no salvation from the decanter.

One of the most recent who drank the swirling, hot, red potion lay motionless on the sidewalk outside the Ponce de Leon after sunset, when the night was still in its infancy; lying still and motionless, eyes closed, and the blood still dripped from his mouth.

But he was still as if dead, eyes shut tight, and the young man, and his unkempt hair and sullied clothes, did nothing to represent the individual he had been in life – for he had once been quite fashionable. The torn, dirty pants, should they have been removed, sewn and cleaned, would be seen as of the latest fashion, and could be seen hanging in one of the upscale boutique shop windows that were a mere few steps from where the man lay.

Above where the man lay stood the one who wielded the decanter, who appeared to be a man – a 'Hooded Man' in a long, flowing, dark cloak – who would visit, shortly before death (as it was argued). Here, above the motionless, bloodied man, the 'Hooded Man' stood, watching and waiting, as the white mist that swirled around him abated. As the cloud retreated, so did the man. He walked without motion, with no bending of the knee; as if he were floating or levitating along the ground, and once his duty had been complete, he left.

He was the one who had crossed the world for decades, undetected until recently, the one who had been, for so long, a mythical figure who was thought to bring life eternal, and now was found to bring death.

It was a time in Hades that he was originally found, but by whom, and for what reason, remains a mystery.

The motive was unclear.

There was a man who had been crawling amongst stones, in search of flowing water but finding none, there was a man – dehydrated yet sweating, macerated yet still living. Searching. Reaching out in desperation.

There was an eternal dryness to his surroundings; the clouds above – painted black, flowing wisps in a blood red sky – did nothing to deliver water. And the sea which was so close to him, as he hugged the gravel, felt so distant. But he could see it – a somewhat blurred vision of blue against the stark palette of burnt orange and fiery red. His arms were macerated. Veins protruded through the dirt on his skin. His frail, fragile naked body lay in the sand, as the cotton feeling in his mouth, his desperate thirst, would never be quenched.

He closed his eyes as he heard footsteps crunching through the gravel. And then, a deep, mysterious and masculine voice.

"I can bring you water."

He hung his head low and rested on the gravel and closed his eyes. The heaviness weighed on him like boulders; he tried to lift his head, look up at the owner of the voice, but could not. "Yes….water…" He felt a giant hand on the side of his head, and he felt a closer presence. He opened his eyes and saw a pair of feet in sandals, and very muscular legs, stooping next to him. "The water comes with a price," the voice said. "If you drink from me, you will be mine throughout eternity."

Those words had sounded familiar. The man thought, back to a day when he had heard those words play into his mind before.

You will be mine throughout eternity.

Had there been a turning point?

There were the days that he tried to remember – blurred images and bright figures rushing past. Bright sunlight. Yes, he remembered that much. The bright sunshine, the cloudless sky. Hot pavement burning his feet. But the visions remained so soft, so delicate, so out of focus, like he was looking through waxed paper.

And then the vision turned dark.

He felt like he was descending, like he was levitating, down a set of stairs. The darkness permeated, but there was a blurred light off to the left. And then the vision started to sharpen; wooden beams off to the left and the right; there were dark cinder blocks in the distance with light white grout; a wooden worktable against the wall; and the blurred light was a hanging incandescent bulb casting a yellowish glow.

He could remember now.

Those days in that basement were the days after Gaye had died. And as he traveled through, he stopped just under the hanging light. Newspaper clippings were scattered about the wall. "George Stanley Investigated" read one line; and on another newspaper clipping, "Four Young Men Missing" hung a few feet from the other. And then he looked down at his hands. They glowed with translucence.

He snapped his head to the right when he heard a chain rattle in the corner. But what seemed like an instant turn of the head was a very slow transgression from one point of the room to another. There was a certain heaviness to the room; a thickness to the air, breathable, yes, but almost like he was in a fluid, with slow moments.

But he saw the corner. Yes, it was all coming back to him now. It was the same basement that he remembered. With the cages in the corner. Four of them, lined next to each other, to be exact. There was more clarity now. His head was starting to clear. He could even remember the rusted padlocks on each one. They were still there, still locked. And then he was directly in front of one of the cages, in an instant. He hadn't even tried to move, as he had when turning his head.

There was a dark, cloudy figure inside each cage, somewhat out of focus, but there was movement.

And then felt a deep thirst.

"Where are you!?"

The clarity blurred and darkened. He was no longer standing in the basement; the cages were not there; there were no newspaper clippings, or a hanging incandescent light bulb.

Just darkness.

"I understand now!"

And then the darkness faded, as the stones came into view. He was lying on the same beach that he had been. The same beastly, muscular demon was hovering above him. "Do you see why I cannot give you water?"

He closed his eyes, and felt the incredible thirst. His mouth felt dry as fresh weaved cotton. And he looked upwards to the demon. His face looked familiar. The snout, green skin, muscularity, and horns from the head. All like a silhouette against an unfamiliar sky. "Will you let me drink?" he said. "I don't care about the consequences. Just let me drink."

And the demon poured cool, refreshing water down to his mouth, as he lapped it up in earnest.

The 'Hooded Man' came to town before Douglas Kahn had dreamed of Ponce de Leon littered with bodies. And before the night when Douglas found himself sitting inside a long, black limousine, reaching forward, towards the front seat.

"Jim! Jim! Are you alive?" Douglas pounded on the button, and slapped the smoked glass divider. He could see Jim's silhouette in the front seat, staring forward, unresponsive. Douglas sat back in the seat, raised his leg, and kicked the glass.

Nothing.

He did it again. Nothing again.

He flung open the mini-bar cabinet and found an unopened bottle of champagne, and hurled it at the glass, which shattered in tiny pieces on the floor and seats. "Jim!"

But Jim did not move.

Douglas hoisted himself forward and peered around the front seat.

But Jim was just as dead as the bodies that littered the sidewalks. His eyes were gouged out, and his mouth was dripping a white pus down his chin. Drained, dried up. Macerated.

Like he had been decomposing for years.

Douglas fell back into the back seat and covered his mouth. His eyes welled with tears, as the overpowering stench of rotting human flesh powered against him like an invisible wall. He reached for the door handle and tugged at it, and spilled out onto the sidewalk.

And then the sun assaulted his eyes.

There was a time when Douglas remembered the sun. When the sun fought its way downwards on the Boston college campus, in the midst of the summertime heat, when he had walked with Sheldon between classes. Sheldon looked over at him, his hair hanging low down the sides of his face; the dark frames of his glasses contrasted to his pale complexion. "Did you see the look on Laramir's face when I brought up that stuff on the astral plane?"

Douglas nodded. "You'd better watch yourself. Your controversy is coming before its time."

Sheldon scoffed and looked up at the sky. The sun was shining brightly, and the clouds looked like giant balls of cotton. There were several blossoming cherry trees covering the sidewalk that they traveled on. Sheldon shook his head as they approached the student center. He stopped short of a glass door. He placed his hand on the silver handle, and looked over at Douglas. "How will I ever achieve what I want when you are holding me back?"

Douglas sat on the sidewalk. He looked down at the body next to him. The eyes were cloudy, open, cloudy and without sight. He reached down and closed the eyelids. The rigor mortis had already set in, and the decay ate away at the skin; he noticed the teeth through the jawline; there were several fillings – the older kind, with the metallic shine.

And then, as he looked down Ponce de Leon, he thought he saw movement in the setting sun.

Doug stood up and waved his arms. "Hey!" he called out. He jumped up and down. Yes, he *did* see someone on the far end of the block. Walking back and forth, what seemed like a zig-zagging, back...and...forth, appearing lazy, or drunk. Doug stopped waving and squinted against the setting sun. As it came closer, Doug was able to decipher the movement – which was more like a slither. The zig zagging wasn't erratic walking in the slightest. And the movement wasn't made by a man. Doug's mouth fell open as he saw the giant, pulsating white worm, slowly gliding across Ponce de Leon, heading towards several dead bodies across the street.

Doug ducked back behind a cement column. He looked down and over and stopped. He focused on the man's chest. There was a fleeting moment – if not just an instant – when Douglas thought the man's chest might have been moving. And this gigantic worm would be headed towards him next. Doug peered around the column. He bent down and dragged the body under the porte cochère, and then looked behind him, at the door:

THE ASTRAL

Integrating Immortals into Society.

He read the frosted lettering and cocked his head to the side. He rapped on the smoked glass, so hard that the interior blind shook. There was no answer.

Doug looked around the building.

The white worm was hovering over the bodies directly across the street. There was a mouth at the end of the large, slithering worm, where the head might be, but the creature was devoid of eyes. It left a trail of slime on the sidewalk in its trail, but the bodies were gone.

He banged on the door again. "Is anyone in there?!" And then he sensed movement at his feet. He looked down, and small, white worms – about the size of tiny earthworms, slithered towards his feet. "What the?"

He raised his feet and stepped back. Douglas stood on the sidewalk, still holding the handkerchief to his mouth. He looked onwards, down the street, towards the setting sun, through the piles of bodies and rising palms, and saw movement towards the horizon.

It was heading his direction, a far larger worm, moving and slithering between the bodies, about the size of a giant snake and growing, minute by minute; the worm was stopping every few feet and devouring a body, opening a mouth in front of the pulsating larvae, and getting larger...and larger.

Doug turned and focused on the door, and banged, several times. The glass shook.

He heard footsteps inside, approaching the door as he slapped his palms against the glass. "Open the door! Help me!"

Antoine and Darius had spent quite a significant amount of time at their Chateau just south of Lyon in France in Darius' final days on the earth. Just before Darius had died, they traveled from Miami to the Chateau so he could live out his last days on earth in the most familiar territory to him – his homeland.

On the day Darius died, Antoine pulled the sheet over Darius, covering his head and body, and pulled the drapes shut to the room. There had just been a quiet summer shower, minutes before, when Antoine had sat in the rocking chair across the room, watching Darius. Waiting. Listening to the quiet falling rain. Looking at the body, covered by a white sheet. But for what he was waiting for, he wasn't sure. Darius certainly was not going to wake. And Antoine was wishing, thinking. He sat back in the rocking chair, listening to the rain, and concentrating on the creak that the runners made on the hardwood floor each time he leaned back.

He sat for quite some time, wishing that the inevitable hadn't really happened. That this had all been a terrible dream. And then he opened his eyes, raised his head, and noticed Darius' eyes.

They were closed.

And it took him back to the very same room, on the very same bed, so many years ago.

It had been in the middle of the night.

Darius was lying in the middle of the bed, in almost the same exact spot that his body would be lying years later. Antoine had wandered in the room, from the bathroom, in a small white towel. It stood out bright against his dark skin. "Darius," he said. "Wake up."

49

Darius fluttered his eyes.

Antoine walked over to the same rocking chair that he would be sitting in years later, and sat down. Darius lay still, and draped his arms back behind his head. Antoine noticed his muscular arms as Darius closed his eyes and sighed. "It's really not the time to be going out, Antoine. Can you see the sun peeking over the horizon? The sky is lightening. Come to bed. Let's wait until tomorrow. I need to rest."

Antoine stood and let his towel drop to the floor.

He locked eyes with Darius and climbed into bed, slid under the covers, and closed his eyes. Darius turned over and immediately went to sleep. Antoine opened his eyes again and looked over at Darius. After a few minutes, his own eyes had closed, and there was simply darkness and silence.

And then he woke to a ringing phone.

He hadn't been sleeping in the bed next to Darius; he had been sleeping in the old, dusty rocker. And Darius hadn't said a word to him. He was lying still, motionless and dead, just as he had been. Antoine shook his head, rubbed his eyes and reached for his phone. He looked at the screen. The exchange looked somewhat familiar. "Someone calling me from Rome?"

Antoine answered the call and brought the phone up to his ear. "Hello?"

The ghosts remained in the Chateau. And Darius, now gone, was one of the many ghosts. But Darius, in his mind, and his essence, was not the type of ghost to remain in the same four walls where he had died. His mind would travel, across oceans and time, and he always would visit his past.

There had been a time, during his life when he was still a mortal, when Darius no longer wanted to sleep. It was during the days of fitful youth and under the veil of perceived immortality; before his transformation and rebirth into darkness, when he had accumulated even more transgressions.

There were days in Darius' youth when his dreams had been wrought with darkness, with fitful dreams of terror and an overcoming sense of dread. One on particular occasion, as he tossed and turned under a blanket, he shot up in bed, eyes wide. He scanned the room, and kicked the blanket off his legs. The sweat instantly cooled and dried, as his heart beat harder in his chest. "Where are you?! Why are you following me?!"

And silence was the only answer.

He looked out towards the window and towards the farmland. In the distance, was the river, glowing pale blue in the moonlight. And then, after lying in bed, night after night, after he pulled the covers up close to his neck, he fought the heaviness in his eyelids and lost, falling asleep once again into another fitful realm of nightmarish dreams.

And then Darius would see the stones. He would always dream of the stones.

The same stones that rose from the misty waters that he saw each night that he had the dream, small stepping stones leading into darkness and misty oblivion. And the same mysterious voice.

"I have been waiting for you, tonight as I have each and every night."

Darius looked down at his feet.

They looked pale and translucent against the blue light. He stepped on each stone with care – first drawing his right leg out, reaching it upwards and over the rising mist, and finding the next stone – roughly a foot or slightly more across – and then straddled the two stones. He looked up at the mysterious man, who easily navigated the stones, despite his heavy, muscular frame.

"Why do I follow you each night?"

He turned and looked at Darius, and held out his arms. "I am Tramos," he said. "I have been sent for you."

Tramos stood before him each night in the same repetitive dream. Darius started to recognize the long, golden hair, the muscular torso, and remembered his powerful grip. Tramos grabbed Darius' wrist and did not let go. "I have brought you here once again to show you. To show you your origin, your blood ancestry. Come with me and I will take you."

Darius shook his head and pulled back, but Tramos tightened his grip. "You are part of the blood ancestry, Daruis. It is meant to be. You must do what is willed, what is written."

"What must I do, Tramos? What is written that I am a part of?"

Darius looked up. There was a sadness to the sky.

The clouds meandered across a rose tinted sky, and as Tramos turned forward, he scaled the stones. "You will know in time, dear Darius. You will learn, gain knowledge, you will make mistakes and learn from them as well."

Darius had no choice but to follow. "The mist is a concealer," Tramos said. "Beneath lie the bodies of lost souls. This is a desolate swamp. This is the land that leads onwards into Tartarus. You do not want to become a lost soul, Darius. You do not want to wind up below that layer of mist. You must find some meaning in your life."

"And why are you showing me this, Tramos? Why do you come to me? Night after night. Why do you come?"

Tramos stopped, and they each stood on a stone that rose from the misty waters. "Because I have told you. And I will tell you again. You are destined to be part of the blood ancestry. And I am destined to make you a part of it. And here, I am leading you into our world, to show you your heritage. You are mortal. I can only come to you in your dreams. But when you wake, you will remember. And I will come to you again."

There were the mornings when the demon had visited him. It was after nights of the dreams of darkness, when he would travel through barren wastelands fraught with meaninglessness. Traveling amongst stones – it was always amongst the same stones – as he would look at his arms, they would always appear translucent, as if he were not completely there, somehow. But each and every night, as they approached a giant, angry, sea, Darius could very clearly hear screaming coming from the sea.

And it would always play out the same way. He would look up at Tramos, as his heart quickened. "What are those screams?" His question would always be the same. And during one of the dreams, Tramos would answer: "They are the screams of the lost souls."

And during a subsequent dream, Darius would ask the same question at the same point in the dream. But Tramos would have a different answer: "You do not want to be one of them, Darius. Remember what you hear. Keep it with you for eternity."

And the sky would turn violent, with winds roaring, black clouds racing across a virulent sky.

And at that point, Darius would always awaken.

The sunlight would finger its way through the curtains, brilliant and bright, bathing the room in light. But as he lay in bed, on the next morning, he saw the monster standing over him, looking down on him. All his vision would allow him to see was a silhouette of a powerful demon, horns rising from its head, heavy, deep breaths, and powerful, muscular shoulders and arms.

All he could do was lie completely still. Frozen under his covers, hardly able to take a breath.

The demon moved closer, and reached its arm over to Darius' chest. "I have come for you."

Darius shuddered and took a deep breath.

Tramos reached for the blanket, as Darius lay motionless and shivering.

"It is time to do the deed…"

And then the blanket was whipped away and tossed across the room, and Darius felt a chill in the air. His sweat dried almost instantly, and he felt a coldness that became more intense as the demon move closer to him, hovering over his body, his powerful arms reached around Darius' small body, the roping muscle taught against his back. The demon pressed Darius' head back on the pillow, as he sought his neck.

Darius cried out as he felt the piercing on his neck, and the heat of his blood running downwards towards his chest. The demon drank, as Darius felt the room spin. He opened his eyes, looked over towards the window, and saw multiple square lights.

Don't look into my lights…you will certainly go mad.

It was madness and isolation that Darius felt when the demon was in the room with him. The light from the window looked like a filter had been flung across the window, a strange, blue tint; tiny snippets of darkness permeated the room, as the crescendo built.

Enter my chambers…take my hand and follow me. Do what is written, do what must be done…

As the suckling continued, he closed his eyes, and saw rivers of blood, seeping across an uninviting sky. He thought at one point that he rose from the bed, but could not be certain.

For he floated above dry carcasses and cracked muddy beaches in an unforgiving land, in unexplored and unfamiliar territory, looking down and seeing a sea covered by a swirling white mist. He could see the demon in a shadow, the beastly muscular profile, and then he felt the roping muscularity of the monster's arms wrapping themselves around him.

The sensation of being carried followed, and he opened his eyes, but all he saw was blackness. Utter and complete darkness. He held his hand in front of his face, but saw nothing. He listened for sounds in the noiseless black, but heard nothing.

But he could still feel the power of the roping, muscular arms, holding him close and tight to the monstrous chest.

Feel my arms, protecting you. Feel my power as it develops within you. Feel me in you...

The arms fell away, and he was floating, feeling alone.

Like in some seismic, extrasensory cosmic existence.

But as he looked downwards, there was a pinpoint of light – far from where he was floating; it looked like a tiny star. For a moment, he floated above it, and as he gazed down upon the light, he noticed it growing larger; it expanded across, a tiny white beacon that grew, expanded and widened. Then he noticed that it was not the light that was expanding, but that he appeared to be floating down towards it. He drifted further downwards, yet there was never the sensation of falling, nor of distress or of a threat – just impenetrable isolation.

And once the light expanded to a massive proportion, enveloping him like a dome; as he levitated towards it, the colors multiplied and stretched over where he was floating, and for some time, they were blurred. He thought he could make out shapes; lengthening dark orbs, floating and stretching before his eyes, until he was standing on the same stones he had been on in his dream.

Tramos stood in front of him, with a smile beaming across his face. "You see, Darius? Do you appreciate what I have done for you now?"

Darius looked downwards as the mist lifted. The water brightened and he saw the bodies. A mass grave, filled with the dead; all ages, male and female, their bodies bloodied and dirty, some limbs missing, others intact, but all eyes closed and faces expressionless.

"There is no hope for them, Darius. But there is hope for you."

Darius looked up at Tramos. "How can you say that? That there isn't hope for anyone?"

Tramos led Darius over to a clearing at the edge of a forest that bordered the lake. He touched his shoulder. "There is hope for you, Darius, because now, when you wake up, you will be immortal. I have come to you, to transform you, because there is hope for you. You are now part of the bloodline. You were always meant to be part of this blood ancestry. And now you will be for eternity. There is no going back. It was as it always has been written. You were chosen – since before you were born."

"And what about them?" Darius gestured over to the lake.

"You don't want to wind up there, Darius. You don't want to wind up lost in a mass grave, drowning in a barren seascape. It's just one step from the anger of Hades."

And then Darius woke up in a pool of blood.

The sheets were stained bright, crimson red, and the sun was shining through the curtains. He winced at the pain on his neck.

He propped himself up on his elbows, and looked around the room. The demon was gone. No sign of anything, except for the blood. Did he dream of the assault?

And then he looked down at the blood-stained sheets.

He touched the sheets with his fingers. The blood was real.

Outside the offices of The Astral, Douglas cowered and hunched over as a tall man with sandy brown hair swung open the door as the winds picked up in force. "You need to get in here, now!"

Doug pleaded with wide eyes, pointing down the street. "There's a young man lying in on the sidewalk down there! I think he is still alive!"

The man craned his neck around the side of the building and looked down the street. "Ethan!" He ran towards the young man and knelt down next to the body. He looked back up and gestured over to Doug. "Get over here! I need your help!"

Doug rushed over and picked up the young man's feet, and the two carried the body inside the offices and slammed the door. They set the young man on the floor and then the tall man went to the door, clicked the lock, and peered through the blinds. Doug joined him and looked out the window as well.

The white worm slithered down the opposite side of the street, now the length of a full city block, and several feet wide.

"The worms come every night, just at sundown," the man explained, as he rushed to a small break room behind a cluster of empty desks. He opened several cabinets and fished out a small, white towel, and ran it under the sink.

"Anthony Peterson," he said, extending his hand as he returned to the waiting area. He knelt down below the body and folded the towel into thirds, and laid it across the young man's forehead. He placed his index finger on the side of the man's throat and looked at his watch, and a few minutes later, looked up at Douglas.

"I'm Douglas, sorry." He looked up and out towards the window. The white worm had expanded further, the circumference reaching outwards halfway across the street. It pulsated and moved. Douglas gasped. "Are the people in there...*alive?*"

Anthony joined Douglas next to the window, as Douglas stood, shaking his head, saying nothing. Douglas looked over at Anthony who moved back to check on the young man. "Those worms clean up everything," Anthony said, as he checked the man's pulse again. "They pretty much eat everything and cleanse the city for the next day."

"I...I just simply don't understand this, Anthony. It sounds like a horror novel. Or Science Fiction, maybe."

Anthony nodded. "Yes, to you it probably does. But I have seen others who have crossed over, like you. Somehow, you got here. In this alternate reality. It looks the same as the world you are used to...only different. Somehow, you got here. And usually the ones who have just arrived don't initially understand the way things work on this side." Anthony took the towel and dabbed the young man's face gently. "And for this man – Ethan here – we have to get him down below. And get him some medical attention."

"So you know him then."

"Yes," Anthony said. "I rushed to his side because I know this man."

Anthony wasn't the only one who knew the dying man on the sidewalk.

Darius had also known the man who lay dying on the sidewalk next to Doug on *Ponce de Leon*. He remembered the young man, from his days in Miami, centuries after he dreamt of Tramos, and of the bodies. The young man had been a shopping partner, and there were days that he recalled long martini lunches; as the two laughed together, he could still see his tight cropped brown hair, the sunglasses which he always wore on his forehead, and how his eyes seemed so large, so brown and inquisitive. And as the young man would stare at Darius with lust in his eyes, while sipping on his martini in the bright afternoon sun, there always seemed to be a question even if a word was never spoken.

Darius smiled, and brushed his hair behind his shoulder with his hand. "You know I am so happy that I transformed you, Ethan. You have so much *joie de vivre*…such a zest for life. Panache. That's what I like about you."

Darius could tell that Ethan was smiling, even though the oversized martini glass concealed the lower half of his face.

"And I invited you to this luncheon so I could review the blood ancestry with you. And I can explain to you our bloodline. You can meet those who have come before you, and you will meet two others today. Antoine and Delia. They are part of your bloodline."

Ethan nodded and smiled. "I trust you will let me dine with you alone later tonight?"

Darius smiled at Ethan, and then looked upwards, over Ethan's shoulder. Ethan set his drink down and looked around his shoulder.

Darius beamed. "Antoine!"

Antoine approached the table arm in arm with Delia. The contrast between the two was striking – Antoine tall, dark, dressed in a black pressed suit; and Delia, small, frail, aged. Her stark-white hair was tied back neatly in a bun, save the few strands at the crest of her forehead which had escaped. Antoine nodded at Ethan and the two joined the table. Darius rose from his seat and pulled out a chair for Delia, and Antoine flashed a bright, white smile at Ethan, whose mouth hung open and could not take his eyes off of Antoine.

Darius noticed Ethan noticing Antoine, and smiled. Antoine shot Darius a glance and winked. As they took their seats, Antoine leaned over to Darius. "Interesting new catch," he said, concealing his mouth with a cupped hand. "Interesting indeed."

Darius nodded. "Where's Roberto?"

Antoine didn't answer as the waiter approached the table and took drink orders. Delia paid no attention to the subtle interactions between the men at the table (and, as she had been seated next to Ethan, she also did not notice his puppy dog eyes shifting between stares at Darius, and then Antoine, and then Darius again).

Ethan ordered another martini, and Darius raised his eyebrows, but said nothing. Antoine smiled. And Delia got down to business. She extended her hand to Ethan.

"Welcome to the family," she said.

The young man set his drink down and covered his mouth, giggling. "I…thank you…"

Delia looked over at Darius. "Has Darius informed you as to why we are having this luncheon today?"

Darius shook his head, and Antoine raised his eyes, looking over towards Darius, but did not move.

"I see," she said. And then she looking back at Ethan, who faced her, sitting forward, looking directly at her.

Delia sat up straight in her chair and smoothed her blouse. "I am Delia. I am your maternal figure, if you may. I remember, years ago in Paris, when I knew Darius." She looked over at Darius. "Do you remember? Certainly you do. Those days when I was in Vaudeville. Oh wow, were those days something!"

Ethan's eyes widened. "You did Vaudeville?"

Delia nodded as the waiter set drinks down at the table. "Yes, I certainly did. I was a vixen. I used to wear bright red lipstick. When it first came to Paris." Delia raised her chin, just a little, and lowered her eyelids, and smiled.

Ethan chuckled and nodded. "I can see it! You were probably a knock-out back then, right, am I right?"

Delia looked over at Ethan and smiled. "I still am."

Ethan took a sip of his fresh martini and, just after he swallowed, looked around the table. "So, is this our entire bloodline?"

Darius looked over at Antoine as Delia sighed. "No, I'm afraid it isn't."

Ethan's face shifted. "I don't…you're afraid it isn't? What does that mean?"

Delia looked over at Antoine. "You care to fill him in, or should I?"

Antoine shook his head and looked up to the sky for a moment, and then back around the table. He looked directly at Darius. "Darius, you are the reason why she is following me. She has a death wish against me."

Ethan sat motionless, and stared at Antoine and Darius.

Delia shot a glance over at Darius. And then Antoine. "Both of you shush!" She pointed her index finger like a school teacher, and looked at Darius. "I did not create you to fight with your offspring like this!" And then she looked to Antoine. "And you, for all you have done lately…The Astral…the interviews with that ridiculous fat, old man…I would expect a little more panache from you! Both of you! It doesn't matter who did what at this point. It's time we told him about Claret!"

Antoine and Darius both sat back in their chairs, and there was an awkward silence which lasted only a few seconds, but seemed like minutes. Ethan, as he took a sip of his martini, looked over at Darius, and then Antoine, and then Darius again. And then finally at Delia, who was shaking her head and scowling.

She exhaled, exasperated. "Well then. I will explain the story myself." She looked over at Ethan. "I told you that I was a Vaudeville performer in Paris. It was the late eighteen hundreds...Vaudeville had just started around then."

Ethan nodded.

"Burlesque mainly," Delia said, smirking as she took a sip of her wine, laughing into her glass.

Darius rolled his eyes, as Antoine remained quiet.

"Anyway," she said. She placed her glass down. "There is a reason why we are selected for the mission that we are on. Why we have been selected for immortality. Just like you. And why Darius selected you."

Ethan smiled and his eyes widened, and looked over at Darius. "Why did you select me, Darius?"

Darius shrugged.

"Oh come on!" Antoine leaned forward, on his elbows. "I know why he selected Ethan. Isn't it obvious?"

Ethan smirked.

Delia raised her eyebrows. She looked like a china doll as she replied, so quiet that she could barely be heard. "No, it isn't quite obvious, Antoine. That's why we are here. I called you all here so we could be on the same page. There is a rumor of a great threat to us, to our kind, and we must all be in unison to survive it."

A silence permeated the table, as the tone shifted.

Antoine spoke first. "A threat?"

Delia looked down at her wine. "It's something I have been meaning to tell you. And, I know you thought this lunch was about you introducing Ethan to me, and bringing him to our bloodline, but this luncheon is really about us saving our lives."

Ethan's mouth hung open, looking confused. Darius and Antoine spoke to each other, inaudibly, as Delia drew Ethan closer to her, as she whispered to him. "You don't really know who I am, Ethan. Or why I am here. But they know." She pointed at Antoine and Darius, waggled her finger, and they stopped, both looking at Delia.

Delia placed her hands on the table, and looked downwards, then back up at the three men. "There is a man," she said. "And he is thought…I want to repeat…thought to be on a mission to exterminate us. But I want to stop now and tell you – these are rumors. Simply rumors. I believe them to be untrue."

Darius interrupted. "Wait a minute. Who are you referring to?"

Delia looked up at Darius. "A man in a hood. Very dark. Comes from the shadows."

Darius took a deep breath and looked down at his lap. His face shifted. "Shadow demons?"

Antoine put his arm around Darius as if on instinct. "What is it, Darius?"

Darius hung his head low. "I know about shadow demons."

Antoine looked Darius in the eyes. "Shadow demons? What happened to you, Darius?"

Darius shook his head and closed his eyes. "That's another story, for another time."

Delia interrupted. "We are talking about this Hooded Man, Antoine. Not shadow demons."

Darius opened his eyes and looked over to Delia. "I know who you are talking about. I saw him last night."

Delia's eyes widened. "You saw him?!"

Antoine craned his head around to look Darius in the eyes. "What is it Darius? You saw this man?" Ethan bit his lip and looked on.

Delia sighed and then looked over at Darius. "So you know what he is capable of, then, right?"

Darius returned her glance, and he looked at her straight in the eyes; they held their stare for moments, if not minutes and then, finally, he answered. "I do."

Antoine slammed his palms down on the table and looked over at Darius. "What are you talking about? She is saying that someone is out there looking to exterminate us and you say nothing? You tell me nothing? What happened with this man?"

Darius paused and there was a silence that permeated the table once again. Ethan looked down at his lap.

Darius finally answered. "Yes, I encountered the man, and yes, I drank from the decanter."

Delia pursed her lips and look off to the left. Antoine sat back in his chair, leaned his chin on his hand, his elbow on the arm of the chair. He kept shaking his head back and forth. "Of course you did," Antoine said, taking a sip of his beer.

"He promised eternal life. The blood is the life...is it not?"

All at the table fell silent, until Darius spoke, looking directly at Delia. "Are you to tell me that these are merely rumors? For I can, for certain, tell you that the rumors are true."

And it was Darius who had closed his eyes, later, after the lunch out with Delia and Antoine, at home alone, after he had made love to Ethan. He couldn't get the previous night out of his mind. He looked next to him, and Ethan was sleeping soundly. And when Darius closed his eyes, he saw that night. The same night, which would replay in his mind, over and over.

Come with me and drink from the blood decanter.

It was after, much later, that Darius saw the 'Hooded Man'.

After the cloud of mist came.

After the streets were silent and the streetlamps hummed, in the wee hours of the morning, after the nightclubs closed and just before the tiny fingerlings of light started to emanate across the eastern sky.

I have been waiting for you, Darius. I have been watching you…and following you.

Darius dropped his keys in the grass.

The two dead cops lay at his feet in a pool of blood; a flashlight lay, shining its light on the bright lake of red stained blades of grass. He could still make out the powder blue shirts, he noticed the shimmer of a steel wedding band, and several partially healed scratches on the officer's left hand.

But as he was kneeling in the grass, searching for his keys, he noticed the mist. He saw the fingers of white vapor reach inwards from the street outside the park; he saw the cloud roll across the turf and through the rising hedges and reach its way for him.

He looked over towards the park entrance.

"Is anyone there?" His voice sounded small and uncertain against the quiet of the night.

Oh yes, Darius, I am here. I am here with my decanter. I am here. Come and drink from me.

My blood is the life.

Darius watched the mist cloud billow and grow, and saw it reach upwards towards the sky. The air was still, yet the vaporous cloud moved as if the winds were powerful and intense; a certain feeling overcame him, as he watched, motionless and circumspect; the drawn out period was not one of awe or reverence, but rather an episode of hypnosis. For when he watched the cloud, all he could feel, at that very precise moment, was a sense of doom.

And then it was certain.

The mist carried the one who wore the hood; the one who carried the decanter, the one who stood before him, holding the decanter in his right hand; his hands extended downwards, almost overly so, as if disproportionate.

I bring you my decanter. My sweet blood decanter. Drink from me and salvation will be yours forever.

Darius did not take his eyes from him.

He knew his keys still lay in the grass; he could still feel the cool, damp earth; he knew the mist was still enveloping him; but his awe of the man before him was overpowering. The intensity was increasing, and he felt a tingling coming from deep within his body when he saw the decanter.

He did not need to move his eyes to notice the neck soaring upwards from the bulbous vase, reaching upwards towards the man's hand; it looked like the same type decanter one might use for whiskey or wine.

But inside the decanter, the glowing potion, the crimson liquid, reached its way up the neck, and churned. Boiled. Watched. Waited.

And spoke to him.

Drink from me.

Darius felt a pressure release from his neck. "I..." he croaked. "I can speak..."

But you try to speak. Don't you see that you must listen?

The man removed his hood with a swift tug from his free hand, and Darius fell backwards on the officer's body. He felt the warmth of the blood, which now was wet and somewhat cooler that it had been before. As he lay back, he saw the silhouette against the swirling vapor; the man who was a beast, the monster that stood before him. But he could not see a face; the man was concealed by darkness and the swirling mist.

"You have come for me?"

The man did not answer.

Darius squinted. "You wear a hood...you have no face...but I can hear your breathing. So I know you're alive..."

But Darius could see, his vision became so much clearer, so much more perceptive, when he simply closed his eyes and listened.

It felt like he was floating; like he was ripped from his body, not unlike those who have a near death experience. He was floating, he was certain of that, and looking down at the park. He did not see the 'Hooded Man', but saw the cops splayed in a pool of blood.

And then the vision changed.

It felt like he was flying; leaping through clouds in a dark, starless sky, as the clouds raced past him, he looked downwards, seeing lights pass beneath him at such a ferocious speed that he couldn't tell their origin; they flashed in a blur, in an instant, his eyes unable to focus on them.

And then he stopped. He recognized the cape from the man's arm, which extended, and he saw the same river near which that he met Antoine. He floated to the ground, and it was the same, blue moonlit night that he had remembered so long ago.

Looking towards the north, he saw the small café, its tiny windows reflecting warm light into the chill of the dark night. "Why did you take me back to this night? Of all nights, why this one?"

He raised his right arm, holding the decanter up in plain sight. Darius look directly at the decanter. The mist swirled around it, rounding the base, reaching upwards around the neck, and circling the mouth. And the angry crimson potion swirled inside.

Drink from my decanter. Drink from me. Live eternally. Take my potion, and find your salvation.

And then Darius paused for a moment.

"Am I to believe you are showing me the night that I transformed Antoine to show me that I have salvation? That I will not burn in Hell for all of eternity?"

The Hooded Man moved closer towards Darius, and blocked the vision, as the decanter seemed to come into a much more clear focus than anything else Darius saw. The white mist swirled around the approaching man.

His trance was broken, and he looked down at the bodies of the policemen. He looked over, several feet away in the bushes, and saw the body of the young Hispanic man who he was originally waiting in the park for in the first place.

And then he felt a twinge of regret.

Darius looked at the man, and searched for his face, but beneath the hood was only darkness. Darius closed his eyes. "I cannot be saved."

Oh, but you can, my son. Darius. Drink from my decanter, and all will be forgiven.

"I am too evil," he said, drawing his legs up to his chest, and hugging his knees inwards. "I am not like Antoine. I have always been like this. I have this innate need inside me to kill. I always have. I don't know when it started. Probably when I was still mortal. I don't know where it came from. But it's there."

The man moved closer, as the mist swirled around the bodies. Darius looked down, and saw the vapor at his ankles.

Darius looked at the man and saw that the mist moved inwards, catching his robe, drawing it apart.

Drink from the decanter, Darius.

Darius looked at the Hooded Man – levitating towards him, coming closer, as the mist parted and revealed darkness…but no face.

"You have no face…" Darius said, leaning back and starting to crawl away. "You have no face…"

And it will not matter that you kill. Drink from me, and your pain will wash away.

"No…no!" He crawled backwards, facing forward; his hands led the way behind his back, his legs following. But he could not take his eyes off of the decanter. The crystal decanter; it's bulbous base, the lines cut in glass, appearing so much more in focus that everything else he saw on that dark night. He stopped and stared at the decanter, as the red hot potion inside swirled, as if speaking to him.

Drink and feel the hot blood course its way down your throat. And treasure the sweetness of the blood.

"And what of me? Why have you chosen me to drink from the decanter? How am I worthy of this salvation?"

We are all worthy, Darius. Every immortal. Every one of you.

Darius looked at the decanter. There was an unusual elegance to the neck, the crystal bulb. And the man's hand. His hand grasped the basin as with long, slender fingers, flawless skin.

74

Darius paused for a moment.

The mist held back, swirling around the man, and the decanter, as if taunting him.

Beckoning him.

And there was a certain point where he didn't think that it was something real. But he looked at the man, he saw the flowing robe, the dark silhouette of his head, and then he caught himself at a point where he could not look away.

The 'Hooded Man' stood tall, towering over Darius, and remained motionless.

Darius raised his head and looked upwards, deep into his faceless hood; further into the darkness. "Come to me, give me your salvation…"

Yes, he was there.

He was there to bring him the blood life.

This man carried a decanter, so stunning and beautiful that it was like a crystal vase, and then, the blood inside was supposed to bring him life eternal, and banish his sinful life. "Why have you chosen me?"

The man lowered the decanter closer to where Darius sat, holding it close to his face.

I bring it to you because you have been chosen. You have been chosen to live.

Darius looked up. "Chosen to live? Will I die?"

The man brought the decanter closer to his face, and then Darius could smell a sweet, intoxicating aroma coming from the neck. A vapor in and of itself, rising upwards from the swan neck, reaching out for him, as if coaxing.

You will if you do not drink. Drink from me. Live forever, Darius.

And then it happened.

Darius did not know if it were something that his mind willed himself to do, or if he was acting under the man's spell. But at that point, nothing else really mattered. Darius looked at the red, swirling potion, treasured its sweet, floral scent, and then nothing else did really matter.

For there was a moment, if only a fleeting moment, where the darkness lifted. There was no longer a veil over his face — just a simple walk through a field of roses, underneath the bright, shining sun, walking under bright blue skies and puffy, cotton-white clouds.

There were no dark, angry clouds painted on a fiery red sky. That had been the difference; and when the potion hit his lips there was a sense of familiarity. He felt as though he had tasted it before.

My sweet, hot blood.

It slithered down his throat, hot and sweet, delicious and luscious.

Blood.

He sensed the taste. He remembered the same sweetness, the same viscosity, the warmth. He drank, swallowing it all down, tipping the decanter to get every last drop, as a drip of blood traveled down his chin.

"Yes!" Darius exclaimed, jumping to his feet. "This is blood! This is the *blood*!"

Come with me and drink from the blood decanter...

Darius closed his eyes and saw a river of blood, flowing fast and with purpose, and he saw himself standing on the edge of the river, filled with blood, amidst the same stones he once dreamt of.

He looked down.

His feet were bare; his toes were surrounded by the smallest stones. The thick blood lapped at the stones, and he knelt down on one knee. And then he felt a rising in the pit of his stomach. A stirring, a fluttering, and he felt his throat tighten. He fell forward and caught himself with his palms. The blood river quickly filled the holes in the sand and Darius felt the heat. His stomach heaved, and he vomited bright red blood onto the stones.

The 'Hooded Man' threw his head back in laughter.

The man pulled his hood back over his head as Darius closed his eyes and moaned. "Yesssss....."

And he sat down, slowly, and laid back on the grass, and that was when he realized the softness of the lawn; how he could once again feel every blade; he could hear the blood draining from the police officers' wounds; every drop that dripped from their dying bodies. As he opened his eyes, he could see the 'Hooded Man', still standing at the park entrance.

He bent over and picked up the decanter from where Darius had left it on the ground, and turned, as the mist started to retreat.

And after Darius thought that he had closed his eyes – just for a fleeting moment –

The man was gone, the mist was gone, and he was left again, in Flamingo Park, as the eastern sky lightened. He looked around at the mess he left.

Had he really been there all night? And where were the rest of the police officers? They did not search for the fallen two? But Darius knew something had changed in the fabric of time, the instant the mist came, and something changed again when he drank from the decanter.

He looked at his hands.

They were clean, almost glowing against the darkness of the night.

His arms were fit and muscular; skin smooth and supple. He got up to his feet, and relished the fact that he did not feel any pain; despite his immortality, there was always a sense of pain at times. This time, there was a feeling of no sensation; of benign numbness. His body felt stronger, far more muscular and powerful than he had ever been; he stood and smiled.

"Perhaps this truly can be my salvation…"

TWO

During the days after Darius had died, Antoine moped around the chateau; even his loyal servant Giovanni could not get Antoine to retreat outside and enjoy the fresh air and scent of the lavender. The days were bright, sunny, warm and inviting, but Antoine chose to view it from a window, until the doorbell rang on the morning that Darius would be buried.

Antoine sat on the sofa, his arm draped over the side, staring out the window. He sighed as Giovanni walked in, using his cane to feel his way through the room. "Who is at the door?"

Antoine shook his head as Giovanni turned around and felt his way through the foyer step by careful step.

Delia entered Antoine's Chateau after she had knocked for several minutes. She had tried the doorbell but it appeared to be broken. Giovanni opened the door, dressed in a long, white t-shirt and black pants. He had a white handkerchief folded and covering his eyes. She placed her hand on his shoulder for a moment and walked inside.

Her heels clicked and clacked on the stone floors. Antoine walked over to the front parlor, sat on a sofa, and stared out the window. "Oh, hello Delia." He sighed and looked out the window. Delia sat in the chair opposite Antoine, and looked over at him. She looked well beyond her years today. Despite that, she had decided to wash the grey hairs out with a hair coloring kit. She normally embraced her age, but this particular morning, she felt the need to appear younger. In theory, it seemed appropriate to her. But in actuality, she appeared older, for her face was awash with worry. The lines in her skin appeared darker and deeper, and her forehead was wrinkled as her mind was cluttered with concern. She watched Antoine as he leaned forward and looked into the fire.

"You cannot sit around all day and stare at things, Antoine. It's time to bury Darius. You need to bury your thought of him, everything. It's time to let him go. Time to move on."

Antoine looked over at her, and into her eyes, and then back at the dying fire. He got up and stoked the embers. "Delia, what I am about to do today is…"

She got up and walked over to Antoine, and placed her arms around him. "I know. I know it's hard. But it's something that we must do. We must experience it."

Antoine looked over at Delia. "I don't think you understand what I am about to do."

She nodded and hugged him tighter. "Oh yes, I know what you are about to do, Antoine. Oh yes, I know. It's something you have done before, right? But do you think you can call Asmodai this time around? I don't think so. Darius died as a mortal. That's a different death. How can you resurrect him this time around?"

Antoine closed his eyes as a tear streamed down his cheek. "But we are supposed to be immortals. We are not supposed to experience death!" Antoine threw the stoker on the floor with a crash and flopped down on the sofa. Delia followed and sat down next to him. She placed her hand on his knee. "Darius tried, so very hard, to live."

Antoine looked over at Delia, shook his head, and turned away, and closed his eyes. He was fighting back tears. His voice quivered with emotion. "I don't think he did. I don't think he fought hard enough."

Delia looked down. "I know he was, Antoine. You were gone, remember. Please don't forget that. I saw Darius through his entire decline. And he tried so desperately to live. He searched for Claret. Far and wide. He knew he had to drink from that cup. But he was not able to find it in time."

Antoine opened his eyes. "The cup. *The* cup?"

Delia nodded. "He believed that if he drank from the cup – *The Christ Cup* – that he would be given the gift of immortality."

"Yes, we know that is true. But it must be genuine. The true cup. There are so many imposters…"

"Like this 'Hooded Man'," she said.

Delia leaned back and looked over at Antoine. "Darius came to me before he died. And when we have had this whole thing with that man in the hood coming about, that's when I started putting things together. Darius shouldn't have died, Antoine."

Antoine looked down, and ignored the fire. He closed his eyes, and covered his face with his hands. After a few moments, he dropped his hands to his lap, and looked over at Delia. "So why did he die then?"

Delia sighed. She sat back on the sofa and shifted away from Antoine. "You remember our lunch on Miami Beach, right?"

Antoine's face shifted. He shook his head, looking upwards towards the ceiling. "Our lunch?"

Delia leaned forward and looked over at Antoine. "Yes. Try hard. Think. Please. It was a while ago. You and Darius were there. I was there. And so was Ethan. We talked about the 'Hooded Man'. Do you remember, Antoine?"

Antoine paused, leaned back into the sofa and remembered. He remembered the luncheon. The toast was burned for his Ruben sandwich. Yes, he remembered the day. "Ethan? That's a blast from the past. Good God…where has he gone?"

"Not really sure," Delia said. She crossed her legs and fidgeted. "He was last seen recently not far from the *Ponce de Leon*."

"The hotel or the street?"

"Hotel."

She shook her head and looked down. "I don't know where he is, Antoine. I'm surprised you *haven't* seen him."

Antoine raised his eyebrows and looked over at Delia. She was still fidgeting. "No, I haven't seen him."

There was a time when the one who was sent to collect the immortals had once been human. There was a time when he didn't wear the hood.

There were fleeting images of days past, growing up as a young boy, into a young man, and onwards towards adulthood, which fingered their way into his mind. He could still remember those days, the days before he was plunged into darkness, before he kept the four young college men in his basement in a cage for each –

But the cages, in his basement, were something that entered his life decades after he had started the downward spiral. It wasn't long after Gaye died that he eventually entered a quick and steady downfall. And shortly after that, he sat under heated lights, his hands in bright, steel cuffs, which caught the light and reflected it on the opposite wall every time he moved his wrists. "I remember the four young men. I remember them quite well. Especially Neil. He was my favorite. I remembered watching him mowing the lawn at his tiny, little house across the street. He was so tanned. So athletic. His muscles would glisten with sweat in the afternoon sun. Loved his hair. So scruffy! Tanned, a perfect specimen."

He looked over at the detective. He remembered the detective quite well also. Martin Jenson. Standing right before him now. Not just three months prior, he had been over to his house for dinner and drinks. Used to be a friend.

Not anymore.

It looked like the cop had put on some weight. Mustache was untrimmed. Pretty big set of luggage under his eyes, too. But his apparent exhaustion did not phase the man. He leaned forward and looked him directly in the eyes.

"George, you need to walk me through this, step by step. Where are they?"

George leaned back in his chair, and winced at the hard, wooden back. "Who is *they?*"

Detective Jenson took a seat opposite George, and motioned for the deputy. The cop placed a steaming cup of coffee in Jenson's hands. The detective took a sip. "The four men. Where are they?"

George shook his head and look up towards the ceiling. "I already told you. They're gone. I don't have them anymore."

"You have four giant cages in your basement. Chains. Leather masks. So you did at one point. What did you do with them? Was this some sort of weird sexual game?"

George paused for a moment and looked down at the table. He studied the hairs on his arm, and took a deep breath. He held his breath as he looked at Detective Jensen and shook his head.

Detective Jensen continued. "But if they are alive, they are still missing. Where did they go?"

He let his breath out and fell back into the chair. He looked up at the detectives and raised his eyebrows. "She has them. I told you already."

The detective pulled a manila file folder across the table, and opened it. He fished through a few papers, studied some photos, and paused for a moment. "Yes I see here from your initial statement. You say an 'immortal' came and took them. Some Claret? Seems pretty far-fetched if you ask me. She just flew in and grabbed them?"

George nodded and shrugged. "That's what happened."

"So we have four dead bodies. There was a widely publicized funeral with all four bodies. It was televised. Do you remember? If those bodies weren't buried in those coffins, then who was?"

"I already told you, Detective, she came and got them. She had me befriend each young man, I drugged them, as instructed, and carried them down to my basement. Then I locked them in the cages."

"And then what?"

"She came to see them. She took each one. And then they were gone. My part was done. She even had me dig up the caskets to check and make sure that the bodies were gone."

Detective Jenson scribbled some notes on his legal pad. He looked back up at George. "And they buried empty caskets?"

George looked down and examined his hands. "Yes, the caskets were empty." The dirt was still underneath his fingernails. He remembered. He remembered being on his knees, in the darkness in the dead of night, tearing at the cool earth and tossing the dirt over his shoulders.

"Keep digging!" Claret had said as she leaned down next to George's head. He looked over at her; she scowled. "Dig now!"

As he dug, and every time scooped a small amount of dirt, he tossed it over his shoulder. He dug for hours, until a pile formed next to them. Claret walked to the edge of the hole and stopped. "Stop. The casket will be just below."

George sat back, and wiped his forehead with the back of his arm. He looked up and over at Claret. "Do you want me to continue?"

She lunged forward and grabbed his neck. "What do you think the answer is?!"

And George continued digging, until all four caskets were hoisted from the earth, slammed on the ground and caked in dirt.

George opened the creaking lids, one by one. Claret looked down into the empty coffins.

"You see? There are no bodies."

And George opened his eyes and looked back up at the Detective.

The morning rays of the sun crept into the window. Detective Jensen rubbed his eyes. "Look, George, we have been here all night. We aren't getting anywhere. We're going to place you in a holding cell and continue questioning in 24 hours." The questioning concluded as George was cuffed and led to his cell.

But George didn't live to see the next round of questioning. His body was found in his cell, hung from a self-made noose, the white sheets twisted and tied around his neck from the rafters, his face swollen purple and eyes bulging out of their sockets.

He was soon after thought to be a monster.

A hooded demon, sent from Hades, to call the sinful beasts back to Hell.

And there was one immortal, in particular, who drank from the decanter, who was arguably aware of the 'Hooded Man' and his presence, and who was actually quite well respected in the community, but was enamored by the spell of the gift.

Darius Sauvage.

It had been on the same night Darius had prowled the parks in Miami Beach, looking for a sexual adventure. He walked towards the rusted gates, which rose above a broken sidewalk around a smattering of untended and overgrown trees. And when Darius had leaned against the fence on the side of the park, looking over at the parked cars, he did not realize that he was being watched.

He did not know that, just a few minutes earlier, when he was walking along the broken sidewalk, that in the amber circle of light shining down on the corner of the sidewalk a block away, a tall, hooded figure in a long, flowing robe appeared out of the darkness, and stood in the center of the light, watching Darius lean against the fence and take his place.

Darius didn't notice the Hooded Man – as he was to be known eventually – who made an appearance on that fateful night, when Darius chose his ultimate fate. As a young man approached Darius, and stammered, the Hooded Man stood and watched and waited. It wasn't until after, that Darius had felt his demon within rise. And that the Hooded Man rose in his mist cloud.

And it was Darius' death that caused a stir in the immortal world.

Those who had the gift started to panic, wondering how one could be stripped of immortality. And although Darius lived for years after he drank from the decanter, he eventually died as a simple mortal, and, because of that, there eventually were rumors quickly spreading. Through the immortal communities in Miami – initially – those who were familiar with Antoine Nagevesh and his work, along with his affiliation with Darius, and started talking about how something like that could have happened.

For when Darius died, no one knew about the decanter. Or what was really the purpose of the decanter. And when Darius became mortal again, he chose not to speak of it. Shortly after Antoine had brought Darius to Lyon to live out his final days, signs were seen, and pamphlets were distributed in underground bars that read:

BEWARE OF THE HOODED MAN.

That was all it said.

A small, black business card with bold, white block lettering was placed on every table with the same warning. The immortal community of Miami was getting the message. The materials were distributed to all the immortals who would venture out in the night, for weeks, if not months, until Darius was the subject of stories around bars and cocktail tables.

There was one table, a high-top cocktail table, not far from the service bar, where several sat, having a quiet conversation amidst the thumping music. The four huddled over the table, staring downwards into their drinks.

After the group sat in silence for some time, a pale-skinned woman, with voluminous red hair, spoke, as she looked around the table. "We all have to be wary of this decanter. Of this man. Darius was no accident. Why would he suddenly be selected for something like this?"

She looked over at her fellow immortals. One was an overweight, middle-aged man with an unshaved beard and a receding hairline. The other two were younger men, possibly in their middle twenties when transformed, a blonde to the left, and on the right, dark-haired and olive skinned.

The olive-skinned immortal looked up from his drink and spoke first. "Darius was out of control. He was on a rampage after Antoine brought him back. Perhaps that was why he was selected."

She immediately noticed his piercing blue eyes.

And then she looked down at her drink for a moment, and considered what he had said. After a short while had passed, she looked over at him. "Paul. Listen to me. This not one of those stories. Darius did not get selected because of his behavior. He acted normally for *Darius*." She looked around the table, at the blonde and the middle-aged man. "Do either of you remember when Antoine resurrected him? He opened a doorway. He called Asmodai. Ever since then Antoine has been running."

The table sat in silence for a few minutes.

Then the music in the bar stopped playing, and each of them looked up and over towards the bar. The bartender was still mixing drinks; the loud chatter of the clientele sounded indiscernible.

The front door swung open, and two men, dressed in flowing black trench coats entered without a word. They walked towards the center of the bar as the chatter died down.

The bartender stopped mixing drinks, and all eyes were focused on the two men, including Paul and his companions. The two men were tall – one perhaps six feet or more in height, light skinned, dark hair which flowed down each of their shoulders. One man had a small scar under his left eye, and before long, he spoke. But the one who spoke first was shorter, heavier, with silver, thinning hair.

"Good evening, everyone, I come to you from Rome. We have received some distressing calls from Miami at headquarters. We are aware of the situation and are dealing with it."

The bearded man snapped his head over towards Paul. "Is he talking about the hooded man? Who called Rome? Antoine did this?"

She shook her head, but Paul did not answer, simply shrugged his shoulders. Paul sipped his beer and his eyes remained focused on the two visitors from Rome.

The man standing in the middle of the bar continued. "Some of you know that there is a 'Hooded Man' who has been appearing to some of you and others in your bloodline. We have come here to address this issue and preserve our species."

The man continued as all eyes remained on him. He set a briefcase down on one of the cocktail tables as his fellow man sat in one of the chairs.

The bartender, a heavyset, muscular man, paused, holding his shaker above his shoulder, and looked straight at the man. "I lost my ancestry. Almost completely. We're almost wiped out." His eyes pierced the room.

The man turned to the bartender and held his hands up. "I understand, sir, and my condolences."

He then looked around the room and continued. "All of you, I'm sure, are familiar with Delia Arnette. She flew to Rome last week and met with several of the members of the board. She is fully aware of this crisis. But for the time being, you must *all* be prudent in your self-preservation. If you see the 'Hooded Man' the main objective is to flee. Get away from him before he takes a grip over you. Do not make any attempts to speak to him. Do not attempt to fight him. Just leave. Quickly."

A tall, dark-skinned man stepped forward and set his beer glass down on one of the tables, and crossed his arms. "And what are we supposed to do if he spots us? Word on the street is that once he sees you, it's too late. Like he puts you under a spell or something."

The heavy man nodded, and smoothed his silver, thinning hair. "Yes, yes that is the commonly held belief. You are responsible for leaving before he can cast his spell." He then turned back towards the crowd. "And I have no reason to believe that it's a misconception. You all are responsible for your own survival. My mission here is to put an end to this. But in the meantime, you must heed my warning. Do not let this man spot you. If he does, it may already be too late."

Paul and the woman looked at the man, who paused for a moment, and was looking around the room. The crowd remained motionless. The man then looked over to where Paul, the woman, and the red haired immortal were sitting. He walked over to their table and looked directly at Paul. "I recognize you, don't I?" He leaned down closer. "You have been here with Antoine, correct? Correct me if I'm wrong, please. But he had mentioned a woman and three men under his tutelage. Am I right?"

The woman looked downward as Paul looked the man directly in the eye and answered him. "We work for Antoine, yes."

The man shoved his hands into his pockets, looked up at the ceiling for a moment, and then back over at Paul. "Who has been calling Rome? I was sent here because of your calls."

The four looked up and over at each other, but no one spoke until Paul stammered and shrugged his shoulders. "We are dying. We need help."

"So you called?"

Paul shook his head.

"Antoine called then?"

"No," Paul said. "As far as I'm aware, Antoine has been in France for the past several months, since Darius died. We have not seen or heard from him."

The man nodded. "I see." And then he stood again, and looked around the room. "All of you here need to be aware of this situation if it hasn't affected your bloodlines yet. We all know about Darius, and the rumors surrounding his demise and death." The man looked over at Paul and the group and raised his eyebrows. "We do, right?"

They smiled and nodded, and returned to the center of the room.

The man continued as he looked around the room. All eyes were focused on him. "There is a 'Hooded Man', as I said. There are rumors that he is approaching those immortals who are near death, who may have lost their way, or lost the gift, I don't know. But these are rumors." He looked around the room. "They are just rumors. They never happened."

A petite woman stood in the center of the room, slammed her glass down on the nearest table, and placed her hands on her hips. "Rumors? You just warned us. Is this man a rumor or not?"

The room erupted in chatter.

The heavyset man raised his hands up, as the other, younger man stood aside and looked on with his hands clasped at his waist. The heavyset man continued. "Please, please everyone. Quiet please! I am addressing these rumors with you, and I called this gathering as we all know very well where we stand right now after the events in Miami. I will not have this sector's reputation tarnished any further than it already has been. As far as anyone outside our sect is concerned, these are just rumors. But my warning directly to you all is this – take this threat seriously. I do not know enough about this 'Hooded Man' to give you anything but a warning. And I'll say it again – you are all responsible for your own survival."

Paul started to raise his hand, his index finger raised. "Forgive me…we know you are from Headquarters. But you haven't introduced yourself." Paul nodded around the room. "And I know many of our other followers here, I'm sure, have questions too."

The heavyset man nodded and stood, and looked around the room as he spoke. "Yes, everyone. We are from an organization called 'The Inspiriti'. Perhaps you have heard of us. I am here from Rome, as I said. Not all of you, especially the newly transformed, will remember our organization. But we were formed over a hundred years ago, and your founder, Delia Arnette, has currently returned to this area. She has been here for a few years now, and she has been addressing the rumors behind Darius' death. What you may not know, is that she is also a member of the High Council. And we are in town now investigating this matter."

The room erupted in chatter as the heavyset man raised his hands. The talking died down. "I am Monsignor Harrison. Next to me, here, is my assistant, Ramiel. We are both members of the High Council in Vatican City."

Paul and the two others looked at each other. "I have seen him before," she said, taking a sip of her wine. "There is something about this man Ramiel. Is he Italian?"

Paul looked down at his beer. "Whatever his ancestry, he is immortal. Could they be demons? Or are they angels?" Paul looked up and over at the two men. He couldn't make out what they were saying. But in his mind, he replayed the scene when he and Ramiel first met, over and over again.

And he saw Ramiel looking over at him. He could feel the heat of breath, the pierce of his eyes. Such a profound stare.

He thought he knew the man from somewhere.

And then it took him back to his days in Rome, when he had spent time on holiday, for a few weeks, decades ago; Ramiel's face appeared in his thoughts. He was still the same Ramiel he had been so long ago. His smile was still warm, his teeth still gleaming white with perfection, his hair was still slicked back with small tufts at the collar.

When the Monsignor finished his speech, Paul looked over towards Ramiel, and tried to get his attention. But he dared not call out his name. The Monsignor and Ramiel were moving their bags, placing them on a long table that one of the barstaff brought to them, and unpacking manila envelope packets, spreading the contents on the table. Paul continued watching Ramiel; watching him remove his jacket, smile and interact with the fellow immortals. Paul sipped on his lager and watched.

He remembered now.

It was the same Ramiel at the lounge in Rome.

He saw the same smile then, as Ramiel had sat at the bar, laughing and drinking a glass of red wine, chatting with the bartender. And in a fleeting moment, Ramiel had set his wine down and looked in Paul's direction, as Paul stood at the bar patiently waiting for a drink.

Paul remembered Ramiel's astonishing blue eyes. So rare for someone with such dark hair. But Paul remembered how striking it had been.

But it wasn't just in the immortal community in Miami that the rumors were spreading. Cities across the world were buzzing with activity after the sun crossed the horizon. There was a society of Immortals in Rome that initially made a call to Miami, once they learned that Darius had been stripped of his immortality.

THREE

Delia Arnette pulled her tiny BMW coupe into the parking lot at The Cathedral of the Gardens the following Sunday morning after she, Antoine, Darius and Ethan had met for lunch and discussed their concerns regarding the 'Hooded Man.' She swung her silver sedan into a small parking space, and then checked her appearance in the rear-view mirror. The lines around her eyes were pronounced; and her silver-grey hair was stringy with the humidity. She looked far beyond her age, but death would never come to her, unless the 'Hooded Man' came for her.

She shivered and shut the door.

Balancing on her cane, she headed across the parking lot in the relentless tropical sun. She looked up and saw the tired, old priest holding the giant wooden door open at the top of the stairs, waving to her with earnest.

Father Bauman had been a priest at *The Cathedral of the Gardens* for well over a decade.

In the span of that decade, he built relationships with a great deal of the parishioners. He formed a bond with each and every one of them that returned to hear his sermon each Sunday morning; he married their sons and daughters, he visited the hospital when family members would fall ill, and he presided over their funerals and burials.

It was after the conclusion of Mass one particular Sunday, over a decade ago, that Father Bauman met a certain individual – one man who would figure into his life with much significance, become a close friend, like a brother. And that was how Father Bauman chose to remember him, despite how his final days progressed.

Father Bauman stood outside the Cathedral's side entrance with the small, grey haired woman, and fished a cigarette out of the soft pack in his breast pocket. "Buried good ol' George in this cemetery right beside the church," he said, with the flick of his lighter. The wind blew the lighter out after an instant. "Damn. But yes, he went down a slippery slope after his lost Gaye. His house was raided. Spent time in prison."

"Those four missing young men?"

Father Bauman nodded. "He was arrested and questioned. They kept him all night. Till the sun came up. And then they sent him back to a holding cell to get some sleep. Plus I think the Detective needed a rest too. But just a few hours later, they found him hanging on a noose he made from his bed sheets."

Delia nodded. "I remember the news stories."

He took a deep drag on his cigarette, and he ushered the woman over to the rusted iron-gate. He held his arm outwards towards the cemetery, holding the cigarette between his pursed lips, and let the woman through. "What did you say your name was again? I'm sorry, ma'am, I'm just not the spring chicken I used to be. My memory escapes me quite often."

"Delia." She extended her hand. "Delia Arnette."

"And who do you represent?"

She reached into her purse, looked downwards as she rummaged through its contents, and back up at Father Bauman, and down again. "I know my card is in here somewhere..."

Father Bauman shoved his right hand into his pants pocket and used his left hand to draw on his cigarette. Delia handed him a business card as he below out a cloud of smoke. He took the card from her and examined it, turning it over a few times, looking at the front and the back. "Says here you are the founder?"

She nodded.

"Founder of what?"

She took a breath as she spoke, and looked upwards at him directly. "We are a group – an organization, rather – that is in place to govern the society of immortals on the earth. We have been in place for many years, Father Bauman. Backed by the church, actually."

"By the church? Are you sure about that?"

She nodded as they walked into the cemetery. Father Bauman continued dragging on his cigarette, holding it close to his lips as he spoke. Delia looked upwards and over at him repeatedly, and nodded as she listened to him.

"I am quite sure, Father. We have many members who are also members of the church. Not all immortals are evil, Father."

He paused for a moment and looked upwards at the sky. "You have good monsters?"

Delia scoffed and then smiled. "We are not all monsters, Father. We have many, in fact very many very good members of our society. There are immortals on this earth who are in place on a mission. Some of them are angels. Others are vampires, and some are demons. But not all are evil."

"And you said you governed immortals?"

She nodded. "Yes. All immortals, good and evil. We are a representative of their best interests."

The tired looking priest flicked his cigarette into the grass as a stream of smoke flowed upwards through the blades up towards the sky. "Damn thing won't go out." He stepped forward and stamped his foot on it. He continued speaking as he walked back towards Delia, who was standing next to a large grave maker, taller than she was. "What I don't understand is why the immortals need this representation. Especially the demons. They are pure, insidious evil. Exorcists have died trying to rid people of demonic possession. Why, in all of heaven, would you try to protect them?"

She walked closer to Father Bauman and smiled. She looked like a sweet old lady. Her hair was somewhat mussed, but tied back in a neat bun. She appeared to be at least eighty years old; the wrinkles along her cheeks and around her eyes signified wisdom and experience, and her warm smile was accentuated by brilliant red lipstick. Father Bauman thought she might have been someone who had tried to hold on to her youth for many years after she had lost it. "Because I am one of them," she said, placing her arm on his, touching his forearm with the soft, gentle touch that only an old woman could do. "I am weak, Father. I am old. But only in appearance. Only physically. I am immortal, and I won't die. But I can assure you…when I became old, I was quite young."

Father Bauman found a bench and sat. Delia sat next to him, never taking her gaze off the priest. Father Bauman looked down at the gravel path that they had been walking on, and shook his head. "I'm afraid I don't follow. When you became old, you were quite young?"

She nodded. "Yes. I am an immortal, Father Bauman. And before that, I was mortal. I was a human just like you are. And I was chosen for this. I was found by the one who made me, gave me this gift – or this curse, however one chooses to receive it – and I was young. A young woman in her early twenties."

"And when was this?"

"The late nineteenth century, when I was living in Paris."

Father Bauman shook his head, and looked over at Delia, who was sitting on the bench, looking downwards at her lap. Her tiny hands were clasped together, fidgeting. She closed her eyes for a moment, and then looked over at the priest. Her eyes were wide and pleading. "We need your help, Father Bauman. We need you to go to the church. We need help. We are dying, Father."

He paused for a moment, his face shifted and he cocked his head to the side. He closed his eyes for a moment, opened them back up, and saw Delia's eyes were still wide, her face shifted in a look of concern. "And so you come to the church for an absolution? For forgiveness for your evil doing? Just accept the Lord and Savior as your Christ and you will be granted forgiveness, my child."

Delia closed her eyes and shook her head, looking downwards. She then looked back up at him. "Father, many of our kind are dying. There is a man – I don't really know if he is a man or a monster – but he is going after immortals, both good and evil. They are losing their gift of immortality and dying a quick and final death. On to damnation."

Father Bauman sighed, and looked over at the troubled old woman. "What is happening to them, Delia?"

She sniffled, wiped her eyes with her sleeve, and stared out at the cemetery as she spoke. "There's talk of a man. A monster in a hood and robe. Someone who is making themselves out to be a savior. But he's not, Father. He's not."

"The teachings say that there will be many imposters. What is he doing to the immortals?"

"He comes at the point where the astral plane – the dimension where the spirits live – and reality as you and I know it – meet. It's a very chaotic place, Father. A horrendous gateway, where evil runs rampant and good is fleeting. When the sun sets, a green mist moves through the city to cleanse it for the next day. People typically drop dead. And monsters are unleashed. And these horrid, disgusting worms that devour everything."

Father Bauman's face shifted. "I am not liking the sound of this. Is your organization satanic? Devil-worshipping?"

She shook her head and looked back down at her lap.

"Witchcraft?"

"No, Father Bauman. We are not witches."

She looked over at the priest directly in his eyes. "Certainly you know about the supernatural, right? You are a priest. You should be more open to these things than the average person. Am I right?"

Father Bauman nodded. "I have performed the rite of exorcism, Ms. Arnette. I know very much about the presence of evil. So what is this 'Hooded Man' doing?"

Her eyes lit up and she smiled. "You see it! I knew you understood. That's exactly what we all have been calling him! So you do understand our kind. I knew I went to the right person."

Father Bauman smiled. "I am calling him the 'Hooded Man' because that's how you referred to him. Tell me more."

"This 'Hooded Man' lures immortals to drink from a decanter, a decanter filled with blood that he claims is from Christ, which will redeem them and bring them eternal life. But he is an imposter. The decanter is not from God and does not bring life. It brings a swift and final death. Damnation."

Father Bauman watched Delia wipe a tear from her cheek. Her running mascara created a dirty patchwork over her wrinkles. He searched for a tissue in his pocket and handed it to her. "There will be many false prophets," he said. *"Thou shalt have no other gods except Me."*

Delia nodded and took the tissue, and blotted her cheek and wiped her eyes. "We are being wiped out. Exterminated."

Father Bauman sat back on the bench. "I don't understand. If they are immortal, why would they need to drink from the decanter? They already have eternal life."

Delia looked over at the priest as she dabbed on her nose. "He targets broken immortals. Those who have either lost their immortality for some reason. Or those who are questioning their purpose. He places them under a spell of some sort. It's like they see the decanter, and all they want to do is to drink from it. Nothing else matters."

"Broken immortals? Questioning their purpose?"

She shrugged. "We have problems just like you humans. Just because we are immortal, or demons, or vampires, or what have you, doesn't mean we are perfect. And it's a common problem – especially among those who have not been immortal for very long – to question their purpose. And we can be destroyed, Father. There are ways. And this 'Hooded Man' has found a way, and a motive, to exterminate us."

Father Bauman nodded. "And you came to me. What makes you think that I am an expert in these matters? I have experience with the occult, as I said, but this is sounding otherworldly."

"I came to you because of Darius," she said. "He spoke about you quite often."

The priest's face lit up. His eyes widened and he smiled. "I have not seen him for so long. How is he?"

Delia looked down at her lap, and her lips started to quiver. Her voice shook when she spoke. "I'm afraid he is gone. Very recently, too."

His mouth dropped open and his eyes squinted. "Oh Delia, I had no idea! When did this happen?"

She looked up and out at the cemetery again, and there was a long pause. She closed her eyes, looked back down at her lap, her small hands holding the crumpled tissue between her legs. "You see, Father? This is why I need you. The one you call the 'Hooded Man' got to Darius. I have reason to believe he drank from the decanter. He was lured by this imposter and now he is gone."

"Oh Delia, I am so sorry. I had no idea."

She nodded.

Father Bauman shifted and sat up straight, placing his arm around Delia's back. He looked down at her, like a loving father. "How can I help you, dear child?"

Across the ocean in Lyon, night was falling.

The treetops blew in a light, passing wind, as the temperature dropped to a chilling cold. Antoine rubbed his arms, shivering, and waiting for the sun to completely set before beginning his task.

After a short while, it was time.

Shrouded in darkness, Antoine was able to enter the woods and drag the casket towards the center of the cemetery, where he had prepared the grave.

Darius, I am burying you with the same diligence and reverence that I did so many centuries ago, when I had first put you into the ground. So long ago, after that night in the foyer, when I plunged the dagger into your chest.

Now it is so different.

Tonight seems so prophetic; it is igniting memories which are centuries old. Like a candle which the wax has dripped down the sides, spilling out and over the candle holder until the candle itself is merely a small stub. The candle has been lit once again. How long will it burn?

He paused for a moment as he felt a cool breeze. He looked over toward the swaying treetops, and peered into the forest for a few minutes.

I am burying a human, mortal body.

It's so different.

Before, you were ash. You were a beating heart. Now, you are a full, human body, already in a state of decomposition and decay.

I am so confused. So perplexed as to how I can bring you back. Or even if I can at all.

Antoine pushed the casket into the ground, and it tumbled into the grave with a thud. He stood above the threshold of the earth, looking downwards, his face sullen, his eyes looking downwards. "I will miss you my Darius. You were my guiding light. Where has my light gone?"

Antoine looked around the cemetery, noticing the same soaring trees on the perimeter, the same small markers that rose from the ground from many centuries ago when he had first buried Darius in the same spot. It seemed that nothing had changed.

"Are we going through a cycle, Darius? A continuous cycle of change? Of death, and life and death again?"

Antoine gathered his equipment. His shovel and bag, and hoisted it over his shoulder. It was to be a very cold night. Record cold in Lyon for this time of year. There would be hot soup in the kitchen at the Chateau, Giovanni would see to that. But the Chateau…so big and quiet now. Darius was gone. The drapes and windows even seemed too large. The furniture, most definitely too much for one.

The sun set and ushered in the night.

The darkness shrouded Antoine, but, when he had finished with his homage to Darius, and the grave was filled and things were completed, he returned to the Chateau. Now it was time to wait. And shortly thereafter, to journey to the west, across the dark waters of the Atlantic, to the Americas, back to Delia and the city and region he once had been able to control.

But even later that evening, while sipping a glass of red wine and sitting in the front parlor, Antoine could not get the images of his death out of his mind. The bleeding altar, the flames which he still felt searing this skin. He could still smell the thick, noxious smoke.

He shuddered and set his wine down on the coffee table. He closed his eyes and lay his head back on the edge of the sofa. "Who is this man with this decanter?"

His question reverberated against the silence of the room. Giovanni had traveled to Paris last week to meet with a team of Doctors interested in repairing his eyesight, and Antoine had the Chateau all to himself, for several more days at a minimum. He got up and went to a large, full-length mirror and looked at himself.

He was not the same Antoine he had always been.

Once dressed in clean, neatly pressed dark suits, he now wore a tattered and stained white t-shirt and dusty jeans. His eyes looked puffy and tired. He leaned closer to the mirror, and opened his bloodshot eyes.

"Who is this man with the decanter? *Who is the hooded man?*"

He turned around and wandered across to the kitchen and started opening random cabinets, examining the dishes. And then he paused and looked around the kitchen, up at the hanging copper pots hanging from the soaring ceiling. The Chateau felt so big and lonely when he was there alone. And tonight, shrouded in darkness, and with Darius buried across the property on the other side of the forest, there were far too many ghosts.

THE HOODED MAN

The deeds of faithless men I hate; they will not cling to me.

Men of perverse heart shall be far from me;

I will have nothing to do with evil.

-   PSALM 101:3

ONE

In the beginning there was a great war between the angels and the demons.

It was a war that had waged and continued since before time had existed, and before man had walked the earth. But this war, this unholy and unearthly battle, this war during which beasts would draw flaming swords, and angels would chorus through the skies surrounded by legions of light and dive downwards to cast the demons away, was taking place through space and history and time, in a dimension that was very little known to those who did not live in it; this enduring battle would cause earthquakes and fires and explosions, but essentially was undetected by those whose perception did not create an awareness of the spiritual beings.

But the war did, at a certain time in a certain city on the earth, make its presence known with humanity. For the war was not always just that of the beasts, or the angels.

Others would join the battle.

There had been a point when the humans would come. They would stand on the edge of the angry sea, standing pale, naked, and staring straight ahead, with expressionless, blank stares, as if stripped of their life force.

And, in a sense they had been.

For the war was taking place in the place – or, as many have argued, in the space, or dimension outside of the reality that these humans had once been accustomed to.

There eventually were these humans which would involve themselves – the souls of the formerly living that would be cast into a dark, burning sea; in an ocean of sorrow, burning with flames of despair and torment.

There was much turmoil and a constant veil of sadness; there was an eternal fire that burned in the sea of souls; the flames covered the water and burned, seemingly without a source, but strong and commanding, a leash of insanity, pulling on the crying, filled with despair, sadness and loss.

In a sea filled with faces, desperate souls looking upwards with unseeing eyes, limbs reached upwards from icy waters in search of air, but finding none. Wide eyes saw nothing, bleeding ears heard nothing, and skin, which was pasty white and covered with ulcers, felt nothing.

The bodies did not feel the frigidness, nor the chill of the waters.

Their numbness was benign.

Their black fingertips, rotted with gangrene, some to the point where fingernails had fallen off and skin cracked and bled, did not feel the cold, nor the pain that would have normally been associated with failing skin.

The waters of the sea were always frigid, always writhing with bodies, always agitated and screaming.

And the war waged on, for what seemed like years, but there was no sense of time. There was no timekeeper in eternity; no hourglass with sand tipping from one globe to the other; no sun, no clocks or anything indicating that the war should stop.

Just a red sky painted with black clouds.

And on the shores of the sea, the rocks were assaulting, rising through the sands like pointed mountains, which dug into the unprotected feet of those who stood on the sand, waiting to be banished into the sea.

And it was the monstrous demon who stood on the edge of the shoreline that cast the evil sinners into the sea, to be swallowed by thrashing limbs and screaming. He held a pointed spire, shooting flames into the sky, a sky from which only drops of blood would fall.

"Do not pass here!" The demon raised a muscular arm, pointing his spire towards the sky. A small group of people huddled together on the beach, not far from the demon; they all looked in horror over towards the waterline, saw the angry sea and the white foam crests of the waves, revealing the thrashing limbs and arms climbing and grabbing and pulling.

But despite the order of Hades, despite the new arrivals at the shore of the sea that was very consistent and steady, the war waged on. And during that war, there was a focus, and that was on one particular demon.

It was a demon who looked that of a man who knelt on the shore, his head hung low, his arms in shackles. He was not monstrous, muscular nor did he have wings or horns.

He was a man who had long, dark hair, twisted locks that hung down from his shoulders. He was dragged from a group of towering rocks towards an altar in the center of the sea, which stood in the center of the waters upon giant boulders that rose upwards towards the swirling, angry clouds.

He was dragged along the sand by two muscular men, his feet bloodied, broken and limp. Upon his shoulders was the heavy, wooden top of the cross; about five feet long, tied to his arms – wrapped around the massive wooden tree with chains wrapped around his neck.

The beasts dragged him to the altar.

They walked on water as the man was not privy to floating on the surface; he could feel the limbs reaching for him, grabbing his legs, fighting to drag him under the water.

And then the largest of the beasts spoke.

He looked down at the man, watched as the two men strapped him to the altar, covered him with stones, and paused for a moment. "Do you have anything to say to me? Do you seek atonement?"

He opened his eyes and looked up at the demon. "You have forsaken me. I brought you into this world. I gave you the immortal gift. You would one cry on my shoulder, your face awash with tears. Why have you betrayed me?"

The beast leaned down, closer to the man's head, his face twisted. *Can you hear me? Can you hear my thoughts?*

The man looked up at the demon. "I know you are still in there, Roberto. You may be a shell of who you once were, but you are still in there. You still exist."

The demon looked at the man straight in his eyes. *Yes, Antoine, I am still here.*

I still exist.

Antoine struggled against the weight of the stones that the two worker demons were piling on top of him. But he did not break his gaze upwards towards the demon. "Why have you betrayed me, dear Roberto? Do you remember how we met? Do you remember?"

The demon did not respond – but instead was forced to remember.

There were thoughts that had originally permeated Antoine's mind. And Antoine, using his gift, was able to project his thoughts to the demon. The demon looked down at Antoine, as his gaze shifted, noticing the telepathic delivery to his mind.

And then, after a moment of convoluted noise, the demon closed his eyes and started to gain clarity. Images of a busy street at night, a street lined with pastel and stucco buildings that rose from sidewalks crowded with people, walking back and forth.

And then more images came to his mind.

There was the sweet smell of car exhaust; the squeak of car brakes. Occasional spotty laughter, doors opening, the chill of cooled air as it passed outwards in the stifling tropical heat.

It was summertime in Miami, one of the hottest times of the year, in the middle of the night, at which time the humidity became stifling, and the sweat would continue and worsen against his skin.

And then, he looked downwards at his hands, dirty, brown, the skin hardened calloused from work.

He opened his eyes.

And there was Antoine, who had been standing at the corner on the other side of the block. His gaze was fixated upon Antoine's tall, dark stature; his long, dark locks, and alluring eyes.

"Do you remember me, demon?"

But the demon did not answer. His eyes were shut and closed tight. There was not much that he remembered after that.

There were bits and pieces, tiny fragments that flowed into his mind like pieces of a puzzle. But the puzzle remained apart, and the bits did not fit together. Much darkness. Nor did they make any sense.

My mind is swimming in particles that don't make sense, Antoine. Why are you sending me this?

Antoine struggled with the weight of the stones around him. "Continue, keep your mind open."

The demon continued his vision.

It was after that night, after Roberto and Antoine had met for the first time and forged a relationship, that Roberto had any type of recollection.

Later on the same night after they had met, they had sat together in Antoine's front living room suite. Antoine had stoked the fire as Roberto sat back on the couch, and stared at the small stemmed glass. He studied the green liquid, his face grimaced. Antoine returned to the sofa and sat down. "Have you ever drank that before, Roberto?

The look on Roberto's face softened and he raised his head and looked up and over at Antoine. "What is this? Some sort of potion? Are you trying to put me under a spell?"

Antoine laughed, shook his head, stood, and walked over to the bar. "No, Roberto, no."

"You practice witchcraft?"

Antoine smiled and brought a small decanter over to the couch, containing what appeared to be more of the same cloudy, green liquid. "No, Roberto. I am not a witch."

Antoine placed the decanter on the coffee table and continued. "This is absinthe. It's not a potion, but a very potent liqueur. It is distilled from the wormwood tree."

Roberto picked up the glass and held it close to his eyes, examining the green, cloudy substance. "Wormwood you say? Never heard of the stuff."

"A taste similar to anise, to black licorice. Take a sip. Feel it on your lips. On your tongue. Let *La Fée Verte* grasp your soul and caress your heart…"

Roberto set the glass down. He looked up at Antoine, who had now sat down. "La what?"

"The legend of the Green Fairy," Antoine explained. "It goes back many years in the history of absinthe. The Green Fairy is said to live in the absinthe. She wants you. To possess you. But I will not let her…" He leaned over and put his arm around Roberto's shoulders. Roberto snapped his head over to find Antoine sitting right next to him. "You were just over on the other chair, right?"

Antoine smiled, and tugged at the side of Roberto's hair. He took a deep breath and held it for a moment, and then exhaled.

Roberto looked down at the small glass with the green liqueur. It sat directly in the center of the coffee table. "Do you remember why I spoke to you that night on Washington Avenue?"

Antoine looked over at Roberto and paused for a moment. He smiled as the fire popped. "Yes, I remember." Antoine stood, and walked over to the fire, grabbing the stoker. He poked at the logs as the embers brightened and tiny orange specks rose upwards into the chimney. "From what I recall," he continued, as he focused on the fire, "is that you were looking for drugs. A high, I would imagine. A trip? A journey without going anywhere?"

Roberto scoffed and shifted on the sofa. He shook his head and exhaled through pursed lips. "You really think it was that?"

Antoine nodded as he returned to the sofa. "Yes, Roberto, I do. Don't you think that I haven't completed my research?"

Roberto picked up the tiny, stemmed glass that was still sitting in the center of the coffee table. He held it up towards his nose and sniffed the glass, and recognized the harsh scent of alcohol. And then it brought him back. To the mornings when he would lie still in bed, waiting for the house to quiet.

For it was on those mornings that his father would wake early and make himself a morning cocktail. And many times, it was those mornings that his mother would lie in bed, crying softly, drawing the covers up over her head. He remembers those mornings, standing outside the master bedroom door, watching her sleep. Listening to him downstairs. Waiting for the sound of the garage door. And then, he would knock on the door.

That much he remembered.

Roberto sat forward on the couch, his eyes glazed over and staring straight ahead. Antoine sat opposite him, his elbows on his knees, looking over at Roberto, as he broke his trance and looked up at Antoine. "No, I don't remember. You didn't want to pick me up?"

Antoine shook his head.

"No," he said. He picked up his glass of absinthe, and lay the slotted spoon down on the table. "The sugar should be dissolved now. Take a sip."

Roberto brought the small glass to his lips, and could smell the heat of the alcohol as he brought it closer. He looked over at Antoine as he brought the edge to his lips, and tipped the green liquid towards his mouth…

…and then he doesn't remember if he fell asleep or passed out, but he remembered waking up.

And he remembered waking up in a long, earthen hallway, and he didn't remember emerging from the labyrinth.

And it was such the same sweet horror.

A ride down a dark highway with no destination. No vision. Just a vision of darkness, madness and regret.

For Roberto would always remember the little demons that would pry his mind open. The little monsters that lived inside his closet, preyed on the grey matter and caused his torment.

He remembered the silver coffin.

He remembered standing in a stone room, in a room with nothing else save a coffin on a stone slab in the center.

There were the flames, which burned underneath the floor...

...The demon opened his eyes and looked down at Antoine.

Yes, he remembered the orange glow around the perimeter of the room, emanating up from the floor. The flames. He still could see their reflection against the silver exterior of the casket. I am remembering everything, Antoine.

"Do you remember, Roberto? Do you remember what you did? What your life had become?"

And then the demon saw himself as Roberto, he saw himself opening his eyes, still sitting on Antoine's sofa. The green liquid had been drunk; a clock ticked in the background. His eyelids drooped, almost completely closed.

Antoine glided over to the couch and sat next to Roberto. He brought his hand to Roberto's cheek, touching it with the back of his hand with such softness and precision it would appear that he loved the young man; but it was still the first evening that he had known him. And then, he saw that Roberto's eyes had closed completely.

The effects of the absinthe had taken over completely, and Antoine then sat back, watched the young man, examining his eyelids, watching his eye movement underneath the thin layers of skin.

Antoine opened his eyes and looked up at the demon. "I remember the night with the absinthe."

Antoine stopped his projection, closed his eyes and pictured the night for himself. He traveled through the memory of his mind, and looked closely at Roberto, who lay back on the sofa, and was sleeping soundly. The fire crackled in the background, along with the dull, fleeting sound of thunder moving farther away. And the pelting of a soft falling rain on the windowpanes.

Antoine stood, but continued to fixate on Roberto. The handsome young man. So youthful; vibrant, muscular, tanned and athletic.

But Antoine's mind had been racing.

Racing with questions that could not be answered until the effects of the wormwood wore off, until Roberto awoke from his slumber. Until the demon interjected and tore him out of his memory.

What are you dreaming about?

And then Antoine closed his eyes. "I am remembering, demon. Remembering. That is what I am doing. Do you remember the night that I transformed you?"

The demon did not answer.

And Antoine saw himself standing in a long, dark earthen hallway. He looked down at his hands, and at close examination, he could tell they were not his.

He could feel the rough skin on the palms of his hands. Had his skin been that rough when he had been a mortal? He tried to remember. But he could not.

And then he saw the same moss-covered walls, and the same doors that Roberto had entered; the same silver casket and orange flames. For he knew that Roberto would be scouring a sullen past, dreaming the nightmare that he was always destined to experience.

But it had been for the wrong reasons.

And Antoine looked down at Roberto, sleeping on the couch. He picked up the glasses and brought them back to the bar, and placed the decanter of Absinthe in a cabinet and locked it, placing the key in his pocket.

"Sleep now, my dear Roberto. Sleep and relinquish your demons."

And then Antoine opened his eyes, he saw Roberto – the vision of the masculinity that he had remembered so fondly; the image of the man hovered above him, surrounded by an angry, red sky.

Roberto stood above him, looking down on him, the same olive complexion, the same muscular arms, the same smile and the familiar feeling swept over him as he leaned down, closer to where Antoine lay.

As Roberto got closer to Antoine's face, there was a veil of uncertainty, where the vision became blurred Roberto seemed to fade away, and transform back into the demon.

And then the demon drew his arm down, after the cairn of stones had been built over Antoine's body, and the demon's hand caressed Antoine's face. Antoine could smell the noxious gas emanating from his mouth as the demon drew his lips close. *You didn't ever really love me.*

Antoine made an attempt at eye contact, but his irises burned. After a few minutes, the demon looked down at him. Antoine looked up and spoke to the demon once again: "Did you know what I was trying to do for you, Roberto? Did you understand? Were you wise enough, and capable of understanding? What Hernan did to you and your mother? What type of life that you were leading? What I took you out of?"

The demon leaned forward, close to Antoine's ear, he could hear the grunts and a deep throated voice. *Yes, I remember…now do you?*

Antoine closed his eyes and saw the entryway to his estate. The large, double mahogany doors, the soaring columns, the ornate black steel and glass Gaslamp above the doors hanging from a network of matching black chains. It was just as he had remembered it. And then he saw himself standing outside the door on the expansive front porch; the lights were burning insides, but the shears were closed.

He saw movement.

A shadow…a man. Yes, the figure moving about on the inside was a man.

And then the door opened.

He sighed as the door opened, revealing Roberto, his young Latino conquest; shirtless and muscular, wearing a pair of grey sweatpants. Sweat dripped down the center of his chest and glistened in the evening light. "Antoine I was waiting for you…" And then Roberto's face shifted and he stepped forward, reaching out to touch Antoine. He reached up and caressed Antoine's cheek. "Are you alright? Why are you so silent? What has happened?"

But Antoine was far from alright on that particular evening. And Antoine sensed that Roberto could sense it, for Roberto instantly transformed into a caregiver, putting his arms around Antoine, ushering him deeper into the house, taking his bag and placing it on the side bench.

Antoine knew he could not control his emotions. His voice quivered when he spoke. "Darius came to see me this evening. He said he saw a man in a dark robe over on Alton. Near the park. A faceless man with a hood covering his head. A real dark figure. A silhouette of a man. Lived in the shadows." Antoine paused in front of the foyer mirror. He stared at himself, as the light from the chandelier made his hair appear lighter.

There was a distinct difference in Antoine's appearance. Once confident and proud, he now had tired eyes. He was not aging, he still possessed his gift, but he felt as though some part of him, deep inside, was no longer alive. The part where Darius resided. He examined his complexion with wide, concerned eyes, and a tired, haggard face.

Roberto moved behind him and removed his coat. "Let's take you inside. And you can tell me all about it."

Roberto ushered Antoine in and put his arm around his shoulders. Antoine couldn't help but notice the heat emanating from Roberto's body, and the feel of the roping muscle in his arms pressing against his back and shoulders. But he brushed the feelings off and continued sniffling as they walked together, arm in arm, towards the kitchen.

"Why are you so upset?" Roberto asked. "Is there some sort of prophecy surrounding this man?"

Antoine closed his eyes for a moment. "Darius had been doing his usual…routine. Which is not unusual for Darius, at least. He is so enamored with the bloodlust. That young man didn't have a chance, from what he told me. He even killed a couple of cops that came by to investigate the disturbance."

"What happened after he killed them?" Roberto sat Antoine down at the table, and walked to the adjoining room to retrieve a fleece blanket. He wrapped it around Antoine and went over to the cabinets and fished two porcelain mugs out and placed them on the counter. "This 'Hooded Man' you spoke of? Where does he figure in to all of this?" Antoine looked over towards the kitchen prep area, where Roberto stood, looking over at Antoine. Roberto raised his eyebrows. "Well?"

Antoine rubbed his eyes as Roberto shook his head and filled a pewter pot with water from the faucet and placed it on the stove. Roberto returned to the table and grabbed a white t-shirt that was lying on the counter opposite the cooking area, and pulled it over his head. Antoine stared at him the entire time, watching the muscles in his arms flex as he pulled the shirt down over his torso. And then Antoine looked at Roberto, directly into his eyes, once the young man took a seat on the other side of the table. "So are you going to tell me? What's all this talk about this guy in the hood?"

Antoine shook his head. "You don't understand, Roberto. What we found out today – from what happened to Darius – is that we are being hunted. This man in the robe is not a friend. He's a warrior. And I don't know who sent him. But he's coming after us."

Roberto leaned forward. "Us? Me and you?"

"Immortals, Roberto." Antoine's voice had an edge to it. "Do you remember the night in your bedroom? When your father walked in on us? That was not a random night that we spent together. It's who we are Roberto. We are immortal. And this man...or demon...or angel...I don't know what he is...this man has some vendetta it seems. But whether or not he does, his purpose is unclear." Antoine lowered his head into his hands.

"So we don't know his purpose, and he apparently has no motive."

"Other than to exterminate us." Antoine looked up. Roberto was fidgeting and drumming his fingers on the table. "Why are you so nervous?"

Roberto leaned back in his chair and looked over at Antoine. "I just don't understand this."

Antoine lowered his eyes. "There is nothing to not understand, Roberto. But let me start from the beginning. This man – this dark figure – has been appearing to immortals around the globe. But now, currently, he has been rumored to be appearing to those of us around Miami quite frequently. And he is said to put us under a spell, or an incantation of some sorts, and has us drink some sort of a potion."

The teapot wailed on the stove, and Roberto went over to prepare their tea. As he was dipping the teabags into the steaming water, he shook his head and sighed. "You know Antoine…" And then he paused, his face shifted, and he continued dipping the teabags into the water, looking downwards.

Antoine raised his head and looked over towards Roberto. "What is it, Roberto?"

Roberto stopped steeping the tea. He flung the used bags into the sink and raised his eyebrows. "I really wish you would give me a little more credit. You always speak to me like I am a child. Like I have no idea what's going on. You're always explaining things to me."

Antoine leaned back in his chair. "I don't…"

"You do. You just did. I know that we are immortal. I know that. And yes, I haven't forgotten the night you transformed me in my father's house. It all plays very vividly in my mind. But when are you going to start treating me like an equal?"

"You've got to be kidding me. We are going down this path again?"

Roberto sighed and carried the two cups of tea over to the table. He placed one in front of Antoine and took the other to his chair and placed it on the table. He sat, placed his elbows on the table, and cradled his chin in his hands and looked over at Antoine, eyes wide open. The two sat in silence for a few moments, before Roberto scoffed and flung his arms outwards. "Yes, we are going down this path. Again."

Antoine focused on the demon as he felt the heat of a flaming torch next to him. And then there was a moment, one very precise point in time, where Antoine no longer felt the heat of the flames. He was no longer overpowered by the smoke. Had the sky been clearing?

He looked upwards. The clouds were parting but the sky remained red. He rose from the altar with ease; feeling light and bodiless, he turned and looked down at the altar.

Ashes.

That is all that remained. The embers still burned, some red hot and orange, amidst a sea of ashes, the greyish, dark dust from whence we came, and to which we shall all return.

TWO

The man named George Stanley, the one who received a message, which came to him, in the back of his mind, and spoke to him, was so often waiting for the deliverer of the message to show himself.

Or herself.

He never even acknowledged the voice. At least, that's what he thought.

For years.

But it was the voice that caused his downward spiral, and he never really understood its purpose. It was the voice that had an essence of power in his daily actions; it was the voice that talked to him, very softly, in the snippets between waking and sleeping, those small tears in time…buried deep in his subconscious mind which was inaccessible in his everyday waking life.

George never blamed the voice when he was arrested and questioned – for he didn't know, at that point, that the voice even existed. And if he had, he wouldn't have understood its purpose. For the voice, over the years, changed it message, but one thing always remained the same: the voice had chosen him.

It started as a small voice in his head, as his wife, Gaye, lay in the back room dying of a virulent cancer that ate her alive from the inside out. As he would sit in the driveway, downing another can of beer, he would still hear the voice in his head. As he sat and watched Neil. The glistening sweat. The roping muscles in his back, flexing as he restarted the mower after it died.

And George would always reach for another beer from the small igloo, repeating the same ritual each and every time that Neil mowed the lawn across the street. And there were the days that Neil sat with George, sharing a beer, and, many days, George would watch Neil as he would walk across the street, shirtless and glistening with sweat.

There were days that Neil knew that he was being watched; George could tell, because George, plopped in a lounge chair in the center of his driveway, sitting next to a cooler of beer on ice, had no particular reason for sitting there other than to watch Neil.

And on one particular Saturday, as he sat with his small, Styrofoam cooler of canned beer on ice, he reached inside the cooler, popped another can of beer with a hiss, and shoved it into his huggie. He then leaned over the side of the lawn chair – almost toppling over onto the pavement – and grabbed the bag of half-melted ice and poured the remaining cubes into the cooler, slammed the lid back on, and flopped against the back of the chair, exhaling deeply.

There were once crisp and sharp lines; now everything was blurred and starting to spin. But when he looked across the street, he was still able to focus on Neil, despite his drunkenness. "Hey Neil!"

The young man stopped fiddling with his mower and turned towards the man.

"Hi Mr. Stanley!" He waved and called over to his neighbor, returning to the task of putting oil in his lawnmower.

"Why don't you come on over here, Neil?"

But Neil didn't come across the street – at least not that particular day. Later that day, when coming to, George didn't even remember calling out to the young man. For his eyes closed moments after calling out to Neil, as drool spilled out the side of his mouth.

George could still smell the chicken boiling in the kitchen. There was a certain welcoming scent that permeated his nose, as he dropped his backpack on the foyer floor. "Mom? I'm home!"

But the house remained silent.

He followed the scent of the boiling chicken. It was calling him to the kitchen. He could still hear the television in the other room, with some afternoon talk show on, and when he entered the kitchen, he could hear the boiling of the water. The pot was at a rapid boil; drops of water spilled out over the pot and sizzled on the stove, as a copious steam cloud billowed towards the ceiling. He raced to the stove and turned down the heat. "Mom? Are you here?"

His footsteps sounded foreign as he walked to the other end of the kitchen. There was an unfinished crossword puzzle on the long, wooden table, and mom's purse was on the accompanying bench. George looked back up and into the family room. He could see the glow from the television against the dark carpet, and reflecting on the pictures on the walls. But mom was nowhere to be found.

He walked into the living room and flipped off the television. And then the house was in a veil of silence; for when he called out, now a third time, his voice truly reverberated against the silence.

It wasn't until later, in the hours following his arrival home, when he would lay on his bed in the fading daylight, as the chicken spoiled in the cooling water on the stove, ever so slowly as the toxic film formed on the surface of the water, he lay in his bed, unable to close his eyes, staring upwards towards the window, unaware of the passing time save the setting sun.

And then he heard the garage door open, a faint rumble from across the house, and then there was darkness. But first, a brilliant, white light blinded him, as he covered his eyes with this hands. And then, when the light faded, he stood in darkness. He could still feel the hardwood floor beneath his feet, and sensed that he was still in his house – at least somewhat – but there was a changed sense. A sense of crossing over.

His eyes adjusted to the shadows. The table was still there in front of him. But covered in moss and dirt, and overgrown shrubbery. Out towards the back TV room, an earthen floor led to thick oak trees, with bent trunks, fingering their way across the moss and bushes, forming a wooden furniture set dotted with green leaves.

He took a few steps closer to the TV room. "Hello?" His voice sounded shrill and lonely against the silence of this strange forest. Through the darkness, he saw a small beacon of light, a tiny white light, which grew larger, ever so slowly, and as it grew larger, it seemed to pulsate. But as the light got closer, he saw a flowing, white gown, blowing in an unseen wind. A woman approaching him, with long flowing hair.

It was mother.

George tried to run, but his feet would not move. His mother floated closer, and he could recognize her long, flowing brunette hair. She had the same brilliant red lipstick that she always wore. He looked up at her as she stopped just short of where George was standing, and levitated above the ground. She looked down at him and smiled. "George, do you know what your destiny is? Do you know what you have been chosen to do?"

He shook his head.

"You have been chosen, dear George. My sweet little boy. My sweet little angel. You have been chosen to be the one. You will have so much power."

"What have I been chosen to do?"

She drifted downwards, as her long, flowing white skirt billowed out, and looked him directly in the eyes. Her face seemed to brighten. "You will bring salvation to the damned."

George took a step back and shook his head. "I don't know what that means, mother. The damned? Who are damned?"

She held her arms out, and George leaned over and rested his head in the crook of her arm. It was the same warmth and softness that he always remembered. "My dear, dear sweet George. You always come home, always come looking for me. But I am never there. Do you remember the day that you came home and I wasn't there?"

George craned his neck and looked up at her. She looked down at him and smiled. "Yes I do," he said. "Yes. I remember the day. You left chicken boiling on the stove and I couldn't find you."

She nodded. "Yes. Yes. But I was upstairs in the bathroom. Did you search there?"

George shook his head.

"You should look there. And then, when you find me, you will understand why you are seeing me here. And why I am delivering this message to you."

George closed his eyes for a moment, and when he woke up, he was again alone in the darkness. The softness that he felt was simply a thick carpet of soft moss. He sat up and looked around. "Mother? Are you still here?"

But there was no answer.

I am upstairs in the bathroom...

His mother's words reverberated in his head, as he drew his knees close to his chest, he hung his head downwards and closed his eyes. But the soft moss wasn't soft moss in the least. The darkness, where it may have been somewhat sudden, was a strong presence in young George's life for several years, and when he had thought that he was standing in his kitchen on an afternoon after coming home from school, he was not.

For when he opened his eyes, he saw harsh overhead florescent lighting. The smiling face of Doctor Johnson. His same skinny glasses. He saw the same tiny nose hairs.

George looked around the room. He recognized his father standing in the doorway with several nurses in light blue scrubs. He was talking with the nurses and nodding, and turned his head to look over in George's direction every few moments. His father brushed the nurses away and rushed over to the bedside. He looked down at George and smiled. His hair was mussed and he had stubble on his face. His eyes looked tired. "George! You are awake!" He bent down and hugged his son.

George looked around the room. He saw the stark, lime-green walls, the television mounted on the wall towards the ceiling, the window that looked out towards the nurse's station. "Where is mom?"

George looked up at his father. He looked older than he had ever looked. The lines running down his cheeks looked more pronounced than ever before. "George, she's gone. That's why you're here." George watched his father look over towards the doctor.

"It's common for him to have some form of amnesia after a traumatic experience like this."

His father stood next to the bed and looked down at George. He leaned over the bed and bent down close to his son. "Do you remember anything?"

George closed his eyes for a moment. "I remember the smell of chicken…"

Father looked up and over at the doctor. The doctor looked up from a clipboard he was holding. "Memories will return, slowly, in time."

George snapped awake as he almost toppled out of his lawn chair. "What the fu – ?" The sun had long set, and he looked at his watch, noticed it was close to three a.m.

"Shit! Fuck!"

He ran inside the house, leaving the chair and cooler in the driveway. He struggled with the door handle – a normally quite simple task – and flung the door open and charged into the kitchen. "Gaye! Gaye, are you alright?!"

He ran through the kitchen and back down the hall towards the back bedroom. "Gaye! I'm sorry. I forgot! I was outside and lost track of time!"

He flung the bedroom door open and saw Gaye under the sheets. "Oh, please don't be dead. Please don't be dead. *Please don't be dead!*"

He ran to the bedside table to the pill reminder, and grabbed two small blue tablets. "Gaye!" He shook her motionless body. He shook her again. "Gaye! Wake up!"

After a few moments, she woke up and opened her eyes. She squinted. "What time is it?"

Relief washed over him as he held the blue pills down to her. "I am so sorry, Gaye. You have to take your medicine. I'm sorry I forgot. I'm late with it again."

With great effort, she sat up in bed on her elbows and took her pills. "You were with the neighbor boy again, weren't you?"

And George stood motionless, stunned at her revelation that she knew what he was up to. He turned, said nothing, and went to the master bathroom, and shielded his eyes when the bright lights came on. He turned the faucet and looked outwards into the bedroom. Gaye was shifting herself into a sitting position and reached over and snapped the bedside lamp on. George looked on from the bathroom.

"The neighbor boy? What are you talking about?" He looked back and forth – from his tired face in the mirror, increasingly concealed by the steam that formed on the mirror, to the bedroom – where he saw Gaye finally take her pills and drink a large glass of water.

"Yes," she said, shifting herself in the bed and wincing. "The neighbor boy. Neil, is it? I can't remember anymore. He's a little young for you, George."

He froze and looked in the mirror with wide eyes. Had she discovered what he was doing? With Neil and the others? How could that have been possible? She lies in bed all day and night for Christ fucking sake!

George turned towards the bedroom as Gaye tuned the lamp back off bathing the room in darkness. George could still see the outline of the billowing, white nightgown. He leaned against the door frame. "Young for me, Gaye? What are you talking about?"

"I'm just saying friends that are a generation – actually *two* generations apart are exceptionally rare."

"He's graduated college."

She shook her head as she burrowed down into her pillow. "I see you guys sitting in the driveway and drinking beer together. But what do you guys do when you come inside? I can hear the door opening, George. What's going on down in the basement? I listen to your footsteps going up and down the stairs too. I may be bed-ridden, but my eyes and ears work just fine."

George shook his head. "Gaye, he's just a friend. *A friend.* Yes, he's young enough to be my grandson. But we relate. I relate to him. I see myself in him."

And he closed the door to the bathroom.

His eyes had not quite adjusted from the darkness of the bedroom and that brilliant light was shining in his eyes again; he held up his arms to shield his eyes from the assault of the bright light. And he saw that same shining light when he was sitting in the questioning room at the police station, and he had held his arms up to shield his eyes in a similar fashion.

"The story of the *Four Hoodsmen* will have to wait."

George sat back in the cool, hard, steel chair.

The harsh light above him was making his forehead sweat. He was exhausted; all he wanted was a cool, comfortable bed, with a soft pillow, but here he was, sitting now in the fourth hour of questioning with Detective Jensen. The officer was scribbling notes in a file and on a yellow legal pad.

"Don't you see?" George slapped his hands on the table. Detective Jensen dropped his pen and leaned back in his chair with a smug look on his face. "We can sit here all night."

George shook his head, slammed his fists on the table and leaned forward, looking Detective Jensen directly in the eyes. "They will come for you, Detective! Don't think I don't know about the worms. The white worms. The white *fucking* worms! *The white worms are coming to eat you alive!*"

And then Detective Jensen stopped moving and looked back at George. "I never told anyone about that day."

George smiled and leaned back in his chair. "You mean the day you saw the worm crawl out of Claire's eye?"

Detective Jensen looked down and paged through George's file. "It says here you were hearing voices."

George leaned forward again. There was an edge to his voice. "You didn't answer my question, Detective. You saw the white worms, am I correct? Or am I not?"

Detective Jenson dropped the file and looked at George. "Yes. Yes, I saw a worm."

"And you know what they are supposed to do, right?"

George leaned back and laughed. "Do you think I know something about the worms? About what they do?" He shook his head. "I know nothing more of the worms other than what I've told you – and what she's told me about them. I know that they exist. That's the extent of it. What they do? What their purpose is? That she hasn't told me."

"Yet you knew I saw one? How evil are you, George?"

The bodies that lay on the sidewalks, in their piles of filth and varying stages of decomposition, were what he wanted. It

144

was the cadavers. It always had been. What looked like a cemetery of sorts on the sides of the streets; none embalmed, all dropped dead at the same time, at the same moment. And then, he stood, waiting to speak to them.

But he knew they would not speak.

In fact, the bodies were exactly what he wanted – an army of the undead, to do his evil bidding.

But an army of the undead required one small thing: renewed life. And, of course, he didn't have that. He didn't have what was required for eternal life; and for that, he had to create something. He had to create something – something that would serve as a beacon. Something that would call them out of their slumber. Something that would awaken them.

He had observed many of those who had survived the setting of the sun each evening; it was either those who were somehow lost, or perhaps had crossed over to a different state of existence, or others who were never lost but neither living. It was only one of the two. Either those who once had lived, or those who had not been living for a long while.

Other than that, all were simply dead.

Awaiting coffins, lying on the side of the street, as the sun rose and the darkness faded, he stood amongst the dead, rising from the fallen dead in a long, hooded robe, which reached downwards towards the sidewalk, and then the hooded man stopped, standing in front of a glass door; the glass was broken in the frame, the vertical blinds were hanging outwards onto the sidewalk, and catching the wind as the breeze would strengthen.

But not everyone remembers the hooded man.

He did not always appear at moments where the bodies would pile up on the sides of the streets; he did not always move through time and dimension to collect the corpses; no, it was never that. It never, never really was.

For the dreams were where he would usually live.

He would live on hardened beaches of rock and broken shells, under a red sky painted with black clouds, next to a still and silent ocean. Where the wind would blow, but so very faint, that the sweat would hardly dry on one's face. He was always there, in the middle of a different type of perception, but never in reality.

Until today.

When he stood, waiting to collect the bodies, waiting to wake them from their slumber, waiting to resurrect them from the dead.

For they would want to drink.

They would want to drink from the decanter…

…Anthony and Doug sat in an interior office in *The Astral.* As Anthony reached behind the desk, he pulled out two crystal glasses, and slapped them on the desk. He nodded and raised his eyebrows as Doug nodded.

"Ethan is the man who was lying on the sidewalk out there," Anthony said, as he fished a bottle of scotch from the lower desk drawer. "I just could have known that this 'Hooded Man' got to him."

The Cathedral of The Gardens was packed the morning of the four funerals.

People lines the sidewalks and up the sides of the steps to the Cathedral to get a glimpse of the caskets of the victims that had been plastered all over the local news stations in the preceding days. The sun shined brilliantly down from the sky as each casket was removed from a line of four black hearses, parked one by one, in a row in front of the front steps leading up to the Cathedral doors.

Father Bauman officiated over the funeral, and he stood at the top of the steps in white and black vestments as the caskets were carried up the stairs.

The entire event became somewhat of a spectacle for the city – the four young men who were to be remembered and buried that day had been featured on all of the local television news programs, and, were local celebrities upon their deaths.

Several news vans lined the streets in the shadows of the rising spires on the holy building, their rising antennae's creating shadows of their own on Andelusia Avenue in the midst of the rising, brilliant morning sun. A light rain started to fall from a cloudless sky, but as the service concluded, the clouds started to form and gather above, but copious rays of sun still managed to find their way to the pavement.

The doors to the Cathedral opened and two altar boys held the doors wide as the congregation filed out and lined the steps, leading downwards towards the hearses waiting on the side of the street. After a few minutes passed, a heavyset deacon in flowing, purple vestments, carried a crucifix on a long, steel pole, raising it upwards towards the sky, followed by Father Bauman. Behind him followed each silver casket, in close succession, carried by pallbearers in black suits, sunglasses and white gloves. The men raised the caskets up on their shoulders as they descended the steps, and stopped moving once they reached the hearses.

The deacon, altar boys, and priest followed, and stood on the sidewalk, as each hearse door was opened, the congregation bowed their heads as the priest raised his hands over towards the casket and spoke a final blessing. "Oh, Heavenly Father, guide these souls towards your reward." Father Bauman held a stainless steel thurible – a small handheld incense burner swung by a chain – in his right hand, as smoke billowed from the grooves on the side of the censer. The sweet smell of burning incense filled the air, and remained, as the air was windless that morning. He held the thurible upwards towards the sky, and swung it slowly back and forth, like a pendulum. "In the Name of the Father, and of the Son, and of the Holy Spirt, we commend their bodies to the earth." He walked towards the last casket in the procession. It was placed on a runner with wheels just behind the open rear door on the hearse. Father Bauman walked around the casket, swinging the thurible back and forth around the coffin, as smoke wafted from the tiny holes carved on the side of the steel incense burner. The two alter boys made the sign of the cross and they proceeded to each casket, until each coffin was placed in its hearse and the doors were closed.

Across the street, George watched from afar. There was a distinct feeling of grief that overcame him, as he watched the caskets being loaded. And when the hearses slowly pulled towards the street, he hung his head low.

But George knew that there wouldn't be granted the gift of freedom for much longer. It was only a matter of time. He knew. He watched enough crime shows on television. He left too much of a sloppy trail.

And as the hearses pulled away, and the crowd dispersed for the cemetery, he looked across the street. And he recognized the man who stood in a cheap shirt and tie, sipping on a cup of steaming coffee. And the man recognized him, for he waved at George, and smiled.

Detective Jensen.

George had fallen asleep in the squad car.

He had surrendered right in front of the Cathedral, without incident. As they drove him downtown, he had fitful dreams.

As the car pulled away, he lay his head back on the seat, and thought of earlier that morning, when the phone rang. He had been up late the previous night. His head throbbed, and his mouth was so dry it stuck together. He lay in bed, motionless, wishing the shrill pierce of the telephone ring would stop cutting into his morning sanctuary. And after a few minutes, it did. But as the road rumbled as the car picked up speed, it massaged his thoughts into a swirl of the subconscious.

And George drifted off to sleep –

He opened his eyes to darkness. He was no longer in the safety and confines of his room. He looked down, towards his hands, and held them in front of his face. He appeared to be glowing – as if there were a translucent luminescence. A feminine voice broke the silence.

"And there you are looking at your essence."

George looked in the direction of the voice, but saw nothing. "Where am I?"

"You are dreaming," the voice answered. "You are in the place beyond your physical reality…but not so far inwards as in another dimension. I have come here to speak to you and tell you what I need you to do for me."

"Do what for you?" George felt the spongy consistency under his feet, lifted his legs, and looked over and straight ahead. The darkness was lightening; and in that process, which revealed a barren sky with dark, swirling clouds, rising forests and thick moss and mud below his feet, he saw the source of the voice: her femininity was absolute; she didn't exist yet she did.

"She is gone, George. That ringing phone – means she's gone. You have no other choice but to come with me."

George had lay in his bed that morning that the phone rang, and when he opened his eyes, he saw her. The most beautiful woman he had laid his eyes on, for years. Supple, bright red lipstick accentuated her red hair. She walked around the bed as George looked up at her and followed her every move. "I know it's been a long time for you, George. I have been watching you for many years now."

George swallowed.

"Now that she is gone, you can stop resisting your urges. You can go and be *who you really are*."

George sat up as she sat on the edge of the bed near his feet and looked over at him. "Who am I?" George asked, rubbing his eyes and looking around the room.

"I have been speaking to you for years, George. Have you been listening to me?"

George nodded. "Yes, I have. I have heard you."

"And do you understand your feelings? What they could mean for you?"

George looked down and thought of the night before. The cooler was probably still in the driveway. "I...don't think I have the feelings that..." And then he closed his eyes. Neil was in front of him, tanned, toned and wearing a small muscle shirt. He smiled a brilliant, white smile, ran his hands through his full, stylish hair, and peeled his shirt off.

George opened his eyes.

"I can get them for you. To like you George. Like they never did in school. They will like you. You will be popular. You will always be the popular one. You'll never have to repress who you truly are ever again. All you have to do is follow me and do a task for me."

"What is that?" George asked. He looked over at Claret and she smiled.

"Come with me to your basement and I will show you."

THREE

"The life, the blood, it is the life." A small man paused for a moment before the stacks of books, holding a large book and reading aloud. He had the look like he was once "one of the chosen" – years earlier he had most certainly been a clean-cut, attractive young man – but was now one of the ones who had passed their prime, but remained fashionable, still were attractive enough to be sought after, had salt and pepper hair, and a general youthful and fit look nonetheless.

It was well into the evening, and the library was readying to close. He stood on his toes, leaning against the shelves, reaching upwards and stretching his arm, and his fingers upwards until he found it. "Ah ha!"

A somewhat younger woman raised her eyes and looked over towards him, over her glasses. She pushed the small laptop that she had been typing on over to the side. The man held the massive book in his arms. The book was so large that he seemed to struggle with it, but he managed to heave it over onto the table. "The blood is the life! Exactly!"

The woman sat back in her chair, folded her arms, and raised her eyebrows. "Yes, Hector?"

And then he closed his eyes.

He remembered the day when the sea went dry; when the sun went black, and the winds howled. He shivered and felt a chill pass through his body. "This book…this book reminds me of when I fought them. When he came."

And then she closed her laptop. "Hector, sweet Hector, please stop remembering. You are sweating! Put the book down. Do it now!"

He listened, and stepped back. The book lay on the table, as if taunting him. But the terror subsided. He looked down at the book and shook his head. "*Le Livre De Vampires*. Why does it taunt me so?"

"Don't open it," she warned. "Don't you open that book!"

Hector pulled a chair out and sat. He looked over at the woman, who returned a smile. She reached for her laptop and opened it once again. Hector noticed that despite her youth compared to his age, she most certainly appeared middle-aged, at the youngest. Her eyes, however, sparkled with youth. She seemed that she was still a young woman now trapped in an older body. She flipped her long, blonde hair back over her shoulder, and pulled the laptop closer to the edge of the table. "Thank you for meeting me, Hector. Now, I saw how you reacted to that book. That is why I wanted to have this discussion in the library. I wanted you to see the book. I wanted to see if we could review it and determine how accurate some of the passages are."

Hector leaned back in his chair as some of the overhead lights snapped off. "And you work for The Astral?"

"No, no I do not."

"Who sent you?"

The woman smiled and looked over at Hector. "Here's my card." She handed it to him and sat back as Hector examined it.

GERALDINE ALESHIRE

Founder

"Founder of what?" Hector asked.

Geraldine smiled, and began typing on her tiny laptop. "We are interested in you, Hector. We are interested in your unique perspective. In your survival."

"I don't understand, Geraldine. How long have you been in Berlin now?"

She stopped typing and looked up at Hector. "Long enough. It's not always going to be Rome, you know."

Hector paused and remembered the day that the altar burned. He remembered swimming upwards from the bottom of a dark sea, fighting upwards towards the surface through thrashing limbs, struggling for air. The days when he wished he could understand his purpose.

Geraldine placed her hand on his. "You moved past that, didn't you?"

Hector nodded. "I think so, I hope so. Those were such dark days."

Geraldine picked up the book, and set it down to the left of to her laptop. "So this book has had such a profound effect on you Hector, but we still must examine it. We still must. We must." She thumbed through some of the first pages, and stopped for a moment and ran her fingers along the gold edge trim of the paper. "And now first, I must know more about you, dear Hector. I don't know how so many years you have gone undetected. But you have. Where shall we begin?" She looked over at Hector, and straightened her glasses.

Hector sighed. "It's been so many years since I visited that dark place. I don't even know where to begin."

"When you received the gift once again?"

Hector looked around the library. "They are closing, Geraldine."

She shook her head. "Don't worry about that. Taken care of. Now please, begin, Hector. I am ready to take copious notes, and I am a fast typist. Please. Do begin."

Hector leaned back in the chairs and closed his eyes. He pictured the thrashing limbs again. The struggle to find the surface. The quest to breathe again.

And then, when he had surfaced, the air had been stagnant.

He remembered scanning the area, as he tread water in the middle of the sea, and all he saw was the dark, black water. He looked downwards, and saw the white skin of the bodies writing below the surface, hands reaching upwards but finding no relief.

And then he swam.

He sought a shore that seemed so far away; a great distance through treacherous waters, he struggled to swim.

Let me be your guiding light. When you struggle for the shore, when you swim through treacherous waters, I will guide you to land.

And then he looked upwards towards the sky, to the swirling, angry clouds. Had there been a face, looking down on him, through the clouds, watching him?

But back in the library, as Geraldine sat typing, the two sat in the post-closing darkness; the glow from her laptop screen illuminated her face in brilliant white, he paused for a moment and looked over at the book. "That book is pure evil," he said. "Why do you want me to continue?"

She stopped typing and looked up and over at Hector. "Because you must continue. You must tell me your story. You must tell me why the decanter was so special. Why the dead returned."

Hector looked down at the table.

The newspaper was spread open, and Geraldine pushed a photo towards him. Slowly, he looked at the photo, his eyes never leaving it.

Someone snapped a shot of the bodies. The photographer appeared to have been standing right before several of them, their bodies splayed on the sidewalk, limbs broken like rag dolls; their skin showing the bruising, discoloration, the pooling of blood beneath the skin and signs of rigor mortis.

How remembered how the dead walked towards the houses, to the cars, and sought the living. He closed his eyes and went back to the day that the sky rained the blood rain. He remembered standing in Ascension when the dead returned. He remembered it so very well, like it had just happened.

When the dead rose from their graves and walked the land once again, that was the day the blood rained from the sky. When the wood splintered, and arms clawed their way through the damp earth, the undead tearing their way through each grave, clawing upwards through the earth.

"Hector, are you okay?" Geraldine looked concerned. She looked over at Hector expectantly, as Hector opened his eyes, resting his chin in his hands, and stared at the photo.

"This was the blood rain," he said. "When the dead rose. I remember now. You have helped me remember."

Geraldine started typing on her laptop computer. "So will you tell me then? What happened?"

There was a bang as the remaining lights in the library were shut off and the facility closed for the evening. Geraldine and Hector remained at their small wooden table, surrounded by stacks of books, the light from Geraldine's computer screen reflecting against her face, and the warmth of the small banker's lamp shining against Hector's face.

"What happened after Darius died?" Geraldine sat back and waited for Hector to answer.

Hector closed his eyes, and saw Antoine.

He saw Antoine in the foyer of their Chateau, crying. He could remember that. Antoine had been still covered in mud, his clothes were still caked with dirt, and he stood in front of the mirror, hanging his head low, sobbing.

And then on that same evening, Hector waited for Antoine to stop crying, for his wave of emotion to pass, watching his friend, crying into his arms, leaning against the wall.

There had been no assistance from any others.

Geraldine broke Hector's trance and interrupted his thoughts. "Tell me, what do you remember about that time you were with Antoine?"

Hector picked up a pencil and examined it. "There was a time, when I was with Antoine, for many days, and he used to sit and speak with me for hours. Like he was grooming me for something."

"Grooming you? What do you think he wanted you to accomplish?"

Hector knew.

He could remember the nights after Darius had dropped him off, but those were different days, and those were times when Darius had been a friend, a confidant, but also an enemy. Hector looked down at his lap and shook his head. "Darius had always been quite angry. There were times that I just didn't understand his anger, or where it came from. I don't even know about his past, when he was a mortal, except about Tramos. He told me once about Tramos."

Geraldine stopped typing on her laptop and flipped through a large yellow legal pad. "Yes. Tramos. He was his creator, yes?"

Hector nodded. "Darius told me one night. Out of the blue."

"Could you take me back to that night?"

Hector leaned back in his chair and folded his arms, avoiding eye contact with Geraldine. He sat for a few minutes, looking down at his lap. "Antoine loved his absinthe. It became like an obsession with him for a while. There was a night that I was there, in his house in Coral Gables, and we were all there – Antoine was there, Darius, myself and Antoine's new friend Roberto."

Geraldine started typing again as Hector continued. "Antoine would drink the absinthe until he was intoxicated – his eyes would redden and his speech would slur."

Geraldine stopped typing and looked up at Hector. She adjusted her glasses. "Antoine was immortal. Why would the liqueur affect him this way?"

Hector leaned forward, clasped his hands, and looked up at Geraldine. "Antoine and Darius are affected very differently. They are not like vampires, you see. They have the dark gift – of life eternal – but they do not live on blood. Darius would kill for sport. Had a lot to do with his anger, I think."

"Yes," Geraldine said. "Darius had an anger issue. Which you told me. And I definitely want to explore."

Hector nodded. "Yeah. It was a bit much to deal with. So back to Darius. When he told me about Tramos. Antoine passed out on the couch as the sun started to rise. Darius and I rushed to the windows and pulled the drapes shut. Antoine had those heavy, room darkening drapes – the big, flowing ones – all throughout the house. He had it set up so every window and door could be covered and the house would be in absolute darkness throughout the day."

"So that is a similarity to vampires then."

"It's a similarity, but that's where it ends. Antoine, Darius, Tramos, Claret, Delia – all of them. They can all go out in the sunlight. They don't have that limitation that vampires do. Antoine has been out many afternoons. But it's a choice. They are demons. They have *chosen* the darkness, as opposed to the light. They have chosen to escape the sunlight. At least as much as possible."

Geraldine stopped typing, removed her glasses, and placed them on the table. "Take me back to the night when Darius told you about Tramos."

Hector looked down and fidgeted. "I can't".

Geraldine sat back and scoffed. "Why not?" She shrugged her shoulders and flopped her pen on the table, and crossed her arms.

Hector took a deep breath. He looked down at the table and held it inside for a moment. And then he let it out, and looked Geraldine in the eye. "I can't tell you about my specific relationship with Darius."

"Why not?"

"Because they will find me. And they will discover my disloyalty. And I will be punished for it."

"Who will find you?" Geraldine closed her laptop, removed her glasses and placed them on the table. She leaned forward. "Who will find you, Hector?"

"The Inspiriti."

"You have connections with that group?"

Hector nodded. "Only to a degree. They're all in it. Antoine. Darius. Delia in a member of the High Council. It's supposed to be an organization of enlightenment."

"Can you tell me more about this organization?"

"No. No, I cannot. Because I am a member myself. And I cannot be disloyal. For if I am, I will be crucified."

FOUR

In the Vatican section of Rome, just near the Sistine Chapel, a tall and imposing young man, dressed in a black cassock, stood in a small vestibule as the Sunday morning sun peeked through the stained glass windows, leaving a patchwork of color on the stone floor. He fidgeted with his personal cell phone, holding it upwards towards the sky, as he finally was able to place his call.

He returned it to his ear and sat on a nearby stone bench, and used his free hand to smooth the side of his wavy hair. "Ramiel. Yes, please, I will hold." He paused for a moment, and stared ahead at the statues against the opposite wall as the opening hymn chorused from the far worshipping chamber on the other side of the building.

After a few minutes, he spoke. His words reverberated and echoed against the stone walls. "It's Ramiel, Giovanni. I've been trying you for the last two days. I know you are not there. But I hear of bad news from America. From Antoine and his sector. In Miami. Please give me a call. You need to come to Rome. The Monsignor wants to leave for Miami tonight."

The door next to the bench opened, and a grey haired minister poke his head outside, in full white vestments. "Come in, Ramiel. It's time for the Sunday services." And then the priest disappeared as quickly as he had come.

Ramiel sat for a moment and stared at his small, black phone, resting in the palm of his hand, as if looking at it more intensely would make it ring for an answer.

But the call never came.

And Ramiel stood, shoved the phone into his pocket, and retreated down the hallway, through a soaring set of wooden doors, framed by multicolored stained glass windows. The doors shut behind him silently as he stood for a moment, in a windowless hallway, shrouded in darkness, lined with doors along the side to his right. One of the doors was open slightly, and a finger of warm light seeped through.

Ramiel fished his phone out of his pocket and checked it. He stared at the small, black phone, waiting for a response, while he knocked quietly on the door that was ajar. "Monsignor, may I enter?"

The man who sat at the desk across the tiny office did not look up from his paperwork, but it was he. He hid behind an expansive computer monitor, studying some paperwork near the keyboard.

Ramiel pushed the door open slowly as it emitted a dull creak, and the monsignor looked up at him, and removed his glasses. "Ramiel. Come in." He gestured to the chairs across from his desk. He smoothed some stray strings of hair on his balding, shiny head and placed his glasses on the desk. They seemed lost in the clutter. The monsignor's face shifted as he leaned back in his chair. "I am troubled by the emails and the phone calls I have been receiving from the States."

Ramiel took his chair and crossed his legs, looking over at the monsignor, who was rubbing a small tuft of hair on his chin. Ramiel cleared his throat. "Yes, Monsignor. I received word from Miami that Darius had died in Lyon and should be buried soon. If he hasn't been already. But it appears that the issue goes much deeper than Darius' death. They have been having quite a bit of fatalities over there. It seems the immortals are being targeted."

"By whom?"

Ramiel shook his head. "We don't know yet. All we know, right now, is that there are rumors spreading about a man in a hood."

"A man in a hood?"

Ramiel nodded. "That's what they are talking about over there."

The Monsignor pushed back from his desk and stood. His white vestments did nothing to conceal his hefty stature. His stomach bulged outwards. "Pay a visit to Antoine. I think he is losing control of his area. There is too much at stake here. This

'Hooded Man'. Does anyone know where he came from?" He sat back down.

Ramiel shook his head. "No, I have spoken with Paris, New York and Shanghai. None of them have heard of him, and there is great concern about this man."

"I see..."

Ramiel straightened his legs and sat forward in his chair. He looked at the monsignor directly, who was fiddling with a pencil. "Darius was one of the victims, dear monsignor. He was one of many, I'm afraid."

The monsignor sighed and played with the computer mouse, as he stared intently at his computer screen. He paused for a moment. "I am reading this email from Giovanni. He sent it to me last week. He says that Antoine is at their Chateau in Lyon and burying Darius, who died as a mortal." He looked over at Ramiel with wide eyes.

"That's what is causing the commotion," Ramiel said. "There has been quite a lot of speculation as to how Darius lost his immortality. How he aged so rapidly."

The Monsignor nodded, but did not look over towards Ramiel, who was intently watching the reflection of the computer screen in the Monsignor's lenses. After a brief period of silence, the Monsignor looked over at Ramiel. "This email is quite long. And quite distressing. Giovanni said Antoine is there, in Lyon, and returning to the States soon. He says that Antoine has been talking about resurrecting Darius again."

Ramiel's mouth hung open. There was a silence in the room that seem impenetrable. But the silence was broken by a knock on the door.

"Come in," the Monsignor said, returning his attention to the computer screen. Ramiel again looked at the reflection from the monitor in the monsignor's glasses, and then snapped his head in the direction of the door, as he heard the familiar, dull creak. It was Sister Ignatius. She looked troubled, her face seemed older than her years, and she stared at the floor and stood in the threshold. The monsignor waved her in, gesturing quickly. "Come in Mary! And close the door behind you."

She shut the door silently and took the chair next to Ramiel. She looked down towards her lap. He noticed that she had been crying. The Monsignor spoke first. "So Mary Ignatius, tell me the news."

She looked down at her lap and sighed. "Delia Arnette called me a few minutes ago. There has been another sighting."

The monsignor leaned forward over the desk. "Of who? This 'Hooded Man'?"

She nodded.

The Monsignor shook his head and raised his arms in the air. "Now you tell me there was a sighting. What is this man doing? Who is this man?"

Ramiel stood for a moment, and looked at his phone. The black screen covering the phone reflected the overhead lights from the office like small, white cosmic orbs as the screen awoke and lightened and he saw a missed call. He shook his head. "I'm not sure when this call came in. But this office is a dungeon. It just shows a missed call."

"Where was it from?" the Monsignor asked.

Ramiel sighed. "Miami. It came from Miami."

The monsignor sat back in his chair and shook his head. "Okay, okay. I don't have any more time for these distress calls from Miami. Sister Mary, please tell me what you had to come to say."

She straightened herself in the chair, and smoothed her habit before starting. She took a deep breath. "Well, Monsignor." She paused. "There were e-mails and phone calls coming in from around the world about this 'Hooded Man' – and…"

The Monsignor waved his hand. "Yes, yes, Ramiel already told me. He has been showing up before the death of any immortal. Quite conveniently, I might add."

Sister Mary nodded and looked downwards.

The monsignor looked at Sister Mary directly. "So what is this man doing? He shows up before the death of an immortal – what is his purpose? To kill the immortals?"

"He carries a decanter….this crystal decanter. It's round, and bulbous, and he convinces them that drinking from it brings eternal life. But it takes away the gift."

The Monsignor scoffed and stood again. "The only thing that can bring eternal life is the cup of Christ. And does it? This decanter? What does it do then?"

Her eyes fell, and she shook her head. "It doesn't seem to. It seems to bring death. Like an imposter."

"And why have you been crying?"

She shifted in her seat. "I'm afraid the news from America is not good. Delia Arnette called me just a few moments ago and let me know that Antoine is missing."

The Monsignor slammed his hands against the desk. "You two are giving me different stories! Ramiel just said that Antoine is in Lyon and I received an email from Giovanni who is at the Chateau now. And now you are saying that Antoine is missing?"

She nodded. "Delia told me this morning. When did you receive that email, Monsignor?"

He looked at the computer screen and clicked the mouse a few times. "He sent it at just past four this morning."

Ramiel got up, walked around the desk, and read over the Monsignor's shoulder. "So what has happened to Antoine has happened in the last six hours."

There was a silence in the room that followed, as the monsignor looked at Ramiel and Sister Mary. Ramiel looked over at Sister Mary, who was again looking downwards into her lap.

The Monsignor stood and put on his jacket. "Get Delia on the phone in the conference room. It's time to get to the bottom of this. First this 'Hooded Man'. Now Antoine has gone missing? I don't need this on a Sunday."

FIVE

He drank, lapping at the water with such ferocity and intensity that he started choking. The demon threw his head back in a deep, booming laughter.

He looked up at the monster, who stopped laughing and looked back down at him. "Finish it. Finish it now so the deed can be done."

He drank the rest of the water, at a much more reasonable pace this time, and looked up at the demon, whose monstrous eyes were glaring down at him, glowed with intensity as the monster's muscles were tight, taught and flexing with every move.

"You will be cursed to roam this world. A cloud of white mist will carry you. And you will convince all who have sworn to the darkness to drink from this decanter."

The demon showed him a small, crystal decanter, bulbous at the base, with a swirling, red hot potion inside. "You will take this decanter. You will call the immortals to me. You will hunt them. Convince them to drink."

"It is their salvation." George looked up at the Demon and the monster transformed into same woman who visited him so many times when he had been living. He recognized the same red hair.

She leaned in closer towards him and smiled. "Do you see now? Do you see why you are doing this?"

George shook his head.

"You are doing it because you now belong to me."

BLOOD
LINEAGE

ANTOINE NAGEVESH

LYON

The phone had been ringing but Antoine chose to ignore it. He sat in front of his computer, hunched over, hanging his head. His eyes were closed.

And there was Darius, living in his mind; Antoine saw his smiling face. It was not the Darius that had been the killer, the monster. It was the Darius that was the loving father, the maker, the teacher. His smile was as it always was, bright and gleaming. His face was framed by his dark hair, always tied back behind his shoulder.

And on that particular night, in that particular memory, Antoine noticed and remembered. He was carried back to that same night. It was an evening shortly after he had been transformed, many years ago, when he was just learning the ways of the immortals, when Darius was a teacher. "Antoine, my dear child, what more do you want?" Darius flopped on the sofa. "Do you want me to always hold your hand? Can you manage being an immortal? Did I make the correct choice in transforming you?"

Wake up, sleepyhead.

In Antoine's mind, Darius had been standing right before him, alive as can be. The sparkle was in his eyes, his long hair was clean and combed, tied behind his shoulders and he remembered – Darius smelled of roses. Yes, Antoine could remember that much. Was it his perfume? His clothing?

Darius unbuttoned the top two buttons of his purple shirt, revealing his muscular chest. "I brought you here to do what is meant to be done, Antoine. What has been written…"

But Antoine could not speak.

Antoine looked at Darius, who stood before the front doors motionless, waiting to unbutton the remaining buttons on his shirt. Antoine wished he could speak. He opened his mouth, nothing came out. And he looked around the foyer. There was the large bouquet of white roses in the center of the table – yes, the foyer was still the same. The same smell of the wood floors, the chandelier, everything.

The same Persian rug was beneath his toes. It had the same softness.

And then Antoine remembered.

He looked down at his hands, and saw the same, tiny silver dagger, which caught the same light and reflected back into his eyes.

He remembered the night all too well.

The sweet scent of the roses, the purple shirt, and Darius standing where he had been that same night, the same prophetic evening, had permeated his thoughts like a swarm of insects. That was the night. The first night Darius had died, and his words played into Antoine's mind as if they had been spoken only minutes previously:

"Plunge the dagger in me! In my heart! It's the only way!"

And then the vision faded to blackness.

And then next thing Antoine could remember was the feel of cool, damp leaves under his feet. Slowly he could see the trees of the thick forest rising in front of him, walking under the moonlight as small twigs snapped under his every step.

He felt the heaviness of the body; and then the memory revealed itself to him in totality – for it was Darius wrapped in the white sheet, stained with blood, slung over his shoulder.

Each step was taken with determination – fighting through fallen limbs and broken tree branches, through wet and moldy leaves, through the dampness towards the clearing of gravestones.

But the dream did not last –

The phone rang again.

Antoine opened his eyes to the shrill ring, his head was still cradled in his hands, and he was staring at his keyboard.

He fumbled across the desk for the receiver and croaked a hello shortly after. He reached over to the lamp on the side of the desk and bathed the room in a dull, dim light. On the other end of the phone was a familiar and reassuring female voice.

"I have been calling you for quite some time now."

It was Delia.

Antoine nodded and rose from his chair. "I know they have been searching for me. I have been here the whole time."

"We have quite a situation on our hands, Antoine. I am sure you are quite aware of that."

"Yes."

"You need to fly to Rome immediately. Monsignor Harrison is going to interview you in great detail. He wants to know all about your history, all the way up to the present. He is looking for clues on what triggered this 'Hooded Man' to hunt our kind."

Antoine replaced the receiver without a word. He looked again in the mirror. He spoke aloud, and his words sounded foreign against the silence of the chateau. "Darius, I must fly to Rome tonight. I am going to meet with the Monsignor."

ROME

Antoine arrived at *Leonardo da Vinci Fiumicino* airport in Rome, Italy, and the terminal was teeming with activity. He exited the plane wearing a light suit, a lavender shirt, and dark sunglasses. His locks were tied neatly behind his back. The early morning sun shone through the windows overlooking the tarmac, and as he walked towards the transportation area. He carried no luggage, for he did not intend to stay.

After hailing a taxi outside the terminal, he settled back into his seat for a brief nap. "Sistine, please," he told the driver. "Vatican City. Please hurry. *Andiamo signor!*"

The taxi driver weaved into the morning airport traffic effortlessly as the cab made its way towards Vatican City.

Antoine arrived as several priests, dressed in the traditional black cassock greeted Antoine's car. He was ushered to the Monsignor's office, and sat in the chair opposite the large, expansive desk. Ramiel sat next to him, studying Antoine intently. A clock ticked as the three men sat in silence for several minutes. Finally, the Monsignor broke the silence. "Would you care for a drink, Sir Antoine? I understand that you have a liking for absinthe. I sir, do not have that, but I can assure you, I have some very fine Italian wines."

Antoine watched the Monsignor as he spoke to him, as he rose from his chair, and walked over to a small wet bar that was located behind the desk, nestled between several sets of bookshelves that reached from the floor to the ceiling. The Monsignor fished three large wine glasses from a lower cupboard, and proceeded to uncork a bottle. "Of course, by now, you must certainly understand why I sent for you, Antoine. You are fully aware of what is going on in your territory, and we are quite concerned by the amount of deaths that have been reported. Because of that, I have called you here, so we can find out a little bit more about who you are."

The Monsignor handed a large glass of red wine to Antoine, looked at him in the eye, and smiled a warm smile. "Thank you," Antoine said.

The Monsignor sat back at his desk, and tasted his wine. "Excellent," he said. "I love the bouquet on this varietal. Smell it, Antoine. A hint of roses and chocolate. Love it."

He set the glass down and turned to his computer screen, as Antoine took a sip of the wine. He was pleasantly surprised at its velvety smoothness.

The Monsignor clapped his hands together. "Ah ha! Now I see. I have been scrolling through my emails, here, Antoine, and I found one from Delia. She emailed me three months ago, and explained the situation in Miami. This was right after Darius died, am I correct?"

Antoine nodded.

"Anyway," he continued. "She also said that you and Darius have had some confrontations over the years. You've sent him to the grave before?"

"Yes."

The Monsignor nodded. "Okay, well I would like to know more about your relationship with Darius, but mainly, Antoine, this meeting is to find out more about you."

"Then I need to start from the beginning."

"Certainly."

Antoine set his wine down on a small table next to his chair. "But I want you to understand something. The beginning, in this story at least, is at my end."

"Then begin at your end, Antoine. Start wherever you feel you need to start the story."

Antoine nodded and shifted in his chair, looked down for a moment, closed his eyes, and let out a sigh —

"I was dragged to the altar and burned to ashes. I found my death when I was betrayed; nevermore did I want to discover the darkness from whence I came. For I always knew.

179

I always knew my origins; I could never fathom what my life would become.

"And then, when I was dragged to the altar, my head hung low and my dark locks were dirty and mussed. I was no longer the charismatic immortal that I once had been. I hung my head in shame, my eyes closed and awash with defeat.

"I remember the heat and the smoke.

"The searing flames under a red sky painted with black clouds..."

Monsignor Harrison shifted in his chair, looking up towards the sky as Antoine spoke. Antoine continued his story, but remembered, as he was speaking, his time after the altar.

There was darkness.

He remembered that much.

The darkness was so enveloping, and when he felt that he opened his eyes, nothing had happened. There were no shadow demons waiting for him, poised around him, waiting to drag him to Hades.

There were no Hellhounds, with their acidic breath and torn, bleeding hides.

When he had passed from the Altar, there had only been absolutely nothing – complete and utter nothingness.

The Monsignor interrupted Antoine. "And when did you start to see something?"

"I didn't, your Highness. I saw nothing. I heard nothing. I was in darkness and solitude, and the next thing I remember, was breaking out of my casket when Darius resurrected me."

Ramiel placed his hand on Antoine's arm.

He spoke softly. "What did Darius see? Did he ever share his view of the afterlife with you after you performed the incantation to resurrect him in Lyon?"

Antoine looked into his wine glasses and examined the bubbles that hugged the slope of the glass. After a few moments, he shook his head.

"I see then," Ramiel said, looking over at the Monsignor. "Now that he is gone, we will never know."

Antoine looked up. "I *do* know that Darius saw a Psychiatrist regularly when he was mortal again and dying. And although I don't know all of the details, I know this – "

"What?" Ramiel looked at Antoine.

Antoine got up and set his wine glass on the edge of the desk. "Darius was running. He was always running. And he confided in the psychiatrist, and in Delia. They were very close. All of them. But I've talked to Delia. And I know that Darius was running. Shadow demons, Hellhounds, Asmodai, they were all after him."

Monsignor Harrison got up as well, and extended his hand to Antoine. "Thank you for coming, dear sir. It looks like we will have to contact Delia. The psychiatrist is dead, correct?"

Antoine nodded.

181

"I see…" he walked around the desk and ushered Antoine out the door as Ramiel stood, placed his wine glass on the desk unsteadily, and smoothed his jacket.

Monsignor Harrison placed his arm around Antoine as they exited towards the barren hallway as Ramiel followed silently. The Monsignor held out Antoine's coat for him. "We must meet with Delia again. When are you returning to the United States?"

Antoine looked down and then back up at the Monsignor. He shook his head. "It may be a few days. I still have to try to bring Darius back. I don't know if it will work this time, but we have to get him back, Monsignor. Where he is right now – where he must be – has got to be filled with torture and torment. We have to get him back for his own good, if nothing else. I care about him deeply. And I don't want him in torment."

The Monsignor nodded, and the three men started down the hallway. He put his arm around Antoine again, looked down, tugging at his chin with his index finger. They walked slowly.

"Perhaps we could come with you," The Monsignor said. "Why don't you consider that? We could help you, Antoine. We understand your reasons, and if Darius is being tortured for his transgressions while here as an immortal, we owe a duty to get him back."

Antoine nodded and looked forward. "I cannot tell this same story again. What if I have you come to Miami? What will that mean for me?"

The Monsignor smiled and placed his hands on Antoine's shoulders. "You think about it. Now you have a safe flight back to Frankfurt. We will join you there soon. But let's try to get him back. We're with you on that. He is better here, where we can manage him, then there – where he is tormented."

Antoine nodded and walked out the side door, out towards the Piazza, and towards a waiting black sedan.

Once he was relaxing in the back seat, he closed his eyes. All he could see was Darius – the Darius he had known, back when Antoine was newly transformed, in the days outside of Badulla, when Darius had stayed with Antoine to tutor him in the early ways of an immortal.

Antoine had remembered so many nights, sitting with Darius, staring at the book *Les Livres des Vampires*. One night, early in his days of being an immortal, Antoine flipped the pages as the turning paper rustled against the silence of the night.

Darius placed his hand over Antoine's. "Stop obsessing with who you are. You will blossom, Antoine. That I assure you. Give yourself time to grow."

Antoine looked up at Darius.

Yes, he was not all bad. He was not inherently evil, like he had said before.

Darius had some good qualities.

There was something about this immortal man, this demon who was transformed by a demon in hell, who was now walking the earth. There was just *something* about him.

Something that didn't seem *entirely* evil; nor did seem like he sought bloodlust.

Maybe it found him.

And as the car approached Leonardo da Vinci, Antoine reached for his bag. Yes, despite what he had done – his killing for sport, his apparent loss of respect for humanity, whatever it was – there was a ray of light that was piercing through the darkness. Somehow, somewhere, Antoine had seen it, way back in Badulla when they had first met. There was just something that was inherently *good* about Darius.

And for that, Darius was certainly worth saving.

Not long after he arrived back at the Chateau, Antoine had a gentleman caller. The two sat in front of a freshly made fire.

"But it wasn't…"

The fire popped and Antoine rose to stoke and rearrange the logs. "I cannot retell this story again."

The young man shifted in his chair. His hair, stone cold white, was brushed to the side from his forehead and hooked around his ear. Despite that, Antoine guessed that his visitor couldn't have been more than thirty.

"You are here from the University, are you not?"

The young man placed a small, black shoulder bag on the floor next to the overstuffed chair he was sitting in, and pulled out a small brown leather journal. "Actually, yes, I do go there. But I came on my own."

"I see…"

Antoine sat back on the sofa and fished a bottle of deep red wine from a drawer underneath the coffee table. "Care to join me in a drink?" He grabbed a wine key that had been sitting on a pile of magazines and started to open the wine. "Beaujolais. Do you know much of wine…I'm sorry…what was your name again??"

"Cris. Cristoph Baudin. I'm really sorry for my manners. And for showing up unannounced. I just wanted to meet you. And talk to you."

Antoine smiled and looked over at the young man. Antoine's eyes travelled up and down the young man's small frame, finally looking him directly in the eyes. "Well, you certainly knocked on the right door. So do you? Do you know anything about the fine wines of the world?"

Cristoph shook his head.

"Well, I would be happy to show you. I have found a passion in wines in these last few years. Since Darius died, I needed to find something to be passionate about again."

Antoine finished opening the Beaujolais and lay the cork on the table. He picked up the bottle and walked over to a wetbar on the other side of the room. "I should be able to decant it," he said, while searching through some cupboards behind the bar. "You must always decant it, Cris. It lets the wine breathe. Mellows it out."

"Point taken."

Antoine pulled out a crystal decanter, and placed it on the bar carefully yet with triumph. He stood and looked over at Cristoph expectantly. "Shall I?"

"Of course. But I would love it if you could tell me a little more about Darius."

Antoine stopped pouring the wine.

The deep red liquid had almost reached the crest of the bulbous base, towards where the etching and carving began. "You must know about Darius. Is that where we are to begin?"

"Yes, I must know about Darius."

Antoine sighed and handed Cristoph a glass of wine, and then sat back on the deep, overstuffed pillows of the sofa, lay his head back, and closed his eyes. "Where are we to begin…where oh, where?"

"If you want to know about Darius, Cristoph, then I have to start at the beginning of the story, as I said before, I cannot tell this story again. I cannot put words into sentences and sit on this sofa and regail you with so many stories of adventure and bloodlust. It was not that simple, my friend."

Cristoph set his wine down on a small side table. "And Darius? What became of him?"

Antoine looked over a Cristoph. "He passed away. He was human, Cristoph. He no longer had the gift."

"The gift of immortality?"

Antoine nodded. "Yes, it was taken from him. I was dragged to the altar and burned to ashes. I was betrayed by the one who I created to be my child. I was pursued by a monstrous demon." Antoine looked down and examined his wine, noticing tiny bubbles in the dark red liquid hugging the side of the glass. "And then after, the dark, and the cold…"

Cristoph paused for a moment. "When did you experience that?"

"When I was in the casket."

"You mean you could feel that, despite being dead? You still had your senses?"

And then Antoine closed his eyes, treasuring the warmth of the wine as it travelled down his throat, and he tried to remember…

…the cold, dark solitude of the casket. The experience of the sensation of the cool satin beneath his head, the soft, supple pillow which hugged his ears; he tried to recall the claustrophobic feel as the lid closed, trapping out the light.

I can feel you as the lid closes. I can feel the darkness, I can see the nails hammering into the sides; I can sense being lowered into the ground. The confinement overwhelms me; the blood is determined to consume me.

And then I deploy the silence.

And the darkness is overwhelming. I fight for the light but do not find it; I seek for the journey to understand but I lose my way on the path. I yearn for the transformation I was always promised…but I do not hear an answer.

"Yes, I remember the casket. I remember each passing day. The cold, dark and claustrophobic feeling. Like it was something I was meant to experience. My own personal punishment."

"For wrongdoing?"

"For such is life. It's an inevitable certainty. Completely unavoidable."

Cristoph leaned back in his chair and smiled. "Except for you."

Antoine paused, and then stared upwards towards the ceiling. "Except for me…"

I have no more blood to give. The decanter has run dry.

Antoine stood. "But it happened to me. I spent those years in the coffin…I once thought I had been so innocent…"

And there was, as the sky darkened and the fire continued to crackle, a point in the conversation when Antoine did finally decided that Cristoph may have been right. Death was never a certainty for him. Not for Antoine. But would it be a certainty for Darius?"

As Antoine prepared for bed later that evening, long after Cristoph had left, he kept on thinking of his father. Of the days past, longing for a relationship with the man once again, wishing he could. And then, he looked in the mirror. What was the purpose of that young man's visit? If just to open his eyes, perhaps?

"Have I lied to the High Council? Was there really only blackness when I had been dead? Was there really only the nothingness I claim?" The sound of himself talking out loud to an empty room sounded strange. "Or was there something else?"

He walked over to the bed and climbed under the sheets. "How do I remember? Maybe there *was* something that I experienced while I was gone..."

As he felt sleep overtake his body, he thought, one last time, about his meeting in Rome, and then the subsequent visit in his front parlor.

"I think I was always alive...never dead...always alive...and I never stopped *existing*."

BADULLA

In the days of his youth, when Antoine was still a mortal and still a child, he would spend his days running through the dusty streets of Badulla, assisting in the coffee fields in the farm behind his small house.

He stopped running and Antoine looked down at his feet.

They were covered in mud.

His sandals were heavily worn, and needed to be replaced. He stood in the center of a large clearing of sand and pebbles in the center of a large field of sawgrass, waiting for the sun to set, looking at the horizon, and how the sky changed from blue, to orange and deep red, and finally to purple and black.

He looked over at the barn, inside the barn where he knew his father lay, dead, motionless, waiting to be carried away and buried.

And then he thought of the old woman.

He could still picture her hefty figure, her silver-gray hairs, tied neatly back in a bun, but still, despite that, she had the persona of a hard worker. The wisps of hair just above her forehead, that had escaped and blew freely in the wind, would lend a thought that the old woman did indeed care for her appearance, but placed work before vanity.

Antoine remembered those small details about the woman. But as he stared into the genesis of the evening, into the sky where stars were just starting to reveal themselves, he wondered where the old woman could be.

"Where did she go?" Antoine wandered around the kitchen, later that evening, as his mother hung her head down at the table. "Where did the woman go off to?"

His mother did not answer, but spoke. She looked over at Antoine with red, puffy eyes. "We must get your father out of there, Antoine. He will start to rot and start to stink up the grounds. We must bury him and move on with our lives."

Antoine paused for a moment. "Mama, where is the woman? Can she help me with father's body?"

Mother banged her fist on the table. "Do not worry about the old woman! She does not exist! She is a figment of your imagination!"

Mother stood and walked over to the kitchen.

She looked down at the pots and pans, shifting them around as she spoke, never looking at Antoine as she did so. "I have someone who will come by and help you with the body. But it must be buried before sunrise tomorrow. I am sorry, Antoine, but I cannot help you. You are his first born son, it must be you."

Antoine sat at the table, and crossed his arms. He looked up at his mother, who was aimlessly shifting dishes around the kitchen as she spoke.

"What am I to do?" Antoine asked. He sat back in his chair.

He closed his eyes.

And he saw Father, lying in the middle of the hay-covered dirty floor, in the middle of the barn, out in the cold, dark night. And then Antoine let his breath out. "Mother, please."

She walked over to the table, a small, dirty rag in her hand, and joined Antoine at the table in the opposite chair. She set the rag on the table and looked at her son. "There are many things that you don't understand, my son. Your Father died because he was much more than what you might think. There will be someone coming to the house to help you bury your Father's body, and he will explain to you what I am talking about."

"And what about me? What will become of me?"

Mother leaned back in her chair. The back creaked. "You will do the same that you are doing. You will continue school. You will grow into a man. And then you will learn more. You will become a great leader in Badulla, my son. It is your destiny."

"Learn more? About what?"

She leaned forward, now hovering over the table. "You will learn more about what you are…about who you are. About how you are chosen, just like your Father had been chosen. That none of this is happening by chance."

Antoine looked down at the table and studied the white rag that Mother had placed there. "When will this man come?"

She sighed. "Antoine, my dear, I don't know. He does not come at a specific time. He comes in his own time. What you can do now, is go out to the stables, and prepare your Father's body."

"What shall I do?"

"You shall take his body and clean it up. Wash him down, clean all of the blood off his skin, and lay it out on a large cloth. You will find one out there in the barn. When it is done, come back to me."

Antoine gathered a bucket and some hot, soapy water, a sponge and a towel and placed it outside the barn door. The sun was just setting over the horizon, and the trees were black, everything was dark except for a small slit of light on the horizon.

He looked down at his equipment and thought of his mother's instructions. *Wash off the blood, clean his body and leave it there.*

There was a heaviness to the air; it weighed down on Antoine's shoulders like unseen boulders. He could feel every breath move in and out of his chest. He preferred concentrating on each breath. A child should not have to perform the task he was preparing for.

He looked at the latches to the giant, sliding wooden doors, and reached the rusted, sliding lock.

And then he heard movement in the stable. Footsteps in the hay. He set the bucket down and peered through the crack in the doors. He could see the flash of an arm, perhaps a torso. But he couldn't tell.

"Father? Are you alive?"

Only silence replied.

And in an instant, he was inside the barn. Moonlight shined through a window; a square, pale light on the bed of hay on the barn floor.

He turned around. "Father?"

He squinted his eyes and looked towards the far corner. No body.

And then came the rustling footsteps through the hay. He turned around completely, scanning each dark corner, seeing nothing.

Then the short creaks. Was someone climbing the ladder?

He turned to open the sliding barn doors but they were locked. He could feel his heart beating faster in his chest, and wiped the sweat from his forehead.

When the creaking stopped, he looked up towards the hay loft. He squinted, it was difficult to see in the darkness. He turned and grabbed at the doors with all of his strength, but they would not open. "Mother! Mother help me!" He called through the crack, looking outside, seeing the coca leaves blowing in the breeze.

The rustling in the hay was louder; the footsteps were getting closer – leading to a thump. He dared not turn around. It was approaching and getting closer…he could feel the chill in the air against his skin, as he closed his eyes and pressed his body against the hard, dry wooden door…

The next morning, Antoine woke with a start and felt his wet bedsheets. He rose with the sun and looked out toward the back barn. Had that been a dream?

Mother was still sleeping.

He went to the table, picked up his sandals, and put them on, very slowly, quietly as to not wake Mother who was snoring in the next room. Antoine looked over at the far window, out towards the back of the house. "Are you there, old woman?"

There was a quiet knock on the door as Antoine shot a glance to Mother. She rolled over on her side. He got up and walked over to the door, and pulled the light pink curtain aside. He almost yelped when he saw her face. It was the same grey hair, a wide open smile, the same familiar face. He smiled and nodded, and opened the door. "Shhh…don't wake Mother, please. *She will be very upset.*"

The woman did not enter the house, but nodded.

Antoine stepped outside and noticed a chill in the air. The old woman smiled, placed an arm around him, and guided him down the steps towards the barn. When they approached the door, Antoine looked up at her. "I had a horrible dream last night. At least I think it was a dream. Is that why you come to me? My mother says you don't exist."

They stopped walking and the old woman looked down at Antoine. She had wrinkles traveling down her cheeks from her eyes to her chin. "You don't remember me? You don't remember me there when your father met his death? I was there, Antoine, I assure you, I was there."

There was a light breeze and the coca leaves rustled in the brilliant sunshine, under a bright blue sky.

"I don't care what Mother says. I remember you. She thinks you don't exist."

The old woman smiled. "I only exist to you, dear young Antoine. Only you."

And then he paused. There was a moment that he didn't understand why he would have an old woman watching over him, but then it all made sense. "I remember learning in school about guardian angels."

The old woman nodded and smiled.

Antoine approached the barn doors. They were shut tight. The same rusted lock held the giant, wooden sliding doors together. He shuddered and closed his eyes. Antoine looked over at the old woman. "Why do I have to do this?" She nodded.

"Because I must show you."

He pulled the doors apart with all of his strength. "Father! I am coming!"

The doors opened with a thud, and Antoine peered inside. The morning sunlight did not penetrate the barn that day, save for the slits at the top on the hay loft, and despite his efforts, he could not see across to the other side of the barn where his Father's body lay.

He thought about his dream. And as he looked towards the dusty corners, they did not seem so dark and threatening as they had been.

"Father?" He called to the empty barn and its silence. There was only the reply of a rooster which called in the distance as Antoine looked back over at the old woman. She stood at the threshold, her arms clasped in front of her and looked downwards, shaking her head back and forth. "He is no longer here, dear Antoine. He lives again, but in the world of darkness. You will not see him again. This is why I must show you."

"The world of darkness?"

She placed her arms around Antoine's shoulder. "His body was here last night, yes, but in that time he transformed. He is no longer here. Look there back in the corner. There is no body there."

"No there isn't," Antoine said. "So why is that?"

The old woman guided Antoine away from the barn, leading him back towards the house. "You will understand in time," she said. "Your father now has a gift, but he is no longer here. You must now be the man of the house."

Antoine looked down and studied the rocks on the path. He kicked a few stones. "I cannot be the man of the house. I am too young."

"You must go out and earn a living, dear Antoine. Your family will count on your support as the first born. Your father is no longer part of your mortal family."

Antoine stood on the steps of Cathedral of the Gardens in Miami, centuries later.

It had been a long time since he had been in the barn from his days as a youthful mortal. Now, he was standing in the same spot where Darius had once waited for Father Bauman.

After a few minutes standing in the afternoon sun, one of the large, heavy wooden doors opened with a creak. Antoine looked over to the open doorway, which opened to darkness. A black abyss. A wall of cool air spilled from the atrium.

The priest stood outside the door, and smiled. He had bags under his eyes, but he looked warm and inviting. He placed his arm around Antoine's shoulder. "I understand that you must be Antoine? You are the one who Darius was missing for those years I spoke with him?"

"Yes, Father."

He ushered Antoine through the door. The chill of the air-conditioned air hit his face like a glacier. It was a relief from the sweltering Miami afternoon heat. Once inside, he looked around, and saw a somewhat muted, dark vestibule, an atrium of sorts with soaring ceilings. He stood for a moment and let his eyes adjust.

"Your friend Delia came and spoke to me a few weeks ago," Father Bauman said.

As they walked into the worshipping area, Antoine saw the same statue – the same *Christ on the Cross* that held him frozen, in its stare, as he had last been in front of the same altar. But those were different days – he was a different Antoine then, and since then, he had felt a lifting of the veil of evil that had surrounded his life since his transformation; there was a time, not long ago, that Darius had spoken to him about the yearning for redemption. "It's a very common thing, amongst us immortals," Darius had said to him, on a night, many years ago, as they had walked together up the sprawling steps to their Chateau outside Lyon in France. "We are inherently evil," Darius had explained. "I know I have told you this before. You need to accept your darkness."

And as Antoine stood in the cathedral, so many years later, he felt, for a moment, that some of the darkness had lightened.

There was hope.

He could feel like, there were comforting arms wrapping around him, holding him tight, swaddling him in clothes; he felt the comfort. Somehow, and in some way, as he stood next to the same, tired priest that Darius had confided in when he was dying, he felt that everything was going to be alright. Maybe not right away. Maybe not in a very long time. But eventually, everything would be alright.

"Darius had always been like a father figure to me," Antoine said as they approached the vestment room.

Father Bauman nodded. "Follow me through here to the rectory. We can sit there."

The priest opened a door that was flush with a stone wall. It looked like it had been added on at some point. Inside, the apartment was furnished with modest couches and shelves, lined with books, and basic living requirements. Nothing posh or opulent like at the Coral Gables estate or the Chateau. They sat on a small, uncomfortable couch just inside the door. Father Bauman turned on a small lamp and there was a warm, yellow glow.

"Your friend Delia came by to see me, as I had said. She had mentioned that your kind needs help from the Church."

Antoine's turned his head to the side, and looked at the priest. "Help from the Church? Why would we need your help?"

Father Bauman raised his eyebrows and leaned forward. "Certainly she has explained this to you? You know about the one who is pursuing your kind, do you not?"

Antoine nodded. "Yes, of course. I just returned from Rome. We discussed it in detail."

"Well then. We are very experienced in these matters, Antoine. Demonic possession. Spiritual force." He got up and walked over to some bookshelves on the other end of the room. "In fact," he continued, "Darius was coming to me on a regular basis because he thought he was possessed by a demon."

Antoine stopped for a moment as thoughts permeated his mind.

Asmodai.

Claret.

He remembered them both all too well.

There were still days when he would walk down Washington Avenue and look behind his shoulder – wondering if he would catch a glimpse of Claret sitting at a café across the street, her red hair catching the wind, a magazine open on the table, and always she would be wearing dark sunglasses. But her eyes would not be scanning the articles in the magazine.

They would be focused on him.

Antoine shivered, and rubbed his arms. "It got cold in here, Father."

Father Bauman nodded and brought two glasses over to the sofa with a dash of amber in each of them. "A little whiskey won't hurt," he said. "In fact, it'll help warm you up."

The priest sat down next to Antoine and handed him the whiskey. They both took a sip when Father Bauman leaned back, set his glass down, and crossed his arms behind his neck. "How long have you been running from demons, Antoine?"

"Too long."

"How long is too long, my son?"

Antoine paused for a moment and remembered *Les Enfantes*. The cemetery that had been closest to the Chateau. And the easiest for Antoine to bury Darius in. And in those days, the days when Darius had first died, in the days when the world was not the same cornucopia of communication that it grew into – *Les Enfantes* had been the best burial choice.

He could still picture himself, walking amongst the gravestones, as the night time mist swirled around his feet. And then Father Bauman touched his knee.

"Centuries," Antoine said. "This has been going on for hundreds of years."

Father Bauman leaned in closer and looked at Antoine directly in the eyes. "Well maybe it's time the running has stopped."

Antoine felt the need to bury Darius close to home.

While Darius died in Lyon, Antoine felt that it would be best to have the Chateau closed up for a while and fly Darius back to Miami, have him buried in the family plot in Coral Gables, and consider resurrecting him there. He felt it would always help to have him close by. And, he also considered closing up the Chateau outside of Lyon, or possibly listing the property on the real estate market and selling it.

But, after considerable deliberation with himself, Antoine wound up burying Darius right there, in his homeland.

And Antoine opted to travel the way Darius had when burying his own ashes, and bought a train ticket to travel from Lyon to Frankfurt to have Darius' body prepared by Ned McCracken – who Darius knew and could be trusted. Antoine also bought a ticket from Frankfurt to Miami, as he had not tested his powers since returning from the grave, and did not know if he had the fortitude to complete the long journey across the Atlantic Ocean once Darius had been put to rest.

For Darius, it had been somewhat simpler.

When Antoine was gone, Darius opted to fly to Frankfurt, with Antoine's urn, and to make his way back to the Chateau to bury him there.

Antoine had been burned to ashes, and his remains were contained in the urn which Darius had tucked under his arm and held on his lap the entire flight.

For Antoine, it was not so easy of a transition with Darius' remains.

Darius died in full, mortal human form, and would shortly start to decompose. Right after Darius passed, Antoine immediately called the mortician he knew personally – Ned McCracken.

There would be no embalming.

For if there were, Darius would not be able to be resurrected. He must be in full, organic form.

Ned, of course, worked out of Miami, but flew immediately to Frankfurt to meet him and the body at Antoine's insistence.

And although Antoine had originally opted to have Darius casketed and placed in the belly of the plane, to make the long journey across the Atlantic, back to the burial site, back to wait or wait for Antoine to resurrect him, and to bring him back to immortality, Antoine changed his mind. Ned still agreed to fly to Frankfurt to prepare the body for burial in Lyon. Because it was Darius.

FRANKFURT

There was a loud hiss as the hydraulics on the coroner's van lowered the casket onto the gurney for transport to the hearse. Antoine stood by and watched the two men load the casket and close the door.

He recalled the same harsh winter weather when he went to raise Darius for the first time; but now, as the exhaust from the hearse permeated the wintry air, he stood, huddled in a heavy, wool coat, shivering and noticing the harsh bite of the air snap against his neck during the harsh Frankfurt winter.

The drive took several hours, through the German countryside, driving along the autobahn, cutting through blankets of white, under a cold, barren, sky, through snow and sleet.

Antoine slept in the back seat, as he leaned his head against the window, and felt the purr of the engine, the rumble of the road, and the occasional breaks in the pavement until the car finally stopped.

And then the car started moving again. They were no longer cruising on the autobahn. He felt that the roads were smaller; the car was moving at a much slower speed, and they were getting closer.

He opened his eyes and looked out the window, and saw the same familiar chateau that he had been in so recently. But now, Darius was gone. He had gone to the astral plane, now in a different state of existence, but Antoine could still feel his presence.

Wake up, Antoine. Do you remember me? Do you see me remembering you?

Antoine opened his eyes. "Wha…" He looked around the back of the limousine, and out the window. The same grey clouds blanket the sky as snow fell across the barren, white rolling hills. Tiny houses rose out of the snow like small blocks, but as they approached France, the rolling hills gave way to muted land grades, and countryside, still white with snow, with the same clouds above, the same storm churning above the car, and Antoine broke his trance.

He studied the horizon.

And for a moment, he thought he saw the eyes. The blue, inviting eyes that he always had remembered, somehow looking down on him from up in the clouds, like they were smiling, as if a father watching his child.

And then Antoine started to remember.

He remembered Darius like he were still alive. Like he was still standing in the foyer with wide eyes, directly across from where Antoine himself had been standing, looking on and over at Antoine, holding the shiny dagger, ready to drive his chest through it.

The same blue eyes.

Yes, they were his eyes.

Darius.

The one who loved and created him, who sought to destroy him, who would not beckon his will or admonish him for abandoning his own.

And then Antoine plunged his key into the front door and opened the lock, and with the click and the creak of the door, he looked inwards at the same foyer. He smelled the same mustiness that he had each and every time he had returned to the Chateau; the same dust greeted him on the table in the center of the foyer, but the flowers were fresh on this occasion.

Yet it seemed so cold and lifeless as he stood there, searching for a light switch. But despite the uninviting feel, he remembered the day Darius first died, right on the Persian rug in the center of the hardwood. He remembered kneeling over Darius and looking down at his chest, watching the blood gush from his mouth, looking at his eyes; he still remembered their glassy stare; they had a deadness about them.

He could still feel the cold steel in his hand, he remembered clenching the dagger, so hard that his skin whitened at the knuckles. But the memory that permeated his mind the most was when he knew that Darius was dead.

He looked down at Darius, and Darius lay on the floor with open, unseeing eyes. Antoine reached down and gripped his shoulder, and shook. Nothing. He then picked up his arm, and it fell back to the floor with a *thump!* And Antoine's mouth dropped open.

He scooted back away from Darius as the vision faded.

And then Antoine opened his eyes.

He looked down at the rug, and then back up and around the foyer.

He scanned the area, the same, large marble table was the centerpiece that it had been for hundreds of years. The same chairs with the same red upholstery lined the walls, and the same winding staircase curved around the edge, raising upwards towards a vast, expansive ceiling, into the darkness of the second story.

"Giovanni?" Antoine took a few steps forward and called into the silence. He stopped at the threshold of a hallway, and paused, looking down the hallway into darkness. "Giovanni, are you here?"

Antoine noticed a small circle of light towards the end of the first floor hallway, which initially hovered in the darkness like a firefly, the movement harsh and erratic. "Giovanni?" Antoine took a few steps down the hallway, his heels clicking against the hardwood.

And then he saw Giovanni, but the shell of the man who was before him was not the immortal that he had remembered. The man before him was old, bedraggled, his hair stringy, silvery and vastly overgrown. "Yes, Antoine," Giovanni managed to croak. "Welcome home."

Antoine rushed over the Giovanni's side, and took the flaming lantern from him. He paused for a moment, gently caressing the old man's cheek. "What has happened to you? Giovanni?"

Antoine looked around the hallway as he helped the old man towards the kitchen. "And what has happened here? The power does not work?"

Giovanni leaned against Antoine. "There has not been power for years…Darius was gone…and then you were gone…and then she came…"

Antoine set the lantern on the kitchen table. It cast a warm, flickering glow in the room. "What do you mean she came?"

As Giovanni sat in the chair it gave a creak. He leaned over a wooden table and exhaled. "She came, Antoine. She came after you were gone, and turned me into this."

Antoine shook his head. "I wasn't even gone for that long."

Giovanni looked over at Antoine with unseeing eyes. Antoine noticed that his eyes were gone, that now there was just dried blood, gaping holes where his eyes once were. Antoine looked down at the table.

"She took my sight," Giovanni said, after a few minutes of silence.

"And your life force," Antoine added. "How much time do you have left?"

"Oh, I am still immortal, dear Antoine. That is the curse she placed on me. I am cursed to live old and blind. I am damned to spend eternity as an old, haggard leper!" Giovanni banged his fist on the table.

Antoine sat back. "So you are cursed now, the same way that Darius was? And Stephen?"

Giovanni shook his head. "No, Antoine. My curse is different. You already know Darius became mortal again. For me, I am damned to spend eternity a decrepit, blind old *invalid*!"

Antoine looked at Giovanni as the old man spoke to him. There was something different about him, despite the obvious physical changes. There was something changed about Giovanni.

Had he drank from the decanter?

And then, later in the evening, as Antoine helped Giovanni to his casket, he thought about the first days that they had met, after Darius had died for the first time – the time that he had died in the foyer of the chateau – and he saw that moment. The moment just after Darius had died.

"I understand that your maker has died," Giovanni said, as he stood on the expansive front porch of the chateau. "I understand that you must bury him, correct?"

Antoine had stood over Darius' body, still holding the dagger, his long, dark locks hanging low, covering his face. His chest heaved with every breath. "Who are you? How have you found me?"

Giovanni smiled, a gleaming white smile, his face pointed, chiseled and framed against dusty blonde hair. "I knew Darius very well," he said, stepping across the threshold. "And I knew the precise moment that you took his life."

Antoine looked over at Giovanni, noticing the man was quite young. "He told me to do it."

Giovanni looked down at Darius. "And I knew that as well."

Shed your skin.

Antoine set the dagger down on small table near the front door, and wiped his sleeve on his forehead. "How did you know? How did you know Darius?"

Giovanni walked across the foyer, carefully avoiding Darius' body, and into the adjoining parlor. There was a fire in the fireplace, flickering against the darkness in the windowpanes, lending a warm glow to the room. He took a seat in a high-backed, plush chair, and looked back at Antoine, who stood in the foyer, watching Giovanni.

Antoine hung his head down low, and closed his eyes. "What do we have to do?"

Giovanni sat back in the chair and crossed his legs. "First, you have to transform me. Darius never would do that for me.

Then, we will bury Darius together, once I have transformed, and then you will need to go to Miami."

Antoine looked over at Giovanni, who was looking back at him. He noticed the whites of Giovanni's eyes, stark against the muted warm and flickering light in the parlor. He walked closer to Giovanni, and stooped down in front of the man, who look down at him. "How do you know all of this?" Antoine asked, sitting on the floor, holding his knees close to his chest. "How can you possibly know all of this?"

Giovanni sat back, and looked around the room. "Darius had promised that he would transform me. He had made me that promise before you killed him. And when he was meeting with me, through the months, he had informed me about your stature and organization amongst you immortals. I already knew that he had plans to send you to Miami."

Antoine closed his eyes and shook his head. "This doesn't make any sense, Giovanni. Darius shared every aspect of his life with me. He would have told me if he had a mortal suitor that he was considering for the blood gift."

"Well, he didn't share this particular aspect with you."

Antoine stood and walked over to the fire. He fished a poker from the fire tools and stoked the logs; they flamed up and the flames reignited, bathing the room in warmth and light. "So then, I must get to know you, Mr. Giovanni. I must communicate with Darius. I must verify what you are saying to me. And then, when I have been able to do that, if everything is verified and true, then I will give you the blood gift and we will bury Darius together. Until then, I will have a room made for you upstairs, and you will not leave until you have been properly vetted."

Giovanni nodded.

"Good then," Antoine said. "Until then, we will leave the body right as it is in the foyer."

And then Antoine was carried back into room, back into the present, where he sat with the decrepit Giovanni. A light rain started to fall against the windowpanes. "Yes, I remember that night very well," Antoine said, rising from the floor. He looked down at Giovanni, who started straight ahead with a blank, sullen stare. "And you…shall I help you retire?"

Giovanni waved his hand. "No Antoine, I am going to stay up for a bit, my mind is deep in thought."

"Yes, I would imagine it would be."

As Antoine walked through the foyer, preparing to retire, there was a knock on the door. He paused for a moment, standing just in front of the expansive, round marble table in the center of the entryway, and looked over towards the door.

And then the knock came again.

Giovanni called in, asking Antoine who would be calling at this hour. And as Antoine opened the door, there she was. The tiny woman he once knew, now looking frail and aged. The lights on the porch made her near-white hair seem glowing and brilliant.

Delia Arnette.

His eyebrows raised, and his mouth opened just for a moment, as the two stood in a temporary silence.

"Who is it?" Giovanni called from the other room.

Delia smiled. "May I come in, Antoine?"

"I…yes, sure."

Antoine watched Delia enter the foyer slowly, and with the same elegant determination that he had remembered her possessing so many years ago. Delia certainly had not changed. She was dressed differently now; her stage costumes and bright red lipstick had been traded for a long, flowing dress, with much more natural and muted tones of makeup on her face. But what he could not get over was the gray, stringy hair she now had.

"Are you going to stare a hole in my face, Antoine?"

She smiled.

Antoine let out a quiet chuckle. "I'm sorry, Delia. How long has it been? Decades? Or centuries?"

"It's been quite a while, Antoine. And as you can see, I am in the same predicament as your Giovanni over there."

Antoine ushered Delia in and over to the parlor. He guided her to the sofa opposite Giovanni, and the two exchanged pleasantries. It was after a few minutes of silence that Antoine spoke. "So Delia, to what do we owe this pleasure of your visit?"

She sat back in her chair and stirred some sugar into her cup of tea. "Well, let me start from the beginning. I worked with Darius very closely while you were gone, Antoine, to try to beat his death. But, as you know, the ending was inevitable."

"Yes," Antoine said. Giovanni nodded.

"And I was working with Darius as I have formed a group called *The Inspiriti*, because, as immortals, we need to band together. There are those out there that are set out to destroy us."

Antoine and Giovanni both nodded.

"I can see from your Giovanni here that he has been injured and seems to suffer from as similar curse as I have." She looked over at Giovanni. "Is that right, my dear?"

Giovanni pursed his lips together for a moment, and exhaled. "I am cursed to live old and blind for all of eternity. Sometimes I think death would really be just beautiful right about now."

Delia waved her hand. "Nonsense. Stop with that rubbish. Yes, I see that your youth has been taken from you. And your eyes as well. I don't know how much of your senses you have, but I have a similar curse, though applied differently. I was youthful and my immortality was stripped from me. But I managed to regain it. I regained my immortality."

"But not your youth," Giovanni added.

Antoine took a seat next to Delia and looked over at Giovanni. "And that is how Darius died. He did not regain his immortality."

Giovanni shifted on the sofa. "So how did you regain yours?" He stared straight ahead initially, and when asking the question, but once Delia spoke, he instantly honed in on her voice and faced her directly.

Delia set her tea down on the coffee table with a light clank of china against glass. She sat up, took a deep breath, and exhaled quietly. "There is a cup, my dear Giovanni. There is a cup that is rumored to be the key to life eternal. It is the same cup that was in *The Last Supper*, back in the times of Christ."

Giovanni leaned forward. "And where is this cup? You drank from it?"

"I have."

"And what about you, Antoine?"

"I have not. I was raised from death by a separate ritual. It had nothing to do with the cup."

Giovanni paused for a moment, seeming to stare straight ahead. Antoine thought that he might be deep in thought. "There is a problem with what you say," Giovanni finally said, after a few minutes had passed. "For I drank from a cup as well. I drank and was told that I would keep life eternal. That

I would find forgiveness and salvation. And that the sins of my dark-hood would be washed away."

Delia looked down and her face shifted slightly. "It cannot be the same cup. I know there are very few of us who are so damned that they cannot regain the gift."

"Who are those?" Antoine asked.

Delia looked over at Antoine and nodded. "You know who they are."

Antoine stood and tended to the fire. "I shudder to think," he said. "That you drank from the cup that I *thought* you drank from, Giovanni. We are here because Darius drank from a decanter – something that was forced upon him. He was enamored with this bloodlust. But this event ultimately ended his life."

Antoine sat back on the sofa, long after Giovanni had retired, and considered what Delia had said. If the immortals were truly under attack, then they may just have to join forces. But he has been running from Claret for years. And why would Claret choose to attack her own kind?

He longed for the days of his youth; when he first had partnered with Darius, and they foraged together, when Darius taught Antoine the ways of darkness, those years of tutelage that culminated with Antoine wielding the dagger in the foyer.

But in the days that led up to that incident, when Darius had died for the first time, were some times that Antoine wished he could revisit. The days of being a student. Now, he was the scholar. He was the teacher.

And Darius was gone.

Antoine closed his eyes.

He wished that there was a simple solution to what Delia had said. And Giovanni...he was another worry. When Giovanni had explained to them how his eyes had been torn out of his skull, and how he was now cursed to live eternally blind, this disturbed Antoine deeply. Thoughts of their conversation permeated Antoine's thoughts as he tried to get some sleep.

"She ripped my eyes right out of their sockets," Giovanni had explained as he sipped his tea. The fire had died down, but Antoine did not rise to stoke it any longer. It was far too late at this point. The sun was already starting to peek across the horizon.

Antoine shook his head. "Why would she do something like this Giovanni? What did you do to deserve being robbed of your sight?"

But it wasn't the conversation that bothered Antoine so greatly. It wasn't Delia's warning either. It was the eyes.

Those dead eyes.

He could still see Giovanni walking the hallways.

Watching the chateau.

Serving his duties for the last several hundred years. And he could still see him, dusting the busts, and the marble statues, cleaning the bright red carpets and drawing the drapes as the night would fall on Lyon.

And then Antoine thought there was a light knocking on the door. He couldn't tell what time it was. Maybe past noon. But he heard a faint, muffled voice through the door.

"I am here for you Master Antoine. Do you want your breakfast, dear sir?"

Antoine swung his feet from the bed, letting the covers fall to the floor. "Giovanni? Certainly we can't have slept that long. Maybe we can talk this afternoon?"

"Oh but Master Antoine, I have prepared this especially for you...just look into my dead eyes. Do you see me?"

Antoine opened the door to Giovanni, who had been standing obediently still, waiting for Antoine to rise and acknowledge him. Giovanni was standing with a large platter, with an oval silver cover. You see Master Antoine? I have brought this especially for you. I cannot see it with my dead eyes...but I know it is just for you.

Antoine stepped back for a moment. "Giovanni, I'm not hungry. Will you please let me sleep?"

"Oh but sir, these are especially just for you!"

Antoine shook his head and took the platter from Giovanni and placed it on the bedside table. As he turned back to face his loyal servant, he waved his hand. "Now please, Gio, let me sleep for a while longer. I need more rest. Stay up if you wish, but I must sleep."

Giovanni left and closed the door.

Enjoy, sir.

Antoine climbed back into bed and pulled the covers up over his head. But he could not get the silver platter out of his mind.

He could not fall back asleep. He would attempt lying in one position, holding the pillow over his head, shielding his eyes from the outdoor invading sunlight, but in his mind, there was the silver platter, he could see it despite his eyes being closed, sitting there, gnawing at his every emotion.

Open me!

And then Antoine's curiosity got the best of him.

He flung the covers over to the side, swung his legs onto the floor, and looked down at the platter. He lifted the lid, and instantly dropped it to the floor. He covered his hand over his mouth, agape and aghast.

I see you Antoine! And I am always watching you!

He crawled back under the covers as he heard laughter from out in the hallway. "Go away, go now!

The next morning Darius was prepped for burial.

The sun had been shining with brilliance as the coffin was hoisted into the funeral parlor, and it sat, back in the preparation room, a silver gleaming box with bright chrome handles. Its elegance was a striking contrast against the clinical feel of the preparation areas of the home, but it was a common scene.

The day after Antoine's discussion with Delia and Giovanni, he opted to venture to the funeral parlor to retrieve Darius' body. He knew that this would be one of his greatest challenges. As Darius died as a mortal, many different things have happened. His body was prepped and laid in a coffin. There was a death certificate and record of his passing. And one more challenge.

Time.

Antoine was desperate to get the body away from the funeral home before it was embalmed. The body would swiftly decompose and decay. And if Darius were to be embalmed, the blood would all be lost...

Antoine woke with a sense of dread overcoming him. How long had he slept? He flung the covers to the floor with his feet, and craned his neck, while still lying flat on his back, to look at the bedside table.

No platter.

He looked towards the other side of the room, out the window, at a setting sun. He cursed himself for sleeping the day away.

"Gio!" He called out as loud as he could as he hopped out of bed and searched for his trousers.

Not after long, there was a soft knock on the door. "Yes, sir?" Giovanni stood in the doorway, his arms at his sides, looking over towards Antoine, with a white handkerchief folded in thirds, covering his eyes, wrapped over his eyes and presumably tied in the back of his head.

"You covered your eyes?" Antoine asked, pulling up a pair of tight black pants.

Giovanni entered the room and started to make the bed. "I have no eyes, Antoine. I see nothing. But I could sense both you…and Delia…staring at me many times yesterday. I thought it would be best to cover those ghastly looking holes."

Antoine looked over at Giovanni who had finished making the bed. "Well, it certainly isn't necessary, but I appreciate the gesture. And I'm sure Delia does as well."

Giovanni nodded and headed towards the door. "Are you going to retrieve Darius today?"

"Yes. I must get his body before it's embalmed if there's any hope of resurrecting him."

Giovanni nodded.

"And Gio…" Antoine finished buttoning his shirt and smoothed his hair. "I have something eating at my mind that I need to talk to you about."

"Anything, Master Antoine."

"Did you knock on my door earlier this morning? What happened to the silver platter that you placed on my bedside table? Where did it go?"

Giovanni cocked his head to the side. "Sir?"

Antoine stood next to Giovanni and placed his hand on his shoulder. He leaned down towards the man's face, and whispered. "What happened to your eyes, dear Giovanni?"

Giovanni looked up at Antoine. "I already told you…she took them from me. She ripped them right out of my head!"

Antoine nodded. "Yes, yes I know, Gio. I know that much of the story. But do you know what happened to them after she ripped them out?"

"Yes."

Antoine raised his eyebrows, took his hand off Giovanni's shoulder, and waited patiently.

Giovanni's voice quivered. "I saw it in my mind. I heard her stomp on them. She took her feet and smashed them into a pulp. I felt the floor tremble and her foot squished them. She was screaming. So loud. She kept saying 'you will be forever blind!' and 'you will living eternally with this curse!'"

Antoine shook his head.

"And ever since, I have been living with these ghastly holes in my face, with the skin torn and ragged, and the blood that was dried…I finally washed away. And I healed. But I could never see again."

"And so the eyes were destroyed?"

"Yes, they most certainly were."

"And you never brought me anything earlier this morning?"

"No sir, I did not come calling once."

Once dressed, Antoine hurried out the front door, slamming it behind him. The sun was shining brilliantly when he coasted down the stairs and towards the driveway; he fished a pair of sunglasses from his coat pocket and ran towards his waiting Mercedes for the short drive into town and the funeral home. He slammed the door as the engine roared to life. Fumbling with the heat settings for a minute, he rubbed his hands together, put the car in gear, and peeled out of the driveway.

As he slowed at the end of the driveway preparing to turn, he looked back on the chateau for a moment. He paused briefly as the car stopped, and noticed the approaching dark clouds, and the imposing shadow of the chateau, the darkness and gray-hued spires, reaching from the daunting structure.

The sky seemed to be awakening as the clouds were gathering above. Antoine closed his eyes for a moment, and hung his head, closed his eyes, and then looked at the Chateau once again.

And he felt a chill course through his body.

For when he looked closely, into the clouds, his mouth fell open when he focused on the details of what was appearing above.

The eyes.

The same eyes that he remembered, years ago, looking down on him from the swirling, angry sky when resurrecting Darius before.

The darkness had befallen once again.

And as he drove to the funeral home, he remembered the night when he sought to raise Darius from the dead. So long ago, it seemed. He remembered lying in an open grave, full of putrid water; dark and dank, watching upwards as the dog-faced demon leaned over the edge of the grave, looking downwards upon him.

Asmodai.

Was he returning? Did he know what Antoine was preparing to do?

After a drive of several hours, Antoine pulled into a cold, wet parking lot, next to a stark, grey building without many windows, as daylight was fading. He placed the car in park and got out. The cold air hit him like a brick wall and stung his face.

Moments later, he stood in front of large steel door. There was a small, frosted square window just above shoulder height. Antoine stood up and peeked inside the window, but saw nothing. He banged on the door, and scanned the parking lot. He appeared to be alone.

A light snapped on and Antoine saw shadowy movement on the other side of the frosted glass. Several locks clicked, and the door opened.

"Good evening, Antoine."

It was the first time that Antoine had ever seen Ned McCracken in person. But Darius was familiar with the man, so Antoine trusted him and insisted he fly to Frankfurt to prepare Darius' body for transport back to the United States, and to ensure that he was not embalmed. Now, that Darius was to be buried in Lyon, Ned was preparing the casket for transport via train, and Antoine appreciated that Ned still made the journey across the Ocean.

Always known as 'The Mortician's Mortician', Ned was rather well known through the Miami funeral circuit, and through the local churches in that area, but he flew to Frankfurt for this special reason.

For Darius.

He wore a grin, had warm brown eyes, and slicked dark hair. "Come in, Antoine. I will take you to him."

Once inside, Ned closed and locked the door. Daylight was almost gone, and the sky was taking on a dark blue tint. He led Antoine through a preparation room – past the giant glass cylinders used to mix embalming fluids, past a giant steel table, and into a long, barren, dimly lit hallway. "I'm sorry that you had to drive so far, dear Antoine." Ned led the way, and looked back at Antoine as he spoke. "But my cousin owns this funeral parlor. His family has been living outside Frankfurt for years. And that's why I had instructed you to have Darius sent here. But I have him here for you. All ready to go."

Antoine stopped in his tracks. "All ready to go. You didn't embalm him, did you?"

Ned smiled and shook his head. Antoine nodded. "Thank you, Ned."

They stopped in front of a door which was closed. Ned looked at Antoine expectantly. "Are you ready for this?"

Antoine nodded and closed his eyes, as Ned opened the door and stepped aside. Antoine opened his eyes and saw the open door; he saw the warm light flowing out into the front hallway, but his feet would not move. He looked down at his feet and studied his shoes. They were the same black dress shoes that Darius had brought home to him from Paris just two years ago. He remembered that day so well.

He closed his eyes.

"Antoine!" Darius had called as the front door of the Chateau slammed behind him. Darius was standing in the foyer, in the same black dress shoes, and clicked the heels together. "Look what I brought you from Paris!"

Antoine walked towards the door, nodding. "And you're wearing them?"

Darius threw his head back and laughed. "Don't be silly my little immortal! My little chosen one! I have another pair for you here! Same shoes!" He raised a brown paper bag and shook it.

Antoine took a step back and sighed, and opened his eyes. Darius looked so different now that the life was gone. So still. It was really gone. "Yes, I remember those shoes you have on him."

FRANKFURT-LYON

Once Darius was buried, then it would be time to move on. Antoine decided that he would have the Chateau closed up, the shutters would be pulled shut, the furniture would be covered in white sheets, and Giovanni could opt to head back to Italy to visit with family until Antoine's return.

Antoine just had to get back to Miami.

Just after his visit in Frankfurt, Antoine had settled into his seat on his return train ride, his car safely tucked into a car transport in the rear of the train, and he sat in his First Class cabin as the remaining passengers boarded the train.

He called the cabin steward for a pre-departure cocktail. Once he had his bourbon, he relaxed into his seat and settled for the journey, closing his eyes, waiting for the train to leave, he closed his eyes and thought of the exchange with his unexpected visitor when he had first returned from Rome.

"I cannot tell you the whole story here. I am unable to speak the words that you would like me to say. For there is much more story to tell that I could even comprehend. There were days when I thought that he was the most damned of demons; the killing he did, for sport. And then I witnessed his decay. His death. His rot and stench."

"I see…"

Cristoph sat back in the large, plush, high backed lounger, holding a pen and yellow legal pad, writing furiously, as the dark ink glided across the paper. His eyes were staring with deep intensity through his thick, round lenses, accentuating the wrinkle in the center of his forehead.

And then the fire crackled.

The man stopped writing for a moment and leaned back as his face softened. "So, tell me again about the first few days after Darius had died," the young man said. "Tell me about what happened from the moment of his death…until you buried him in the cemetery in Lyon where he now still lies, correct?"

Antoine shook his head. "No, Cristoph. He has not been buried yet. He is in Frankfurt as we speak. I had him shipped there to be prepared for burial. I am scheduled to go there tomorrow and claim his body."

Antoine had hung his head down low. "I let Darius lie on the bed for several days after he died."

The man sat back in his chair, ran his hand through his spiked hair, and shook his head in disbelief. "What about the stench? Wouldn't his body have rotted at that point?"

"It did. It was fine for a time. Maybe a day or so. It was a transitional season in Lyon then. Not the same wintry weather. The windows were open when he died. It was rainy. I remember that much. And soon after he passed, I shut the windows tight, closed the drapes, and turned the air conditioning system on as cool as it would go. But it didn't matter. Despite the chill I was able to create in the chateau, I was not able to thwart his decomposition."

The man nodded.

"The first night was the hardest. I sat in the rocking chair across from the bed, and rocked back and forth. Back and forth. For hours. Watching his body. From my vantage point, Darius looked as if he could just be sleeping. Like he would wake up. Sit up any moment. Look over at me with his wide, brown eyes, and ask me why I hadn't come to bed yet."

Cristoph had nodded, and watched Antoine. Antoine noticed him adjusting his glasses, and then he look down as he spoke.

"Maybe I was delirious. Maybe it was the effect of the absinthe I had been sipping. But after what seemed like several hours of rocking, listening to the creak in the runner, sitting in the silence of the room, watching his body, motionless, I stood up. I set my small stemmed glass down on the table, took off

232

my shirt, and let it fall to the floor. I unclasped my belt and let my jeans fall to the floor. I stood naked, staring at the body, covered with the sheet. So many times before, I had disrobed and joined Darius in bed. I had to do it. One more time. I had to do it this *one last time*."

The man placed his legal pad and pen down on the desk, and looked Antoine directly in the eyes. "Antoine...you didn't..." He shook his head. "No, I didn't do it. But I wished he were alive so I could have."

Antoine looked around the parlor. There were shelves of books.

He had lived there but had never noticed them before. Books and more books. And then he looked back over at the man. Cristoph. So amazingly delicious.

Yes, that was his name.

Had he forgotten?

The introduction in front of the Sistine had been so brief, so fleeting. And the meeting in the offices so momentary, such a blur. But now, he remembered who this man was. This man who was sitting in his own Chateau. Antoine set his glass down and leaned forward. "This is a follow up visit?"

Antoine opened his eyes and shook awake.

Antoine returned to his drink, and as the train pulled from the station, he remembered where he had first met Cristoph. The Piazza in Rome. Outside the Sistine. When he had first visited there. That was it!

And when Antoine closed his eyes again, he remembered the scene in more detail…

…Cristoph looked down at his pad and jotted notes. Antoine studied the young man. He looked very stuffy in his formal cassock that he wore. But so young. So delicate. So delicious. He clearly was youthful beyond his years. Antoine snapped out of his musing. "It's been hundreds of years. Not long compared to some."

"Some who?"

"Others. Claret. She thousands of years old. Lived in ancient Jerusalem. You know her story, right?"

"Of course. Which others?"

But the others were not who were on Antoine's mind.

For in that moment, the tiny little office seemed to fade into blackness, the young priest sounded farther and farther away when he spoke, like he was hundreds of yards away from where Antoine was sitting, speaking from a tiny porthole in a dark, dank ocean.

And then Antoine remembered the night that he sat in the same rocking chair, rocking back and forth, sipping his absinthe, holding his stemmed glass silently, as the rocker creaked the same creak as he moved back and forth. Darius had been sleeping in the bed opposite from where Antoine had been sitting. But, on that particular night, Darius shot up in bed, his eyes wide.

Antoine placed his glass down. "What is it?"

Darius looked down and shook his head. "I dreamt of him again. I dreamt of Tramos."

And then Antoine opened his eyes. He was back in the office. With Cristoph. The young priest looked directly at Antoine, and raised his eyebrows.

"Tramos," Antoine said. He shifted in his chair. "Tramos is the oldest that I know of."

"How old is he?"

Antoine shook his head. "Don't know. I don't think anyone knows how old he is. Tramos transformed Darius. But even Darius didn't know. Or if he knew, he didn't tell me."

Cristoph nodded. "I see…"

After a great deal of thought, Antoine had decided to visit the priest that Darius had befriended during his short time as a mortal. He returned to Miami, on a transatlantic flight, on a jetliner like so many people would do. It just seemed like the right thing to do.

He landed at Miami International close to midnight in the middle of a light rain. The lights in the city as the plane was descending looked like tiny diamonds in a dark sea, which grew ever larger and more prominent as the plane traveled closer to land. The flight was uneventful, the terminal was the same as he remembered it – cold and stark, teeming with activity despite the late night hour, and the hallways were just as long as he remembered them from years past.

When he was about to raise his arm to hail a cab, he paused for a moment. His estate was gone. It was a burned out shell. He remembered that much. There was no home to go to. "The Biltmore," he said to the cab driver as he slid into the cold, uninviting back seat.

After he showered and changed, Antoine rented a car and drove over to the Cathedral. The now familiar priest smiled when he saw Antoine in the dimly lit church atrium.

Antoine followed Father Bauman down the center aisle between the wooden pews, towards the altar, and off to the left, towards a wooden door. When Father Bauman opened it, Antoine knew exactly which room he was in. The vestment room. The room where priests kept the different colors and styles of vestments.

"Yes, my son." Father Bauman sat behind an expansive desk. Volumes of books lined the shelves behind him. "I had met with Darius multiple times when I knew him. He came by the church numerous times. I was so sorry to hear of his passing…"

Antoine nodded.

"And, if I might add," he continued, "Darius seemed troubled. His face…when I saw him…always showed a state of distress."

"I understand," Antoine said. He leaned forward and looked Father Bauman in the eye. He stopped fidgeting with his pen. "I tried to speak to him to no avail. Multiple times."

"When people die, Antoine, they don't stop existing. They may not be next to you physically. But they are still there. They still exist."

And that gave Antoine pause.

Darius wasn't still alive. He was lying in a coffin in Lyon. But Antoine thought of the days in the Chateau, looking in the mirror, wiping tears from his eyes.

"So Darius is still with me?"

Father Bauman smiled. "Of course he is. That is what we believe. Darius will always be with you. If not physically, at least he will still be with you spiritually."

Antoine threw his head back and laughed. "Do you think that, Father? I'm not so sure about that. I'm fairly certain Darius is in hell."

After Antoine returned to *The Biltmore*, he fell asleep with his clothes still on and dreamed of Sheldon…

…Antoine placed the bottle of Absinthe down on the coffee table, the large coffee table that was in the center of the front parlor. The thunderstorm continued outside, more softly now, as the rain gently pelted against the windowpanes.

"Antoine, this is a very important part of the story. Is it not?"

"It's all important," Antoine nodded, placing a small, white sugar cube on the slotted silver spoon which he lay flat against the small stemmed glass. He reached for the absinthe and poured some of the green liquid into the glass. "I saw him fall from grace. I saw him lose his gift. He was so damned. So remorseful. But aren't we all when we are dying?"

"Yes…yes. We are talking, of course, about Claret now, aren't we? About where she figures in to this whole story. And how she has come to pursuing you."

Antoine paused for a moment and leaned back into the plush couch. "How did you inherit such an organization? The Astral? How did you do it?"

Antoine already knew the answer. The young man was the son of a priest.

Sheldon shift his weight in the chair, and lay his legal pad and pen on the side table. He pushed his glasses up his forehead, displacing his stringy hair like a mop, which grew thin but long from his shiny head, as the fire popped against the quiet evening. "I need to know more about Claret," he said, leaning forward, reaching for his own glass of absinthe. "Why is she pursuing you?"

"Oh, she has found me, and Darius, for that matter, she is coming for us!"

Thunder crashed and Antoine was jolted out of his dream. "Could that be it? Could it be *her*?"

DARIUS SAUVAGE

CITTÀ DEL VATICANO

Back in the days before Antoine returned from the dead, and long before Antoine had met in Rome with the Monsignor, Ramiel and Cristoph, Darius had been there, in the days during his quest for immortality, in that same office, for a very similar meeting. After Darius had his encounter with the 'Hooded Man', Darius had talked to Delia about it, and, since Delia is the Director for the Eastern United States, she felt obligated to report the findings to Rome.

Darius stood outside the conference room located underneath the bowels of the Basilica. The halls were stark and unfurnished; the paint on the walls was cracked, peeling and in no way indicative of the opulence just a level above in the worshipping area. In the secret chambers below, in a non-descript location, in those underground chambers, were the offices of "The Inspiriti".

Darius had heard of the organization but never had encountered anyone of authority with the exception of Delia. And Darius had known her since they were first newly transformed, living together for a time in Paris, in the Vaudeville years, in the late nineteenth century, when Claret would roam the streets looking for those to follow her.

Rome was far different from Paris, when he had been standing in the middle of Piazza San Pietro. He stood in the famous square, in the center of Vatican City, next to the obelisk, and he scanned the area. The soaring colonnades reached upwards on either side, with their Tuscan influence, four columns deep, and framed the gathering area.

Across the plaza, through the passers-by, and the wandering tourists, Darius saw a man in a black cassock waiting for him, next to Maderno's fountain. He could see the young priest walking back and forth in front of the large basin, as cascading water flowed from the rounded top, which Darius thought looked a bit like a large mushroom; but it was so elegant, sloping and exquisite; and the sound of the water was so soothing and peaceful, that it was the most beautiful mushroom he had ever seen. The water, which flowed from the crest of the upper dome flowed downwards into a large inverted basin, and spilled over with such an even, elegant tone, it appeared to be a rain shower, which gathered towards the pool below. How Darius loved Rome, so much, so very much.

Darius approached the man with a quick, determined pace. There was a youth to the man that Darius appreciated, and as the man got closer in view, Darius could make out the man's thin mustache, his receding hairline, and youthful skin. As soon as the man was within a few feet of Darius, he extended his hand. "Sir Darius, welcome, sir. I trust you had a restful flight?"

Darius nodded. The young priest couldn't have been more than twenty-five, near Darius' age, but an oxymoron of presentation – his skin was youthful, taught and flawless, but the hair was graying and receded, so at first glance, the priest could have appeared to be middle aged, but in the physical shape of someone half his age. "I'm Cristoph," he said, as they started walking to the far end of the plaza, towards *Basilica di San Pietro*. [author's note: Saint Peter's Basilica].

Darius watched the priest walk with small, methodical footsteps, and noticed the lower skirt of his cassock catch the passing breeze.

And then Darius looked up, as they arrived closer to the Basilica. He looked up at the rising dome, in the center of the structure, which stood command over the square, as an elegant centerpiece.

"Welcome to Basilica di San Pietro," Cristoph said, turning around to face Darius. "Truly the masterpiece of the Renaissance, for certain."

Darius nodded as he looked outwards towards the massive columns that reached around the square from either side of the Cathedral.

Cristoph looked back at Darius as he led him towards the front doors. "Carlo Maderno designed the fountain I met you by," he said. "But the Basilica, here, has been built by legendary artists and designers – Michelangelo and Bernini, to name a few."

Darius looked up and appreciated the soaring ceiling. "Truly amazing."

Cristoph led Darius into the grand atrium, and down a small, nearly hidden hallway at the far end of the gathering area, towards a small door. Cristoph fished a key from his pocket, and opened the door to darkness. He looked over at Darius. "You are one of the first to come here. To even know about this place. Its existence has been a solemn secret for over a century. So it is expected that it remains that with you."

Darius nodded.

"Very good then, please follow me downwards."

As the two men descended the stairs, Darius could not help but notice the back of Cristoph's head – the neat, trimmed hairline, the salt and pepper look, a sleek style of his hair, held closely with a hair care product, giving it a wet look. And the skin. The supple skin. So youthful in appearance; and then, it carried him back to when he saw Cristoph for the first time.

Sacrafice was open back in Miami, the music was thumping, and the lights were shining lasers across the top of the dance floor.

Darius had been staring into his glass at the bar across from the stage. He looked up for a moment, out across the dance floor, and watched the sweating, writhing bodies in the billowing white smoke. Zahara had been spinning that night. And then a deliciously fine young man walked into his line of sight and blocked his view.

"Hey!" Darius called out. His voice was lost in the pounding dance music cascading across the walls. The man did not move. "Do you hear me?" Darius reached out and touched his shoulder. He turned around, and Darius sat back on his barstool.

There was a certain aura about this man. Youthful yet mature, he had the face of a young, uncertain boy – but the wisps of greying at the temples indicated a more advanced age. "You really have to tell me what you are doing," Darius said, leaning back towards the bar, as he picked up his glass and took a sip. The man's face shifted, but he smiled. "Doing?"

Darius set his glass down with a clank on the marble. "Yes. Doing. You seem so extraordinarily young…but I see your hair. Are you truly youthful?"

The man smiled, looked down, and took a step back. He looked at Darius again. "You are clearly after someone different," he said. "Perhaps a twink? I am not that."

"I know you are not that," Darius said. He stood. "That's why I pointed that observation out to you. And that's why I asked you that question. For you must have wisdom, but what are your years? So I ask what you are doing. Either you have had some experience with the Miami plastic surgery market, or you could share more in common with me than I first thought."

Darius came back to the present, still staring at the back of Cristoph's head, as their surroundings changed. Yes, that night, years ago back in Miami, was when Darius had learned that Cristoph was, in fact, immortal. And that he was far older, and much wiser, than Darius.

Cristoph flicked a light switch and a small, incandescent bulb lightened the yellowish walls. The stairs were wooden, old and creaky, and it smelled of mustiness and mildew. Cristoph had shut and locked the door behind them, and as they descended the stairs, he continued. "The Inspiriti has been put into place to serve as a representative group for all immortals around the world. We have our representation here with this organization. All of us, whether good or evil. We represent the supernatural, the paranormal."

"In what matters?" Darius asked.

"Matters such as this. Which is why we called you here. This hooded man is causing such a great stir, we must put him to a stop. We are in place to preserve our kind."

Cristoph opened the lower door to an open hallway.

And then Darius was standing in the lower catacombs, in the chambers of The Inspiriti. Cristoph had left him outside the conference room, went inside, and closed the door. Darius sat in a small plastic chair in the hallway just outside the door and waited.

Not before long, the door opened.

A large, imposing man, with an equally large gut, exited the room, which appeared dark. "Good morning Darius," he said. "I am Monsignor Harrison. Thank you for coming on such short notice, but we have some concerns about Miami and the eastern third of the United States. Please do come in."

Darius stood and entered the conference room. It was dark; a projector was running on the opposite end of the room, with a large map of Miami projected onto the opposite wall. There were men and women around the conference table; although Darius could not recognize any familiar faces in the darkness, he did see a small chair in the front of the room and facing the table.

"Please sit there," the Monsignor said, gesturing over to the chair. "We need to get started."

Darius took his seat and the Monsignor took a chair at the end of the table not far from where Darius sat. The priest gestured for the lights, and the room was then bathed in stark white light, washing out the projection screen to a blank field. The Monsignor cleared his throat, looked downwards at the papers and files on the table in front of him, and put on a small pair of rectangular reading glasses. Darius scanned the room for familiar faces. Men and women lined the conference table, there would about a dozen, and he scanned, back and forth, until he saw her white hair. And she smiled. Delia. Of course she would be there. Darius felt a twinge of relief.

"Thank you again for coming on such short notice," the Monsignor said. "Let's begin."

He stood and Darius watched the booming man take his place in the center of the room. He snapped off the projector, and then looked around the room. "Darius Sauvage is here with us today. He is facing a challenging predicament – he is mortal again, he has lost his immortality, and is facing a certain and final death if we cannot intervene. The only thing that will save him is to drink from the Christ's Cup – which, at this time, we are unware of the location of the cup or even if it still physically exists after so many years. But that, everyone, is another story for another time. Why we are gathered here today is to determine the how and why Darius finds himself in this situation. Darius here has been so kind as to fly here from Miami on a moment's notice, so we can get an idea of who he is and his origins." Monsignor Harrison took a few steps back and gestured. "Darius."

Darius' eyes widened as he looked around the room.

The Monsignor took his seat and gestured once again for Darius to begin. Darius stood in the front of the room, and looked outwards at the people sitting around the conference table. Delia smiled at him again.

"*Bon Giorno*, to the High Council," Darius said. He removed his jacket and placed it on a nearby chair, and stood again in front of the room, and clasped his hands together at his waist. "I will get right to it. There was an exact, very precise moment when I knew that Antoine would be the one that I transformed into my son. It came many years before I had first spotted in him the café; for I had been following him and watching him all of that time."

The Monsignor interrupted. "And where can we find Antoine? We would like to question him as well."

Darius looked downwards. "I've just flown to Europe from Miami, after the battle at the Sea of Souls. Antoine has just died on the altar at the hands of Nesmaron, the demon that Roberto had transformed into. I'm afraid he is currently not living."

Delia stood.

Darius noticed her stringy, silver hair, and the silver pendant that hung around her neck. "Darius, tell the group about your experience in Miami recently. About the man who visited you. The 'Hooded Man', as he is called. And tell us about what is happening to you now. Physically and emotionally."

Darius nodded and cleared his throat.

"Okay. So as you know, Antoine had resurrected me a few years back. He brought me to Miami and I have been living in that area with him ever since. The demon Asmodai had been following Antoine since the days in Lyon, when he brought me back. Claret had also been pursuing Antoine. And somehow, Antoine was betrayed. Dragged to an altar and burned to ashes."

"When did this happen?" Delia asked, leaning forward.

"Just recently. Antoine was a very particular leader – he was all about charisma and presentation. Miami loved him. But he met someone who betrayed him. Sought his power, I suppose."

Delia sat back and nodded.

Several of the people around the table took some notes on large, yellow legal pads. Cristoph sat at the corner of the table typing on a small laptop. The Monsignor removed his glasses and sat back in his chair. "Go on, Darius," he said. "Tell us more of your story. When did you first encounter this 'Hooded Man'?"

Darius pulled one of the small side chairs to the center of the room and sat. "I had been living in Miami for several years when I first saw this man. A man who wore a hood. I had heard a few people talking about him – in nightclubs and bars, mainly. That's where we would always hang out. Everyone would always talk – about the man in the hood who rode in on a cloud of white mist and carried a decanter. It was a big rumor that was talked about in hushed conversations, but that was about it. The man seemed to be a mythical figure. Everyone I had talked to had heard of someone who had drank from the decanter, so everyone knew someone who was dying, but I knew of no one personally. Well, he came to me."

"And what does this decanter do?" The Monsignor asked.

Darius shrugged as Delia raised a finger. "I have performed some research on this decanter, your greatness. It's a weapon to lure the immortals to early deaths."

The room erupted in chatter.

"Silence!" The Monsignor stood. "Everyone, please! We cannot jump to conclusions. Please be quiet and let Darius finish his story."

After a few minutes, the chatter in the room died down, and Darius continued. "The story on the streets goes like this: a man in the hood visits an immortal shortly before their 'death'. He targets immortals who have lost the gift. He carries this decanter – which has a bulbous base and top, and looks similar to a whiskey decanter. But it has a red, swirling potion inside. He convinces his victims to drink from it, insisting it brings them salvation."

"How does he do that?" The Monsignor sat back down.

Delia answered. "He is very convincing, your highness. So many immortals believe they are damned for all of eternity. This 'Hooded Man' places a spell on the immortals he encounters. He convinces them that drinking the potion will save them and offer them redemption."

"A spell? And will it offer them redemption?"

Darius looked at the man directly. "No, your highness. The decanter brings death. But yes to your other question. He recites some sort of an incantation as he approaches his victim. And what we have been finding so far, is that the spell does not fail. Like it didn't fail with me."

"I see." The Monsignor nodded and gestured for Darius to continue. Darius looked around the room, stood, and removed his shirt. His chest was covered in tiny, red sores. "I am dying, everyone. I drank from the decanter, and now I am dying a quick physical death. I am twenty-five, but how old do I appear?"

Delia looked down at the table, and wiped her eyes.

Darius looked at those around the conference table and no one said a word. Darius was macerated and sickly thin. He placed his hand on his head.

One of the priests at the end of the table stood. "How do you know that you were enchanted? That you were under a spell? And not just simply fascinated by his potion?"

The room erupted in chatter once again.

Darius looked at the man. His small framed barely hovered over the table. He adjusted his glasses as he waited for Darius to provide an answer. The small priest spoke again as the chatter in the room died down. "Darius, we have studied you. Researched your life and how it has led up to that particular moment. We have watched you and how you relate with Antoine, how you have become a cold blooded killer. Do you think that maybe you have become a little lost in your ways?"

Darius shook his head. "No…" He sat down slowly and stared at the contents on the table. There were several books – thick research volumes – and several files. Large photos of himself, as well as Antoine, some other photos of Miami, and another folder that was marked CONFIDENTIAL. Darius reached for the folder as his voice trailed off. "No, not at all…"

Monsignor Harrison gestured for the small priest to sit, and then looked back over at Darius. "I am certain you understand your predicament. And the purpose of this hearing is to help you, not to harm you."

Darius flipped through a folder filled with glossy photos of the park, the dead cops, the young Hispanic man, and himself. There were also copious reports and handwritten notes. He looked up at the board, and then back up and around at the High Council. "When was all of this assembled?"

The Monsignor answered without hesitation. "We have had some operatives in Miami trailing you for some time now."

Darius took a step back and shook his head. He looked down at the files and photos, spread out on the table. "So you are saying…what…I am being watched? For what purpose?"

Monsignor Harrison leaned forward and folded his hands. He raised his eyes to view Darius directly. "Darius, you have been quite a burden for our society. You have drawn attention to yourself for centuries. Your whole tutelage of Antoine has been sub-par. He is lost. A lost immortal, Darius. You have failed him."

Darius felt his heart race and the skin at his temples tighten. His face grew hot. He swallowed, and took a moment to gather his thoughts. "Let me get this straight," he said. "You are telling me that I am what – a failed immortal? What are you trying to do with me? Throw me away? Toss me out with the trash?"

The Monsignor stood. "Now, Darius. No reason to get upset."

Darius grabbed his jacket. His eyes flared. "Just let me be clear on one thing, your highness. Am I being excommunicated?"

The Monsignor sighed. "Put down your coat, my son. Please calm down. And this may help."

Monsignor Harrison removed his glasses and walked over to the dark side of the room, grabbing a small folding chair. He sat directly next to Darius and looked directly into his eyes.

"Sit down," he said.

Darius was still breathing heavy.

"Sit down and calm down," Monsignor Harrison said again, this time more insistent.

Darius set his coat down on the table slowly, and sat. He glared into the Monsignor's eyes.

Monsignor Harrison sat back and a deep breath. "Look into my eyes, Darius. I am going to hypnotize you. You must remember, my son." He motioned to one of the other officials and the lights were dimmed. He picked up a candle from the conference table, struck a match and lit it.

Darius felt his eyelids getting heavier with each passing second.

"I want you to think, Darius. Open your mind to what I am saying. Think about the days when you first were transformed. Think about Tramos. And how he came into your life. Open your mind to me, Darius…"

Darius could not help it, he closed his eyes, and then he was standing in the same rooms that he had so many years ago, when he was still mortal. He remembered the same, small bedroom with the eastern facing window; the same, delicate curtains that hung on the window, and the same small bed in the center of the room.

"What happened in that room, Darius?"

Darius shifted in his seat but his eyes did not open. "He could come to me there...he would visit me...and then he transformed me..."

"Go on, Darius. Take us there. Take us back to Lyon...it's time to remember Tramos..."

LYON

A small spider scurried across the wall, heading up towards the ceiling as a cool summer breeze blew through the window and across Darius' face. He could hardly remember the night before. He picked at the grit in his eyes, and felt the ache in his legs. Had he been running? He couldn't remember, but swung his legs over the side of the bed and padded across the room, shaking the sleep out of his head.

Darius did not always live in Lyon.

He did not venture to the south of France until he was in his early twenties; but it was there, when he had lived in a new city and away from the constrictions of his mother and father, he found a new vision of his life; at which point that he blossomed as a mortal.

Darius also could not remember the last time that he saw Tramos. Once Darius had received the gift, the immortality that he had once so longed for as a young mortal man, he was very quickly abandoned.

Tramos, oh dear Tramos. Are you with me? Tramos, are you there?

During those first days, in the genesis of his new immortal life, he found himself frequently in deep thought.

And it always was about Tramos.

Darius could still see the long, flowing hair as he always walked in front of Darius; he could still feel the roping, powerful muscles in his back, and the commanding way he would carry himself.

But as quickly as Tramos was there, he was gone. It was always that way; Tramos would appear for minutes or moments, but never stay.

There were years of uncertainty long before Darius lost the gift – when he had become a mortal for the second time in his life. For in the beginning, he was not always the confident immortal that he once was; and, as there had been with Antoine, there was also a long period of time where Darius had his own lessons to learn; where he had become the student as opposed to his usual role of the mentor. A time when Darius sought confidence, the quest, the path to freedom; to independence and surviving in this new, foreign world on his own.

"I am going to walk tonight on my own," Darius found saying to himself as he would rise in the evening. He was a young immortal; many would mistake him as a vampire. And to even more, he was appear as that of a vampire. But in such an infantile stage of immortality, the case of mistaken identity was a common one.

"I was never a vampire," Darius had explained, centuries later, to his psychiatrist, Claire Winchester, in Miami, while dying as a mortal. He had started seeing Claire after he lost his immortality. "People once mistook me for a vampire. As they also had with Antoine. But it's a silly mistake. Vampires are mythical figures. They're heroes in stories. Folklore and such. But angels and demons…the supernatural is real. *We* are real."

But in the early days when Darius had become the student, he had been most vulnerable.

The first night, that first terrible night, his eyes opened. He could still feel the grit and dirt between his eyelids, and he instinctively reached his finger towards the edges of the bed and was halted by a solid surface. His head throbbed.

"Tramos? Are you there?"

Only silence.

His eyes were having trouble adjusting to the darkness, but he could sense confinement. Not that of a cage, but more of a box. He shifted his body, and heard a dull creak.

He shifted again.

The same creak followed. But there was still only darkness. And an overwhelming sense of confinement.

Feeling that the grit and dirt were cleaned sufficiently, he opened his eyes once again. He tried to raise his hands, and they were blocked, by an unseen ceiling. Something soft, like a fabric, yet with a hardness underneath, like wood. Soft though, initially, yes. Perhaps fabric. Cotton or satin of some sort. Yes, perhaps that was it.

But it was the solidity of his surroundings that bothered him. And the darkness that would eat away at his mind.

He could feel his heartbeat as he looked to the left, and then snapped his head to the right. "Tramos?! Where are you?"

And then he reached out towards his right. The same softness covering the same hardness. And then to his left. Once again, the same.

He took a deep breath and held it, and shifted once again. The same creaking, like wood on steel, like metal shifting on top of stone, ensued.

What happened to Tramos?

He racked his mind to remember, as he exhaled. He closed his eyes once again.

There had been a small café, although it may have been a bar. He remembered that much. The wine had been flowing freely. He remembered that as well. And when he concentrated, when he tried with all of his might, he could see the wine glass. The deep red liquid, and the tiny bubbles that hugged the side of his glass. And as he raised the glass, he saw the glass rising closer towards his lips, upwards, expanding, as the deep, dark liquid started flowing towards him...

...and then he lowered the glass from his lips, and saw Tramos in a fit of laughter. His teeth were gleaming white and well pronounced. Darius looked down at his wine glass as he placed it on the table, and looked up again at Tramos, who was slapping his knee, and then leaned back in his chair, and stared at Darius intently.

And then, after just a few moments, Tramos shuffled a bit, and regained his composure. He looked over the table at Darius with wide eyes, framed by long, golden hair that reached down towards his powerful arms. He smiled at Darius, and paused for a moment, reaching his arm across the table. "Stop this nonsense, Darius. This is just a replay of this in your mind. You are seeing this again, but you are lying in a coffin. I won't be there, I promise you that. And you will find your way. I promise you that too."

Darius looked up from his wine. "Where are you Tramos? Have you abandoned me? Will you leave me?"

"I have not abandoned you. I have always been, and will always be with you. It's up to you to listen to what I have to say to you."

"What do you have to say to me?"

Tramos looked at Darius, directly in the eyes. He leaned in closer, hovering over the table, and reached his arm out, placing an enormous hand on Darius' back shoulder, drawing him in. "I come with a warning." Tramos took his hand down and placed it over Darius'."

Darius paused for a moment, and looked down at the large, muscular hand covering his. The fingers, he noticed, were large, thick and pulsating. Neatly trimmed nails. Veins spider webbing up a muscular forearm. Clean and powerful, yet soft and reassuring and protecting. Tramos spoke again, leaning in closer towards where Darius was sitting, and spoke again, this time at a much lower level. "A warning, Darius. I come with a warning."

And Tramos reached his arm upwards, and the activity in the bar halted. When Darius looked around the room, he saw the same small, dark tables. But the candles in the center of each table had a flame which was frozen still, and when his gaze drifted off towards the bar, he saw the bartender, holding his arms upwards, holding a mixing glass and shaker, frozen in the process of mixing cocktails. And the patrons, scattered about the room, some at the small, dark tables, others leaning against the wooden columns that reached down from the ceiling to the floor, and even more huddled over the bar top, looking upwards to where the bartender had been doing his mixing – all frozen still and silent in a semblance of a painting.

"My warning is of a great unfortunate prophecy. I have inserted myself into your memory so you can make a difference for our kind. There will be one that will come, and his only purpose will be to destroy us."

"What do you mean?" Darius said.

"I mean there will be an imposter. And he will behave as though he has the key to our redemption. Our salvation. But he won't be one to be trusted. None of it will be true. All lies. There will be many stories that you will learn in your days and years as an immortal, Darius. You are remembering this night. The night I transformed you. But since you were transformed, so much has happened. And now, our kind is being wiped off the face of the earth."

Darius looked down at his wine again and opened his hands. "I am just someone who has been watching you from the other end of the bar. Didn't we just get past first names?"

Tramos shook his head and adjusted his sitting position, looking Darius straight in the eyes once again. "Darius, please understand. Right now, yes, in your mind, you are still an uncertain human, but I am here, everything here has frozen, because I needed to break into this memory of yours and let you know that things have changed. You will accept my gift that I will offer you later after you and I leave the café. You will become an immortal. And there will be others. You will find a son of your own. The 'Blood Lineage' will continue. But my warning will come just but once…"

"Why did you choose now? Why now?"

"Because you will always remember this event. Your transformation into darkness. It's a transition that you will never forget."

"…And your warning…"

"Yes. My warning. I am coming into this memory to give you a piece of knowledge. You see, when the café around us returns to normal, and you are transported back to the moment you were in with me, on the night that we first met you will be somewhat changed."

"Changed how?"

"You will still be exactly who you were on the night that we sat here, in this café, and enjoyed our wine together. And all of the events that happened after that night, will still happen, in the same order and in the same fashion. The only thing that will be different is that you will know that a man in a hood is exterminating our kind. And it will not happen for many, many years after this night that I transformed you. But you will know of it. I am inserting this memory into your mind. I pray you never forget it, dear Darius."

And then the bar erupted in laughter, Darius looked up from his wine, and Tramos was gone. Darius stood and looked onwards, through the boisterous bar patrons, across towards the door. It was slightly ajar.

Darius made his way through the crowd, pushing people aside and excusing himself, but never taking his eyes off the door.

And then, when he exited the bar, he felt the cold sting in the air; he could see his hot breath emit tiny clouds of vapor under the stars, and he scanned the area. A forest to the left. Rolling terrain to the right, fields, with an occasional tree dotting the landscape. It was a bright, moonlit night, and the gravel in front of him reflected a light, blue hue.

He was startled for a moment when two drunk patrons spilled out of the bar door. But he returned his gaze to the field.

Where are you Tramos?

The walk home took a bit, and when he crossed the river and towards his small modest cottage, he paused at the front door. He looked around his shoulder. There was a forest on the opposite side of the small, dirt road that ran in front of his cottage. "Tramos? Are you there?"

But there was no answer.

The room remained silent as the lights were turned back on. Darius, and others, squinted as their eyes adjusted to the assault of the bright fluorescents. Monsignor Harrison took his seat back at the head of the conference table, and rubbed his eyes. Darius looked around the room, and then focused on Delia. Her face was shifted with concern and looked like she was about to cry.

The Monsignor shook his head and sighed. He closed the file and looked back up at Darius. "You were given a warning, Darius. A warning. You *knew* this was going to happen. And you did nothing."

Darius looked down and his hands. They were clasped in his lap. He twitched his fingers. "I did not remember. Not until tonight."

The Monsignor slammed his fist on the table. "Darius, he told you! Tramos came to you! He warned you! We could have known about this *years* ago had you shared this with us. Now we are being exterminated!"

Delia closed her eyes and lowered her head. "Darius, why did you block this? Why did you repress this memory?"

Darius stood and pleaded with the group. He reached his hands outwards. "I didn't even know I had this memory to repress!"

The Monsignor stood and shook his head. "Darius Sauvage. You have lost your dark gift of immortality as you drank from the blood decanter. The hooded man has found you, and sentenced you to a life of eternal damnation. You are now mortal again, and shunned from this group. You will have a short life, and after, an eternity of darkness and punishment. Now, you will leave these quarters, never to return again. May God have mercy on your soul."

MIAMI

There was a time when Darius remembered the moment of his death, and could still remember the words that Antoine spoke to him, as he lay in the cusp of the astral dimension, his soul barely clinging to life: "The dark ones didn't come, my friend. They didn't come."

And then he remembered slipping way.

And rising from the bed. He remembered looking back down at the bed – his body still lay on the mattress, and he noticed that Antoine had pulled up the sheets so they covered his chest, and his arms were clasped over his torso. He remembered walking around the room, the same room in the same Chateau that he had lived in for so many years; the same light curtains hung on the windows, the curtains that had caught the summertime breeze so many times when he lived there, and their blowing served as one of the last memories that he ever had while living.

But now, as his body lay in the bed next to him, the room felt different.

Things felt different. They looked different.

He looked down at his feet. Barefoot, the same small hairs on the top of his foot, the same few freckles…but he could not feel the floor. He raised his hands. They didn't appear as aged as they had before; perhaps some renewal was taking place.

Despite the different sensations, he still could remember his first few moments in the afterlife, and it wasn't what he had expected, not in the least.

Darius could feel the sting in the air; the winter chill had been significant that year, and as he walked closer to the river's edge, he could see each breath leave his body like a cloud of smoke against the glassy air. He pulled his jacket close to his body, and rubbed his arms as he walked, his footsteps, each crunching through the frozen grass, and, as he left the glowing café lights behind him, the warmth of their small booth, and Tramos sitting in the chair, he picked up his pace, as each step in the gravel quickened up the point of a jog.

He looked over his shoulder.

The café lights, as warm as they seemed, grew distant, but despite his speed, Darius continued to look behind him.

You will return, my Darius, my dear, sweet, Darius. You will return.

Darius flung the front door open and did not bother to light his way through the house. He found his door, made every effort of silence, and found the warmth of his bed. But, even in the safety and solitude of his bedroom, the lights of the café far behind him, sleep did not come to him that night. While the early morning hour was already at hand, it was still several hours before sunrise.

Darius lay under the covers, pulled up and over his head, still in his clothing from the night before, smelling of wine and of Tramos.

Darius shut his eyes as tight as he could and covered his ears with his hands. "No, no, no." He shook his head back and forth, realizing what was outside, just on the other side of the wall behind him, standing in the moonlight, a beast as tall as his house, with clenched fists and roping arm muscle.

There was a light, methodic tap on the window. A fingernail rapping on glass.

I hear you, Tramos.

But there was only silence. No answer.

I remember you when you visited me each night, when you stayed with me until the sun would rise over the eastern sky. And when you were with me, drinking wine and breaking bread.

Darius kept his eyes closed, and envisioned Tramos in front of him. His long, golden hair, warm, inviting smile, the beaming bright teeth which caught the light. He remembered that much.

And who was the monster outside his window? Who was the demon in the passing breeze, walking back and forth through the puddles that caught the moonlight in their tiny little worlds?

A giant webbed foot stomped in one of the puddles, setting the reflected moon into chaos. Darius could see that much, for there was one reason why he was lying in that bed, with the covers pulled towards his head. "Tramos I am here! Have you come for me again tonight?" He flung the covers down to his waist, and felt some relief as the cool air hit his face and torso.

There was a connection.

Darius could see the monster, pressed up against his window, just outside. Hovering, breathing deep, grating and raspy. Darius knew what he would see if he drew the curtains apart.

But the monster was coming.

There was a crash of thunder and a bright flash of light. Darius shielded his eyes, and as the thunder subsided, he kept his eyes closed, and heard a light rain patter against the windowpane. But it wasn't the rain that Darius had been concerned with. For he could not open his eyes. He dared not. For in the room, he could hear what he was trying so hard not to hear, the deep breaths and the shuffling of heavy footsteps around his bedside.

He squeezed his eyes closed until they hurt. Until the dull ache behind his temples forced him to ease the tension. But he kept his eyes closed, and easing the force did nothing. For the monster was still there, hovering over his bed. He could smell the hot, putrid breath above him. And then the monster spoke, with a deep precision, from well within its throat.

"Open your eyes."

Darius did as he was commanded.

And when he saw the monster looking down upon him, his tension eased. It was Tramos. The familiar demon of his dreams and nightmares. It was the same monster, the long, pointed fingers, the musclebound chest, powerful arms and torso. And then the demon looked directly down at him with glowing eyes shaped liked prisms.

"*Open…your…eyes!*"

"They are open…"

Darius hugged himself. And looked into the glowing prisms. "Tramos? Is that you? Are you the light?"

The demon moved his head downwards, closer to where Darius lay. "It is I. Now will you rise from that bed and come with me? Will you pledge the same promise you did when we were speaking earlier?"

Darius raised himself up on his elbows. "Why did you tell me again? Why didn't you remind me about your warning?"

Tramos sat on the edge of the bed and looked down at Darius. "My dear Darius," he said. "I'm afraid it is too late. These are all thoughts…just merely thoughts…that are permeating your mind as you lay in your bed, in your Chateau, just after death. Antoine is there. He is watching over you.

Your mind is decompressing. It is downloading your life. You must not think that these things are happening to you again."

Darius sat up and let the covers fall. He stared at the wall, and closed his eyes after a few moments of silence. "I cannot understand this, Tramos. I feel so lost."

Tramos put a muscular arm around Darius and hugged him close to his chest. "You will find your way, Darius. Just like you did when you first transformed into immortality. You will find your way through the spirit world. It takes time. And now you have so much of it."

Darius shook his head and looked up into Tramos' eyes. "Will I ever return?"

Tramos nodded. "Yes. Death is never final, Darius. It's merely a change. Think of yourself as the butterfly."

DELIA ARNETTE

PARIS

Mother was crying.

She knew that much.

As she looked on, watching her mama cry, she stood behind the door and could almost feel the warmth of the tears running down her cheeks, and hear the quiver in her voice as she spoke in broken sentences. The voices were muffled and low, but could see the feet scuffle across the floor. She cupped the sides of her face and peeked through the crack. She had the door open, just a crack, just so much that the darkness of the bedroom was pierced by a finger of light. But she did not dare open the door.

She leapt back and fell on her bum as heavy footsteps barreled down the wooden floor, just outside her bedroom door. She crawled under the bed covers and drew them up and over her head. She knew that Mother was crying. She could hear her sobbing in the other room.

She remembered that much. She could hear the muffled tears emanating through the door as she peered through the crack. Had mother come to check on her? It was late in the evening, perhaps very early in the morning. Delia had gone to bed for what seemed like hours earlier, and then she heard a thump in the house.

"Delia, come here!"

She skittered back into the bed and yanked the sheets up towards her neck.

And then the door opened with a creak, and light spilled into the room.

She lay still with her eyes closed, but could still sense the presence. Footsteps walked slowly towards her bedside and stopped. The scent of alcohol wafted into the room, and she sensed him standing over her bedside.

Father.

There was a time when she loved her father. There was a time, which seemed so far away and unreachable, that the man who was standing over her bed was loving; one that cared for her and mother and had been the protector.

But times were different.

She remembered when doors slammed and china plates were hurled across the room. But then the drinking got worse; and the nights post binge drinking became increasingly difficult for her to endure. She would lock herself into her room, retire early, and lay in bed in a cocoon of blankets, trying to ignore the muffled scuffling in the next room.

But it was always impossible.

And sleep would rarely come without a fitful fight of adjusting the covers; turning from one side the other; holding the pillow over her head to block the raised voices that would be just out in the hallway outside her bedroom door, traveling through the living room and kitchen.

Mother and Father were fighting again.

She could still remember the wetness on her cheeks as she lay in bed with the covers pulled tightly over her head; lying helpless on the hot nights, her legs sweating, her hair matted to her forehead as she dared not lift the covers for cool air.

This night, in particular, it had been worse than usual. She remembered that much. For when she stood at the door, looking outwards through the thin crack of light, she could see, from the corner of her eye, her mother.

Lying on the living room floor in a pool of blood.

Her heart thumped in her chest, but she continued to look through the slit. And she dared not run out to her mother. For he would find her.

And that was when she ran back into her bed and slid under the covers. And shortly after, he was there.

"I saw you get out of bed, Delia."

She lie frozen still, listening to him speak, wishing he could go away. She shivered despite the heat.

"Your mother had it comin'."

And then Delia opened her eyes, and she was no longer in the warm bed. She saw the gravestones, standing in the middle of the cemetery in the late fall, in a cold, falling rain, in a barren, brown and dead landscape. She could feel the sting of the cold air against her cheeks; she could hear the tinny sound of the frozen rain against the dry, cracked leaves and blades of grass.

And then she closed her eyes, as the warmth of the tears cut into the chill on her cheeks, and she listened to the casket being lowered into the ground.

Oh, Mother.

And then she saw the flap of a dark coat blowing in the wind behind a gravestone several rows from the burial service. And she could not stop staring at it.

Oh, Mother, I can still hear your sweet lullaby...

I can still feel the warm touch of your skin...

"But she is going to be down there rotting."

There was a light passing breeze, and a brief clearing, as the clouds increased and tiny droplets of rain started to fall again. She felt a drop on her cheek as she closed her eyes, standing over the casket, letting the wave of emotions pass. She opened her eyes again after hearing the phantom female voice. "Who?" All she could see were the same gravestones and the same rain, dried up and dead grass. She looked to her left, and saw the mourners leaving. The casket was now lowered into the ground, but not buried yet. A mound of dirt still was at the side.

But mother was gone. And the voice, she could not find the source of the voice.

As she stood, she closed her eyes again. She remembered her days when Mother was alive, as footsteps crunched in the leaves behind her, approaching. She opened her eyes and turned around. The woman smiled and removed her large, dark sunglasses. Tiny tufts of red hair wisped out from underneath her beret. "I am very sorry for your loss," she said.

Delia nodded. "Do I know you?"

The woman looked down and moved closer to Delia.

"No, you do not," she said. She took Delia's hands and looked into her eyes. "My name is Claret Atarah."

Claret put her arms around Delia. She looked over at her. "I am here because I have been watching you. I have seen what you have endured. I have selected you because of it."

She looked at Claret. Her eyes were warm and reassuring. There was a slight smile on her face. Delia looked down. "You have been watching me? Do you know me?"

"I do not know you personally, no. But I assure you, I am a friend, and you can trust me."

Delia stopped walking and turned to face Claret. "My mother just died, ma'am. I am sorry, but now is not the time to – "

Claret put her hand to Delia's mouth, very gently. "No worries, dear child. I am here to love and protect you. That is what you need in your life. I am your war angel."

The waves of emotions overtook her, and then she fell into Claret's arms. There was a moment that Delia did not mind that she fell into the arms of a stranger. There were days that she didn't recognize herself in the mirror. For many days, after the funeral, she would walk through the house, tip toeing on creaky floorboards, looking outside towards the fading afternoon sunlight.

"I did not murder your mother."

Delia stood motionless in the hallway, wearing a red, flowing dress, looking at her father. Studying him. Watching his every movement.

"You said she had it *comin'*". Delia glared at him.

Her father shook his head and set the shovel down next to the door. "Yes, I did. And she did. But I did not do it. Your mother isn't the saint you think she was."

Delia turned and stormed back into her room.

And when inside, she kneeled on her bed and looked out the window. The moon was shining brightly, highlighting the city in pale blue and white fade; the buildings in Paris looked like stacked dominoes. But Delia knew that she wanted out. She wanted a different life. She wanted to experience the city, the country, the world. She remembered the days of her childhood. Her mother had always been there for her. But now, that she was gone, Delia wanted to move on with her life. She let the curtains fall back over the window and lay in bed.

And there was a time that she wanted to perform. She looked at the lovely ladies, their brilliant red lipstick, puffy skirts and flawless skin. Under the lights, they were beautiful. Dancing on stage, the music was playing, the lights were bright and hot, and the stage was up and above the crowd.

There was a light knock at the window.

Delia got up and peeked outside the shears. She recognized the woman from the cemetery earlier that day and raised the window. Claret bent downwards to speak. "Have you thought about my proposition?"

Delia sat back on the bed as Claret smiled. She fidgeted for a minute and then looked back up at Claret. She took a step back and looked downwards. "No, I can't. I cannot commit my life to evil. My mother always taught me that. I don't want to go to hell."

Claret reached down and raised the window, and started to climb in. She looked up at Delia and smiled. "Who said you were going to hell?"

Delia looked down, sighed and shook her head. She looked back up. "Isn't that what happens? Something just doesn't seem right about too much success. You become rich, you must be evil."

Claret chuckled as she entered the small bedroom. "Who taught you that?"

A light rain started to fall outside, and Claret came inside and sat on the bed next to Delia. Thunder rumbled in the distance. "A storm is coming," Delia said.

Claret nodded. "Oh it's been here, Delia. It's been here for a while."

Delia nodded.

"So now, when are you going to let me in? Into your life, Delia? When will you invite me?"

Delia paused for a moment as thunder rumbled in the sky above the apartment building. After a few minutes, rain started to pelt against the windowpane, and she looked over at Claret, who was sitting next to her patiently, smiling, her eyebrows raised.

"You seem…evil…"

Claret threw her head back in laughter. "You think *that*? You must really have a hard time reading people, Delia. Look at me. Have I done anything evil to you?"

Delia shook her head.

"So then. Will you consider my proposition?"

Claret smiled, revealing brilliant white teeth. "Good then," she said. "So I will leave you for now, dear one. I will give you some more time. I will return, though, Delia. You are too special. There are too many passages already written about you. You are too special and too needed to pass up."

Claret raised the window as Delia looked on. "I will come to you again, Delia. I don't know when it will be. But I will always remember you. And you will always be the special one that you are. You have the gift that we seek. And one day, I will reappear to you, special one."

Delia escaped to Paris once she was more mature and took a liking to Vaudeville, which had just made its introduction to the area in the late 1800's. She waited in the alley outside the club, leaning against the cool brick wall, and closed her eyes, listening to the muffled music, still playing strong to laughter and applause. She opened her eyes and looked around the corner.

It was well past four in the morning.

The music still thumped inside, but she sunk down the brick wall and lit a cigarette. She blew out a cloud of smoke and looked down the alley, and saw very little pedestrian traffic on the sidewalk towards the street. A solitary drunk couple staggered by. After the show, she was exhausted. She leaned against the wall, smoking a cigarette, waiting for Darius.

She remembered Claret, and the days when she had visited her as a child.

And her mother, how she missed her mother so much.

Over a century after she had stood in the alley in Paris, and remembered Claret as she was waiting for her next act, she was called to Rome as well, and sat in the same office, with the same priests – Monsignor Harrison and Ramiel and Cristoph – to discuss the same issue which was plaguing the immortals.

She had looked up, wearing the same bright red lipstick that she had worn during her Vaudeville nights. Candles burned around them.

"I miss Paris." Delia said. "I miss the Vaudeville nights. The brilliant red lipstick. The smoke billowing from my mouth. The puffy skirts. The hot lights. The dusty stage. Oh, how I miss it all. I wish I could go back to it."

Cristoph shifted in his chair behind the expansive desk. His cassock was tight. The silence was impenetrable, but after a few moments, an organ played in a distant room above in the Sistine. "So that is when she met you? During those nights in Paris?"

She remembered the first night. The night that the mysterious woman came to the show, sat in the center of the seats, and as Delia performed, looking out into the dark seats, she could get a glimpse of her. Despite the shining hot lights in front of her face, she noticed Claret, sitting in the audience, staring directly at her.

Looking like a china doll with her neatly tucked red hair, matching lips, and light skin.

Delia looked down.

Cristoph noticed her pendant, which caught the light, and shined back in his face.

Delia looked up and brushed her silver hair back behind her ear. "No, she came to me long before that."

Cristoph sat back in his chair, and flopped his pen on the desk. He removed his glasses and placed them on the yellow legal pad. "So tell me, Delia. When did she come to you? When did Claret first enter your life? We must know, Delia. Your relation to her is imperative."

Delia sighed and stretched her legs out. She looked down at her legs, noticing the grey stockings she had worn on that day. And then, those were just like the same hosiery that she wore on the same night that Claret had been in the audience, and Delia had been sitting in the same position, backstage, looking down at her outstretched legs. And she'd heard a door creak open near stage left.

She looked up. But she was no longer in the Monsignor's office. She was on the same stage in Paris she had remembered so many years ago. "Yes, may I help you?"

"I watched your show tonight." A warm female voice, slightly raspy, but friendly sounding nonetheless. But she looked over towards the source, and saw darkness.

"I can't see you," Delia said, standing up from her chair. She reached over towards the makeup table for her tiny silver rimmed glasses, but they did not help. The other side of the stage, with its flowing black curtains soaring down from the ceiling, was far too dark.

"I will come out of the shadows," she said.

She shook her head and looked around the room. She got up out of her chair, fishing for her cane. "Cristoph, I really must return to Lyon. Antoine is there, alone. I understand my obligations. But my obligations to him come first before Rome."

Delia rose as the Monsignor looked up at her, speechless.

"So you will not assist us with this investigation?" Cristoph asked, jumping out of his chair. The Monsignor waved and Cristoph said nothing more, as Delia exited. "I will assist," she said. "But you will not get my assistance like this."

Delia waited for her flight in Leonardo da Vinci and considered her meeting with The Inspiriti. She questioned whether the organization was even beneficial to immortals. They had sat her in front of a conference table, asked her about knowledge of a hooded figure that she knew nothing about, and backed her into a corner.

She looked down at her notebook as she heard the rumble of a plane taking off. She looked down and sipped her coffee as someone tapped her on her shoulder.

"Delia," a warm, feminine voice said. "I'm here. Talk to me."

Claret was there. She sat back and smiled. Her red hair was tied back, unusual for her.

"What do you need to help me with?" Delia asked, setting her notebook to the side. She leaned back and looked over at Claret. "And how did you get in here?"

Claret raised her eyebrows and smiled. "You haven't figured out my gift yet? Don't you remember the days I first came to you? And your transformation?"

Delia paused for a moment and looked out at the tarmac. "Don't try to remind me, Claret. You may have given me this gift, this immortality, whatever it may be. But to many, being immortal can be a curse."

CLARET ATARAH

JERUSALEM

"I grew up in the times of Jesus Christ."

"I still remember the day that my captor arrived at the hanging flap that served as my door; when I was sleeping, huddled in my bed, the single, simple and thin cover hugged up tight towards my neck, my eyes shut tight."

Claret paused for a moment, and lit a cigarette. "But I heard his footsteps."

"Thick, heavy on the earthen floor, getting louder and closer as they approached my bed…"

And then Claret remembered.

She remembered the night the 'Hooded Man' came to her, so many centuries ago, in a different time and for a different reason.

"I drew the covers up over my head and listened. The footsteps stopped. But I felt a presence up and over where I lay."

She closed her eyes and was back in the same dusty room. In the small hut east of the market, in the stony sands of Jerusalem.

"Claret…" a deep, rasping voice pierced the silence. "Claret, wake up…"

"But I was awake."

She lay beneath the protection of the cloth blanket, the tattered piece of fabric that secured her from the outside world when she slept, which now would serve as the only barrier between her and him.

"For I remember, now while telling you this, the night when I lay as a child, huddled under the covers, in the chill of the night air, as I covered my eyes with the crook of my arm, and waited."

Claret shifted in her chair, her eyes remained closed, and she continued the vision.

"His breathing was heavy. But he let me lay where I was for minutes. And then the minutes felt like hours, and I watched the edge of the blanket and I waited to hear his breathing. But the night remained silent. And I waited for the covers to be pulled down from my face, waited for his hand to caress my hair, to pull it back from my forehead, but that never happened."

It was a rainy afternoon.

The blinds were open, the sunlight shone through, but the rain dampened it. The day felt like a heavy blanket. Like the sun was somewhere off in a distant place, but the light was still present.

Claret leaned back in her chair. She wanted a cigarette. She started to fidget. Her fingers drummed on the arm of the chair, and she shifted her legs back and forth from one crossed position to another. "So do you understand what I was saying?"

A silver haired man sat in the expansive desk before her. He thumbed through a file. After a few minutes, he reached out and pressed stop on a tape recorder. "This sounds pretty far-fetched."

She leaned back in her chair and let out a deep sigh. "Do you mind if I smoke?"

The silver haired man gestured with his hand and she lit up. He continued to look through the file.

Claret lit up, inhaled, and blew out a cloud of smoke. "Far-fetched?"

The silver haired man looked up from his paperwork and adjusted his tie. "Um…yes. It seems pretty supernatural."

Claret scoffed and took another deep drag on her cigarette. "What am I paying you for again?" She shook her head. "You clearly do not understand any realm other than basic reality."

"Maybe you should try the Church, or maybe a medium, then. Psychiatrists tend to lean towards reality and the human interpretation of it, ma'am."

Claret shook her head and stood, walking over to the door. She looked down at the man who looked up at her. "Well then you recommend some to me," she said. "Because I need some spiritual assistance. I came to you because I thought you could help. And clearly, you don't have the spiritual knowledge to assist in these matters. And by the way – I'll be disputing my credit card charge."

Claret stood outside One Brickell in Miami and thought of her appointment. She dialed her phone and spoke after holding it to her ear for a few moments. "Clearly these mortals are useless," she said, as she lit her cigarette as the traffic roared by. She shook her head. "I don't know why I thought that psychiatry would provide good direction. It doesn't. "

Claret pressed the button to unlock her car doors, but did not get inside. She tossed her purse on the seat and slammed the door, staying outside the car, and leaned against the door, looked up Brickell Avenue towards downtown.

It was a rainy afternoon. The rain was light, and the clouds lent a brightness that filtered the sun, and the wet pavement still shone with the reflecting daylight. She didn't want to return to Andelusia Avenue. With Antoine's estate now a burned out shell, she could not afford to enter through the portal there. But she closed her eyes, the roar of the traffic silenced, and she was there again.

Darkness befell the city of Jerusalem.

In the days when Claret had been newly transformed, after she had experienced the nights with her own 'Hooded Man', she had decided that every immortal should do the same.

The tiny box cutter houses, with their clay walls and straw roofs, rose from the rolling, barren desert landscape like building blocks, stacked neatly against one another, rising up the hills towards the center market square.

It was the same time, the same city, the same Jerusalem that Claret had remembered so long ago; the time when she had been captured in the night, as a little girl, before she was transformed into darkness. But those were so many years ago. In the times when the Messiah – the one they called the Son of God – walked the land, and on the same night that he was betrayed with a single kiss on the cheek.

"The Judas Kiss," she had said to Antoine, one night in *Sacrafice*, in Miami, shortly after the nightclub opened. Antoine had stood at the bar swirling a glass of bourbon and ice.

"The ultimate betrayal, that same kiss, the one that you gave me when you took the cup. When you took it!" Claret slammed her drink down on the bar.

Antoine shook his head and looked at Claret. "I don't have the cup," he said. "It was lost in Cairo, not long after the earthquake. You should have known this."

Claret leaned in closer. "I have been following you for years, Antoine, and I have been watching you. And I know, now, when you are lying to me."

Claret remembered the days when Christ walked the land so vividly, but when she returned, so many centuries later, it was not the same Jerusalem that she had remembered. For so much had happened since that night, her life had taken so many directions, there have been so many descendants, and so many battles fought and wars waged, and now, the battle that she was fighting, she did not even know why she was even waging it any more.

She remembered the night that she first felt the cup in her hands – as she stood on a small, wooden stepstool outside the window, a weathered, white piece of fabric hung over the window, blowing in the passing light breezes, which blocked her view.

But through the tapestry, she could see the figures moving. Hovering around, she could see their movement in the blurred, dark figures through cloth, lined on either side. And when she had peered through the edge of the cloth, she saw the men gathered around a table. It was a small, wooden table along the floor.

And He was in the center of the table, speaking with the men. And He had passed the cup around the table, the bread was shared, and when they adjourned, she climbed up the side and hoisted herself on the dusty ledge, and peered inside.

There it was.

The Cup – the figure of salvation, of eternal life. And she would have it. For the one who drank from the cup and shared called Himself the *King of Kings*.

She must have it.

The 'Hooded Man' demanded it.

And then she hoisted herself up on the ledge, shuffling her weight on the ledge, and rested her abdomen on the stone, and peered inside. Her head was inside the room, and the tapestry hung over her small body like a mosquito net. But her eyes remained transfixed on the prize. The cup. The cup.

And then a hand tugged at her robe.

"Claret! Will you take it? Will you seek its power?"

And then she paused, hanging in the window, and turned her head around. She could see the silhouette of the man's hood and robe in the moonlight. She saw the man pull the tapestry down from the window and toss it to the ground.

She stopped and looked down at her feet. Her dirty toes, her dusty sandals. The cup was inside. She turned to the man in the hood. "What is so special about this cup!?"

"It will bring life eternal, if you drink from it."

She climbed through the window, grunting through the frame. Her long, red hair was dusty, mussed and dirty, and glowed against the fire that was still burning on the far side of the room. The table, a large wooden slab with small pillows surrounding it, was left uncleared. Goblets and plates were sitting at each place, with partially eaten slabs of bread and goblets with bits of wine.

"Come back!" the man hissed. He stood, looking through the window, waving his arm for Claret to return.

CAIRO - 1805

There was a time when Claret did not care what Antoine or Darius did; she knew that they were part of her bloodline, but she cared not at all. But there was a day, when she stood amidst the soaring skyscrapers in modern days, when she could sense that it was time to return to Cairo; to return to the desert.

Claret paused at the corner, north of the market on the dusty streets with the clay houses, the square huts with colorful handwoven linens covering the doors, tapestries propped up with wooden sticks, and little children standing on side walls watching the shopping crowds walk back and forth on the dusty streets. Claret no longer had the red hair that she donned in Miami, for now, her hair was dark, and she was much truer to her heritage.

She dropped the red wig in the dirt below her feet, as she leaned against the concrete, reached for a cigarette, and scanned the crowds. The sun was shining, it was about mid day, and there was no sign of Antoine or Darius.

She waited until sunset.

And then, when the market was closing up for the evening, she saw them. Antoine rode on a Camel right down the center of the buildings, and Darius followed him on his own camel. They paused as a tired, old woman was closing up her merchant tables. And then Claret saw the small, brown satchel.

She waited and watched as Antoine and Darius spoke with the merchant, and then she noticed a smaller man with them – shorter in stature, with sloppy hair and an unshaven face. It could only be Azra. Their pet. Their little immortal who followed them everywhere like a little, obedient dog. Azra was very unkempt, very different from Antoine and Darius. Azra went inside the building as Antoine and Darius dismounted their camels at the side of the building behind the packing merchants. Claret watched them disappear inside.

She walked across the dusty road and stood, watched the old woman hastily rolling tapestries and closing small jars of spices. She looked up at Claret and smiled. "May I help you dear?"

Claret smiled, and took a step back. "Those two men that you just spoke to. I couldn't help but notice them from across the way there. May I ask how you know them?"

"They are staying here." The old woman continued rolling tapestries.

"Staying here?"

"In a room, yes."

But Claret was not able to get the Cup that she sought. And despite crashing through the door and into the courtyard, she felt a sense that Antoine and Darius were not there.

Claret stood on the corner of Washington and 5th and waited patiently, remembering her journey back to Cairo. She leaned against a traffic light, looked down at her watch, and shook her head. The wind caught her red hair, and she reached up and brushed it away from her forehead. She rummaged through her purse and fished out a cigarette, lighter, and hunched over as she flicked the lighter.

"Claret?"

She turned up and saw the boy. His hair was slicked back, as Darius had described. He was wearing an oversized pair of dark sunglasses. "I was told to look for the woman with the red hair."

She nodded. "So you've found me. Now let's go. I need to take you inside."

Claret turned around and faced a red brick building, with cement steps that rose to a set of double doors. She reached into her pocket and jingled a set of keys. "Here we go!"

She unlocked the door, and it opened to darkness. "So your makers have been a thorn in my side for centuries," she said, as she disappeared inside, while Ethan stood for a moment on the steps, looking inwards towards a black abyss.

"You mean Antoine and Darius?"

He peered inside but couldn't see her. "Claret? Are you in there?" As he stepped inside, he felt a chill in the air. It felt like he was standing on cement, or stone, the floor felt hard and cold. He scanned the area, but saw nothing.

Claret appeared from the darkness and he stepped back. "Yes, them. Antoine and Darius. But I know it was Darius who truly is your maker."

Ethan nodded.

The door slammed with a thud. He snapped over towards the door, and reached out and tried the handle, which would not budge. She disappeared into the darkness.

"Claret? Where are you?!"

A torch lit on the far wall, the flames reached upwards towards the ceiling, and bathed the room in a flickering, orange glow. He was standing a circular foyer, the walls and the floors were made of grey stone. He looked onwards, down the hallway, towards the torch, and saw Claret, in a far doorway, leaning against the side. "Let's go," she said. She took a few steps closer towards him, as her heels clicked on the stone. "Step inside my chamber."

Ethan moved forward, lifting his right foot, concentrating on the movement, and then the left foot. There was a certain increased heaviness to his legs, as if his weight had compounded, and each step that he took, towards the massive door before him, took much more strength and effort than walking ever had previously.

Claret opened the door.

Brilliant crimson light spilled out, which fingered its way into the dark, stone hallway, and Ethan covered his eyes. The light brightened the further it reached out from the threshold, and darkened to a deeper red towards the center of the door. "Uncover your eyes," Claret said. "You must step inside and we will go."

Ethan lowered his arms. "Go where?" Claret reached out for Ethan's arm. "This is a doorway," she said. "A portal. The light will not harm you. I am going to show you my origins. You must trust me." She held out her hand. Ethan took a step forward, stopped for a minute, and then stood before Claret, the Demon Princess, and looked at her tiny hand. The bright red nail polish picked up the light in the barren hallway.

Ethan looked up and in Claret's eyes. She smiled. It could have been the history, and all he had learned about her. But he knew, from this point forward, if he stepped through that portal, that he would be submitting to the Demon Princess. For she had the upper hand; he would venture into a world he had never known before, in time and space that he had never previously journeyed to; and the only form of protection would be in the form of a monster he had always been told never to trust.

He stepped into blackness as the door shut behind them; like a heavy stone rolling across the entrance to Christ's tomb, they were sealed. And then there was silence. Ethan could still sense Claret was next to him, but the darkness shrouded his vision so intensely that he could not even see any figments of her fair complexion. "Claret?"

"Yes, Ethan. I am here. You must trust me. Move with me. And do not let go of my hand." He felt her hand take his. The tiny, cool skin. She held his hand tightly as snippets of light flashed around them, moving from far ahead of them, back towards them, and back behind them. Ethan snapped his head in the direction of the passing lights. They looked like lights passing on a darkened highway, but so blurred. So unfocused. And when he followed another passing light, he looked behind them, and noticed that they were much further into the blackness that he had originally thought. There was no door behind them, no large stone rolled across the opening. But a dark infinity; for the lights moved beyond them, behind and into the black abyss.

It felt like they were no longer moving. The passing lights stopped, and the darkness was lightening. Very gradually, the darkness abated.

The stone of the Christ tomb had been far larger; but the stone that covered the entry from the chamber that he had entered from was so much more profound; there was a certain heaviness to it.

A sadness.

Tears that weighed so much more than joy. But the tears always flowed. Tiny rivers on the map of his face. And then the stone turned away, and it was revealed.

LIBERA ME

Somehow the casket must deliver a sense of freedom.

It's constricting, but for many, it's a freedom from the confines of their lives. How many have committed suicide and thought that act would be a deliverance from the ignorance, bigotry and rejection of human life? But the answer they got was a physically confining box.

And the casket is what it is – it's a small, sealed box that contains a decomposing body after death. It's traditionally sealed in a cement and steel vault (to help prevent water contamination – although that is not something that works indefinitely. Water always penetrates; it always finds a way. The insects and maggots always find a way to the body contained inside, no matter what.) So even despite our actions – placing a body in a sealed coffin, in an even more sealed vault, our preservation methods always fail.

Every time, without argument.

No matter how well preserved the body, dig it up after a decade, you'll get a pile of bones. It's only in very rare occasions that a body will last years after death. And that's why we have caskets – and that's why we inter our loved ones shortly after death, entrusting their bodies to the earth.

But where do they go? For if they do not rot in the earth? If they do not decompose in the casket? Where are they truly?

At this point, you probably thought you were rid of me. But I remember you.

You stood outside my door.

Outside my window.

I guided you through, into the bowels of my existence, through the preparation room, past the stainless steel table, the glass chambers that held the formaldehyde.

Do you remember me now?

So at this point, you should see what I am seeing now – it's not just mortals who are coming into my funeral home. My chambers are filled with the immortals – those who supposedly once had the gift, the thought of living eternally, bestowed upon them. But what happened to that gift? And then, the differences in burial. When a deceased "immortal" passes through my preparation room, there are specific instructions.

I should not embalm, not under any circumstances.

And within a day after the arrival of the body, a representative arrives at my funeral home to claim the body of the deceased. And that has been happening, now, lately, quite often. There was a time when immortals were truly what they were.

Immortal.

They had the gift to live forever.

They did not have to worry about death, or disease, or sickness, or aging. But now, with this threat of the decanter, they have been coming into my chambers regularly. When will the gift of being immortal be, once again, what it was truly meant to be?

Or is the gift of immortality really a curse?

Deliver me.

The Morticians Mortician

MIAMI

Darius might still be alive.

Why did that thought permeate his mind this morning? This morning, the first morning after he had returned to Miami, now an ocean away from where Darius lay in his coffin, now encased in darkness, now covered in layers of dirt and earth; no air to breathe, no water to drink, no voices speaking to him. Just silence.

Utter silence.

And Darius would be subject to that loneliness, that isolation, half a world away.

Antoine closed his eyes. He hung his head down. "But you're dead. You're dead and gone." He shook his head.

Until there was a knock at the door.

He opened his eyes, and looked towards the large, oak frame. He stood in front of the mirror, wiped his face with the back of his hands, and straightened his hair.

The walk over to the front door was layered with questions. There had been no one in this house for several years. There was still smoke and water damage from the fire years ago. The crime scene tape was never removed. Windows on the second floor were still covered with plywood.

No one should have even suspected that Antoine would be there. Not a soul.

But there was still the persistent knock. Once again, the short, methodic raps echoed through the foyer, and Antoine stood frozen still, just feet from the threshold, waiting. And listening.

"Where are you Darius?" He looked upwards, at the crystal chandelier they had installed together. It was now covered in soot, a layer of gray ash, and it hung downwards from the ceiling at a haphazard angle, with an octopus of multi colored electrical wires reaching downwards from the ceiling.

But the front door was another matter.

And he managed to take a few more steps, finding the large, brass handle in the center of the doors. He grasped the cool metal, and paused. He could hear the leaves rustling in the trees outside.

But nothing more.

There was a certain time, in the past, when Antoine did not live in such fear. When he was the Antoine who had been known and respected throughout the city, when he was the enigmatic individual that so many had come to know and love.

But then everything fell apart.

When Antoine had been banished, when he had been dragged to the altar, when he had been burned to ashes. And when it had been his turn to wait in the coffin.

For Antoine knew of the isolation. He knew of the waiting, the loneliness. The darkness and the silence.

And now, standing in the burned out shell of his former mansion, that darkness and that silence entered his life once again.

He opened the door to an empty front porch. He scanned the area. The giant columns that rose from the front porch were stained with black soot, but they were still standing, reaching upwards towards the sky.

The porch, which ran the entire length of the mansion, was devoid of any furniture. Antoine remembered when he first had acquired the estate from the Perez family, years prior, and there had been elegant outdoor furnishings lining the porch, enormous palms in ceramic planters, ceiling fans and hanging light fixtures.

No longer was the porch inviting.

But it wasn't the furnishings that Antoine was concerned with that particular day. Throughout the day, he heard the knocking again. He once more would go to the door, open it to no one standing on the porch, and would return to his meandering around the house, to his remembering as he walked the halls, and then there would be a knock on the door again. And the process repeated itself until evening. At the latest moment, he stepped outside, as his heels clicked on the stone, he walked to the edge of the stairs, which led downwards into the gardens, which had once been adorned with hibiscus, palms, birds of paradise and azaleas, were now untended and overgrown with weeds.

But there was no one standing in the front lawn.

Antoine stood on the front steps and looked upwards towards the sky. The clouds were parting, revealing an array of stars, and a crescent moon.

He fished through his pocket for his phone. He held it up to his ear, the glow of the screen shined against his cheek, as it rang. Antoine soon spoke. "I cannot stay here. There are too many ghosts."

There was a brief pause, as Antoine looked over his shoulder towards the end of the house. "I am not sure. I don't know…I came outside to see who it might be, and there is no one here. Like I said, too many ghosts."

And then another pause. "Okay…okay. Good then, I will see you shortly."

Antoine ended the call and put the phone back in his pocket, turned and went back inside, and closed the door behind him. Once inside, he stopped in the middle of the marble floor.

He looked around the foyer.

The soaring ceilings were now burned out and covered in ash. Some of the plaster was water damaged and dripping down from the walls. Wall studs were exposed above the winding staircase, and the floor had crumbled paper and trash strewn about.

And then he closed his eyes.

And then he remembered.

It had been right after Darius had returned to Miami. Antoine had been so excited about the new house. The marble floors were polished and shined. The foyer, with the warmth of light from the wall sconces, was warm and inviting, with a large, round mahogany table in the center, and a silver vase with a voluptuous bouquet of white roses.

And at the end of the foyer, in front of the rear hallway, stood Darius. Smiling Darius. His ivory white skin, framed by his long, brunette hair, standing and smiling, opening his arms and welcoming Antoine.

"Welcome to this wonderful house," Darius said, moving over to where Antoine was standing. "And you bought this from whom?"

"Well…" Antoine said. "It wasn't as much as a simple real estate transaction. There was much more involved in acquiring this house. So much."

Darius laughed. "I know, Antoine, I know about Roberto. I know about Hernan. Don't you think I know what you are doing when I am around?"

Antoine smiled.

And then he was standing, alone, in the darkness. The chandelier was once again covered in soot and ash, the multicolored wires still fingered their way out of the ceiling, and he was again alone.

Antoine stood at the edge of Andelusia Avenue and looked at the burned out shell of his mansion. His mouth hung open and he hung his head in disgust. The soaring columns were still there, but they reached to a burned out second floor; the white stucco stained with soot and ash; the windows were shattered. A white curtain blew in the passing breeze. Without venturing under the yellow crime scene tape that surrounded the property, he got back into his little, silver Mercedes. And shortly thereafter, after driving in shock across the city, he reached Miami Beach, and parked on the side of Washington Avenue. While standing in front of the tall, dark gothic structure that was once *Sacrafice*, the nightclub that he had invested so much time, energy, and passion into – was a burned out shell of its former self.

He ventured up the stairs as the dull hum of the traffic on Washington Avenue roared behind him. He slid his key into the door, and opened it to darkness. The stench of burned wood and ash was overpowering. His footsteps clicked against the stone floor as he walked in a second set of doors into the main dance floor area. The bar was trashed, water still pooled in the corners; tables were strewn about everywhere, and even the stage was partially burned. He stared at the stage; the torn and tattered curtains, and remembered the nights that he and Darius spent in the conference room that overlooked the expansive dance floor. He did not notice the approaching footsteps until they were right behind him.

He turned around and Delia smiled. Ethan stood next to her, and he smiled and pushed his glasses up his nose.

Delia walked to Antoine with outstretched arms. "Do you see now? Do you see what they are doing to us?"

Antoine looked around the room and shook his head. "Extermination." He walked over to the bar and examined some broken glass on the bar top. "That is a word that comes to mind. My house is the same way. A burned out shell. It's like I am being erased."

"They're going after more than just you, Antoine, Delia said, joining Antoine at the bar. "Immortals all over the world have seen the man, and they're losing their gift, Antoine." She looked at him directly in his eyes. "Do you know what that means? We could literally be wiped out."

Shortly after Darius died, Antoine returned to Miami, and not long after that, he received a visit from those in Rome. He knew that *The Inspiriti* had valid concerns about his sector. He had lost control. He had lost Darius. His home, his business. And his sanity. And there was a sense, in the back of his mind, that Darius might still be alive. Somehow, in some way. Perhaps it was a dream. Maybe denial. Or it could have just been a longing; missing him, rotting in the grave, a wish that might have been fleeting, as Antoine looked in the mirror, at his eyes, red-rimmed, puffy. His cheeks fresh clean with streams of tears.

But there was a sense, that feeling which would not let go. It was too much to think this.

He stood in the foyer of a rented condominium not far from his estate. As he stood, propping himself up from the wall, his hands flat against the slate, he hung his head down and dared not to keep looking in the mirror hanging in front of him.

"Why did you take him from me?!" He raised his hands to the ceiling and fell to his knees, hung his head and closed his eyes. "I tried to save him. Put forth all my effort. And then you take him from me!"

Antoine looked over at the door when he heard a car pull up outside. He walked over to the door, and pulled the curtain aside. A long, black limousine stood in the driveway, as a young male driver walked around the front of the car and opened the rear door. And there was the Monsignor. Here. In Miami.

Antoine rushed back over to the mirror, and wiped his cheeks. He grabbed a tissue from the small table underneath, and wiped his eyes. They still looked a little red.

The door chimed, and Antoine took a deep breath, and exhaled. "Here we go," he said to himself.

The door opened as the Monsignor smiled. His silver hair was neatly combed across his shiny head. Antoine first noticed the man's expansive forehead. "Antoine, may I enter?"

Antoine nodded and stepped aside, ushering the Monsignor inside. The priest looked upwards, as another man, much younger, stepped out of the back of the limousine and walked up the steps. "My assistant Ramiel," the Monsignor said, gesturing towards the younger priest. Ramiel nodded and shook Antoine's hand. The driver leaned against the car and lit a cigarette, as Antoine shut the door.

The three men walked into the front living room, as the Monsignor looked around. His eyes stopped for a moment on the fireplace. "Very exquisite," he said. "Italian marble?"

Antoine shrugged his shoulders. "It's a rental."

"You have a very lovely home," the Monsignor said, as he sat in a large, white, overstuffed sofa. He moved several pillows to the side and leaned back.

"Actually I don't. My home is a few blocks that way." He pointed out towards the front window. "It's basically a burned out shell now. This is a rental. Would you care for a drink?" Antoine stood at the bar and held up some glasses.

"Chianti, if you have it."

Antoine set three large wine glasses on the bar top, opened a bottle of wine, and poured a bit in each glass. He placed a glass in front of the Monsignor and Ramiel, and took his own glass and sat in a chair opposite the two priests.

The Monsignor leaned forward. "Let me get right to it," he said. "You know why we are here, correct? Delia has filled you in?"

Antoine nodded.

"Very well then. Here is where we stand right now. Right now we know that this 'Hooded Man' is most active in your sector. I have received some complaints from areas in Europe, but he is most active in Miami and New York. We are stepping in because – if we don't – we are afraid our kind will suffer a great loss. If we lose Miami and New York, we will lose our stronghold in America."

Antoine nodded and sipped on his wine. "Did he burn down my business? And my home?"

The Monsignor shook his head. "I don't think so. We have a team mobilizing as we speak to investigate that."

Antoine sighed. "The cops are all over – both on Andelusia avenue and at the club. Big time arson investigation. I'm all over the news down here."

"Understandably so."

Ramiel set his glass on the coffee table with a slight clank. He stood and walked over to the window. "What type of clues are in that house, Antoine? Evidence of the portal that is there?" He turned to look at Antoine.

"There is no way that they could find that entrance, Ramiel. It's impossible for a mortal to see it without a guide – someone either who has the same dark gift that we have, or a spirit from the other side."

The Monsignor was quiet.

His lips were pursed together, and he rubbed his head and set his wine down. "Antoine, have you considered the possibility that we may have someone on the inside working against us?"

Antoine's mouth dropped open.

"Consider it, and investigate it, Antoine. Act on it with immediacy – our fate depends upon it. And if there *is* a traitor to our kind, their punishment will be swift and severe."

Antoine remembered the charter. "Crucifixion. I remember."

"Warn them, Antoine. Warn all those in your sector. Crimes against our own will not be tolerated. I will spread the word in other sectors. If we have a traitor, they will be nailed to a cross and hung for all of eternity."

Antoine, Monsignor Harrison, and Ramiel sat in silence for a few moments as a giant truck lumbered down the street, rattling the windowpanes. Antoine rose from the sofa and peered out the window. He caught the tail end of a military Humvee, just as it exited his view. "Those have been coming down the streets quite a bit lately. It's like they are mobilizing for something."

Ramiel joined Antoine. "Why would the military be mobilizing for a spiritual war? That is not their area of expertise."

Antoine looked at Ramiel. "Because the barrier has been broken, Ramiel. That's what's going on here, Monsignor. The barrier was broken. There has been so much confusion as to what is reality, and what is taking place in another dimension. It's like rips in the fabric of existence and time. But the netherworld is spilling out – and people are getting lost on the other side."

"Can you please elaborate?"

Antoine joined the Monsignor back on the sofa and Ramiel followed. "There are several. Sheldon Wilkes, Paula Tandy and Anthony Peterson – all paranormal researchers for *The Astral.* Mr. Wilkes was interviewing me for a book that he was writing on my life. They're all gone."

The Monsignor shook his head, took a sip of wine, and placed his glass back on the table. "Of course, we were not happy with the news surrounding Darius, and how he died, and also how you had died. We're happy, of course, that you have returned, but what has happened to Miami, Antoine? Seems like things really got out of hand here in the past few years."

Antoine set his wine down on the coffee table, and looked directly at the Monsignor. The man raised his eyebrows. Antoine's eyes fell. "I lost control, dear Monsignor. When I was dragged to the altar, I completely lost control."

"How do you mean? You had no successor?"

Antoine sighed. He leaned back into the couch and closed his eyes. He had dreamed of Roberto becoming a successor. He didn't understand what had gone wrong. His thoughts carried him back to the night on Washington Avenue that he had first met Roberto. He could still feel the stifling humidity, he could still hear the click-clacking of high heels on dirty pavement, the chatter of friends out having late night fun; the cool wall of air-conditioning still blasted his face as if he were still standing there in the hot Miami night air.

And he could still see Roberto, the shiny penny in the midst of dull and dirty coins, standing at the other end of the block, looking towards him, his eyes calling him, beckoning him to come forward, and then it stopped.

"Yes, yes," Antoine said. "I had a planned successor."

The Monsignor leaned forward and set his glass down. It clanked on the glass table. "Antoine! Are you listening to me?"

Antoine nodded.

"So who was your successor then? Why did Miami fall apart after you were gone?"

Antoine paused for a moment and thought of Roberto. He saw him, standing on Washington Avenue. He saw his pretty features, his olive complexion and dark hair.

Come and see me father. Come and see what I have done!

Antoine snapped out of his musing. Ramiel handed him a tissue and he wiped his forehead. "Yes, I remember. I know now." He looked up at the Monsignor, then at Ramiel, and then down at his glass of wine. "I was betrayed."

The men nodded. "Who betrayed you, Antoine?"

Antoine paused for a moment. He remember the nights that Roberto cried in his arms, when he stood in his room, in the same estate that Antoine now owned, the same house that sat burned and a shell of its former glory – and then he looked at the two men directly. "Roberto Perez. He had me dragged to my death. I was taken through the bodies, through the thrashing limbs in the sea of souls, and to the altar. I was burned to ashes."

The Monsignor waved his hand. "Yes, I know your story, Antoine. We have it in your file back in Rome. But this betrayal – this is something I have not heard before. These 'specifics' surrounding your capture and death."

"What was his motive?" Ramiel asked.

Antoine shook his head, but the Monsignor answered. "It's clear, gentlemen. I have seen this before, over the years. It's apparent that the gift went to his head. Some get spellbound with their newfound power, and become rebels. Those rebels can retaliate against their makers – sometimes in anger, or hatred, for giving them the gift if they didn't *want* it – and others just for the pure pleasure of power and the kill. Domination. That sort of thing."

Antoine looked directly at the Monsignor. "So what do we do, your highness?"

"The answer is clear, gentlemen. We find out who is betraying our kind, and we bring justice for those who we have lost."

"And what about Darius?" Antoine said.

"Darius may still have hope. He has only been gone for a short while. We shall exhume him and I shall perform the ritual. But with even greater importance, we might be able to find out what was in the decanter. What he drank. If we can. We shall try our best."

Antoine grabbed a small bag from the master bedroom closet and flopped on the bed. The sun would be rising soon, and he wanted to be gone before the light peeked over the eastern sky. He opened the chest drawers and fished a few items of clothing out and placed them in the bag. In the bedside chest was his passport; he put that in his jacket pocket and zipped the bag, picked it up, and walked out to the foyer, placing it near the front door.

He then walked back through the kitchen and out to the garage, and to the breaker box. He snapped the breakers to the OFF position, and slammed the door shut. Back in the house, he examined each room. Furniture was covered in stark white dust cloths. The curtains were all pulled tight. The damper was closed. The air conditioning was set at 80 degrees.

It was time to leave for Europe.

Antoine waited in the front driveway of his condominium for the airport limousine. His fished his phone from his bag and dialed Delia. After a few rings, she answered. "I am waiting for the car. We'll swing by and get you next. Are you all packed? Are your breakers shut off?"

"Yes."

"Very good then. Monsignor Harrison and Ramiel will meet us at the terminal. We're all on the same flight to Frankfurt. The plan remains the same – get to Lyon and we'll all hole up at the Chateau. I've already let Giovanni know that we're all on our way. Then after that…"

"All we can do is our best, Antoine. We will try to save him, if we can. The Monsignor is going to try his best."

Antoine shook his head as he saw a long Town Car pull up in the circular driveway. "I just wish there was a way we could still use our powers. I used to be able to fly and cross the ocean in minutes. Now I am cursed to fly in an aluminum tube."

"It's like we are being drained," she said.

"Let me go, I'll see you at the airport. But I'll tell you one thing, Delia. I think there is something bigger going on than we know."

FRANKFURT - LYON

The flight was bumpy, and Antoine attempted throughout the nine hours to get some rest. But it did not come easily, nor without fitful dreams.

Roberto.

Antoine could not get him out of his mind. And the nights they spent together. He remembered the night he transformed Roberto, as he plunged through his neck, drinking his blood, as Roberto's small, muscular frame shook beneath him.

"I will now be the same as you," Roberto had said after Antoine had come down from a state of euphoria. He reached over and turned on the lamp next to his bed. "I am going to be just like you, Antoine!"

Antoine leaned back and reached for his shirt. "Where is the sudden confidence coming from? Just a few minutes ago you were crying on my shoulder."

"That was before I drank from you! Your blood gives me so much confidence! It was exactly what I needed my whole life!"

Antoine raised his eyebrows and looked at Roberto. He was standing next to the bed in a small pair of boxers. His muscles flexed as he spoke to Antoine, such an animated young man. "This gift is *great* Antoine! Now I can be all who I want to be. And I won't have to die, *ever*!"

Antoine stood and held his hands up. "Wait a minute, Roberto. There's a *lot* that is going to happen to you. Especially in the first few days. You can't just go and take over the world from the start. There are a lot of things you will have to learn. About yourself. How to interact with other immortals, everything. And you will need some time to self-reflect, shed your skin, so to speak."

Shed your skin.

"It's exactly what Darius told me," Antoine said, as he watched Roberto pull a shirt on.

"Screw that!" he said. "Thank you man!" He kissed Antoine on the cheek, slapped him on the back, and walked out of the bedroom.

Antoine woke as the jet touched down on the runway in Frankfurt. What a mess with Roberto. Could he be the betrayer?

Antoine waited at the end of the baggage claim terminal as the sun faded. Giovanni was waiting for Antoine with his car and driver, leaning against a black sedan wearing dark sunglasses. His hair was tied neatly in a pony-tail. Antoine looked over at the Monsignor, Ramiel and Delia who were getting into a separate car. Delia looked over at Antoine and nodded.

Once inside the car, Antoine looked over at Giovanni as the diver pulled away. "I wanted to travel separately, Giovanni, so we could talk privately."

He nodded. "What is it, dear Antoine?"

He looked out the window and saw Delia looking at them, shaking her head as the car pulled away. "I had to speak to you about Roberto. How he betrayed me. Do you think he is murdering our kind?"

Giovanni leaned in closer towards Antoine. "Murdering our kind? What has led you to think this?"

Antoine looked over at Giovanni and shrugged. "Look what he did to me, Gio. I mean, betraying one's maker. Isn't that grounds for crucifixion?"

Giovanni shrugged. "I know there are rules. Written by the ancients, apparently. I've never heard of an immortal actually *being* crucified. But I know there are books out there that talk about it."

Antoine shot a glance over at Giovanni. "So is it something we do or not?"

Giovanni placed his hand on Antoine's knee. "My friend, I don't know. Since The Inspiriti, a lot of things have changed."

The Town Car pulled up in front of the Chateau and Monsignor Harrison stepped out in a two piece pinstripe as Antoine and Giovanni stood on the front porch and looked on. Ramiel got out of the car after his highness, and then Delia. Antoine leaned against a cement pillar as the light on top of it automatically turned on as the sun set.

Delia looked over at Antoine and smiled. "Are you ready for this? To see Darius again? You know what to expect?"

Antoine shrugged his shoulders and walked over to the three others. Monsignor Harrison looked at Antoine. "You have the equipment ready?" Antoine nodded. "I have it out in a barn out back. I haven't used it for years, but it's all there, and should be ready to go."

"Good," he said. "Then let's go inside and save our energy. Let's wait until we are under the complete shroud of darkness. I don't want the local authorities to get involved."

Antoine nodded as Ramiel assisted Delia up the front path towards the Chateau. Antoine leaned close to Monsignor Harrison. "I've explained to you my predicament, Monsignor. I am very concerned with going in the middle of the night. It seems the forest is always churning at night."

The Monsignor stopped walking and looked at Antoine. Antoine couldn't help but notice the bags under the tired man's eyes. "Asmodai, I presume?"

Antoine nodded.

"You do have a debt to him, Antoine. There is no getting around that. But I do believe we will be able to defeat him if he comes. But you know, as well as I do, that we must get Darius' body. It is simply not an option. We must find out what the potion is that he drank."

"And what about what you said? The ritual? Can't you bring him back?"

Monsignor Harrison looked at Antoine and smiled. But hesitated for a moment. "Antoine. We will do everything we can."

"And do you honestly think there will be a way to find out about what he drank? After his aging and now decomposition?"

The Monsignor continued on towards the front steps and did not immediately answer. He trudged up the first few steps and turned back around to face Antoine. "If there is any hope for the survival of the immortals who have drank from the decanter and are still alive…then it is our only hope, dear Antoine."

The group of immortals waited for several hours in the chateau before venturing into the night and to Les Enfants Cemetery. While they were waiting, Delia napped in one of the guest rooms, the Monsignor read by a crackling fire, and Antoine and Ramiel gathered the equipment for the exhumation of the body. They went to a large garage in the back of the Chateau, which was several hundred yards behind the main building. Antoine led the way through a path surrounded by tall, old oak trees, as Ramiel followed in silence.

"Do you remember the days before it was this complicated?" Antoine looked back towards Ramiel seeking an answer. Antoine noticed Ramiel's dark hair, how it framed his face perfectly, and his olive complexion which was undeniably flawless.

Ramiel nodded. "I am several thousand years old," he said. "From the sect in Rome. Yes, we have always been embroiled in uncertainty. And things have always been complex. And they have always been complicated."

Antoine stopped walking, turned around and nodded. He looked at Ramiel for a moment, and their eyes locked. He then turned and looked forward. "I feel like a novice."

"We all are at different stages, Antoine. One shouldn't compare oneself to another who is significantly their senior. I have far more experience. I have had more time to gain wisdom. You will get there. I assure you of that. The way you conduct your behavior – from what I see – is far superior to Darius. You will grow much wiser than you are now."

And then Antoine turned to face Ramiel. "Yes. But you appear to be my age. It's very difficult to view you as an elder when you look like a peer."

Ramiel nodded. "I certainly understand. But it is something that you must accept. There are those who will come before you who will have more knowledge than you. Look at Monsignor Harrison. I am a child compared to him."

"When was he transformed?"

"He is older than Claret."

Antoine whistled. "Wow," he said. "Is he the oldest of our kind?"

Ramiel shook his head. "I'm not sure. There are others who say there are older immortals, but I have yet to find one."

They stopped in front of the garage. The building was far less glamorous than the chateau. Rather than grand mason columns, it was a rather small wooden building, tucked in the woods, several hundred yards behind the chateau.

"Do you see the bag? It's hanging on the back side of the barn." Antoine stood in the doorway, holding his flashlight, and shining it inwards. Ramiel walked deeper into the barn, and turned around for a moment. "You're not coming?"

"I would prefer to stay outside," Antoine said. "I have this thing about barns. They don't agree with me. Just get the equipment, and get out."

Ramiel nodded and turned forward. "Just direct me then. Let me know what I am grabbing so we can move the night forward and get this all over with."

"Yes, yes."

Antoine stood at the edge of his own barn and remembered Badulla. And his father. And the old woman. And his mother. And then he turned off the flashlight and closed his eyes.

"Hey!" Ramiel called from the darkness. "Are you going to give me some light?"

Antoine stood with his eyes closed. His voice quivered. "Yes, Ramiel…"

And then a few minutes passed, and there was a rustling of hay. "Hey are you going to give me some light? Isn't this my second request?"

Antoine opened his eyes and snapped the flashlight back on. "Sorry," he said, wiping his eyes. "I'm sorry, Ramiel. Just get the green bag in the far corner. You'll see it hanging on the wall. That's all we'll need."

LYON

After Antoine and Ramiel had gathered the equipment from the barn (which was all neatly organized in the hanging green bag which Antoine had insisted to Ramiel) – they all retired to the Chateau. Later, after dinner, Antoine sat in the study, as the others had retired to their rooms, and sank deep into thought.

Antoine knew that once Darius had passed, things had to be set in motion. As soon as Darius expired, he closed the window and drew the drapes. And then he walked over to the bed and covered the corpse with a blanket.

Antoine closed his eyes.

Darius, here we are again.

He remembered the moments after Darius had passed; they were burned too far into his mind to forget them.

Antoine shook his head and closed the door to the bedroom and let the body lay where it was. He was at a point now, it seemed, in deciding whether the body needed to be burned to ash, which he doubted, since Darius was mortal when he passed. It was so much different now since Darius had been mortal.

Would he be able to return? Was Darius gone forever?

He paused in the kitchen and looked over at the table. Darius had left his cup of tea there. He walked over to the table and looked down at the remaining bit of brown liquid inside of the china cup.

And then he cleared it, placed it in the sink, and went to the study. There were too many emails to sift through, and too many phone calls to make before Darius started to decompose. He knew that he could not venture to the local authorities, and bury a body that essentially died hundreds of years ago.

For the immortals, they leave, they pass away, just like anyone else. Immortality is a myth. But what they leave behind is so very different. Their mortality returns and they die. But what they get – and what so many seek – is their extended life. They live, and they die, and they continue to live when they are dead. But eventually, just like anyone, their time arrives that they must face the astral plane and move on from this world.

Antoine opened his eyes. "Is the only way out truly gotten to by going farther in?"

Antoine thought back to the day he buried Darius. When the sun was setting in the sky, when it was painted red.

The sun sank into the horizon, and painted the sky with deep blues, fiery red and crimson. The purple clouds leapt across the sky and fought their way to the west, across the Atlantic and towards the Americas.

Antoine looked upwards towards the sky, surrounded by the dark patches of forest, holding a shovel in his hand.

The deed had been done.

He looked over towards the grave, under the same tree that Darius had been buried under so many years ago; under the same tree that he himself had been buried under. And then he paused for a moment.

Darius, do you hear me?

Antoine envisioned Darius, lying in his coffin below.

It would be dark, it would be cold. Darius would be lying utterly still, his eyes would remain closed. There would be a musty smell, the odor of rotting flesh, the crispy sound of insects fighting their way into the coffin. But Darius would be lying there, waiting.

Waiting for something.

Maybe to resurrect, maybe just to decompose and lie utterly still in darkness.

But Darius, can you hear me? Can you hear my thoughts? Do you remember? Do you know how to find your way back?

Remember, the only way out is farther in.

There was a sense of familiarity when Antoine visited the same cemetery in the same town that he had so many years before. As he walked down the old, familiar path, and as the gravel crunched beneath his feet, he looked off to his right, and saw the edge of the forest; they were the same trees which Asmodai tore his way through, years ago, when Antoine had visited the cemetery the second time to raise Darius back to the earth.

But this time, things were quite vastly different. For the first time, Darius had died as an immortal. Antoine had plunged a dagger into his heart and he laid Darius to rest, as he was written to do so, in that very same cemetery under the very same tree, under different clouds in a different time.

And then there was the second time that Antoine had visited *Les Enfants*. It was the time that Antoine remembered needing Darius. Longing for his companionship once again. And Antoine had made the journey to the cemetery from Miami, after years of living in that city, building a name for himself, becoming a spiritual healer, finding himself to be a local celebrity and nightclub promoter.

But Antoine had his downfall.

And it was not an event that led to his downfall. It was not an event or the timing of everything.

It was a person.

And that person was named Roberto Perez.

The only way out is farther in.

What exactly did that mean?

There was a certain time when Antoine could remember. He felt the searing heat of the flames on his skin; the hot burning assault, tearing his flesh from his body in a chorus of bloody aspiring mist, as he had burned on the altar. And then, there was the tearing of his muscle, as he felt the rocks underneath him dig into his back, assaulting his inner being. And the smoke, which billowed above his body; a black cumulous dark cloud rising into the sky, into the red sky painted with black clouds, as cries of sadness and despair from the sea of souls fought to drown out his own cries for help.

But the help would not come.

For the last thing he remembered was only darkness.

His eyes closed, and then there was darkness.

There was a certain time when he still felt that he existed, when there was a point that he were still alive, maybe not immortal, but somehow still a presence. That much was for certain, was it not?

"I exist. *I still exist.*"

His words reverberated against the black silence like a metronome. And he caught himself saying it again. "I still exist."

But there was no physicality. There was no body, no muscle, no blood coursing through his veins – even if he were immortal, he still had some physical existence, did he not?

"I still exist."

Antoine waited in the darkness. "How much further should I go?"

And then he woke up. As he opened his eyes, he saw he was in the front parlor of the Chateau, and the Monsignor was staring at him.

"You were talking in your sleep," he said, looking over at Antoine, holding a glass of red wine.

Antoine nodded. "Yes, it was a smattering of thoughts, swimming in my head."

"You were speaking though. I couldn't make out all of the words. But I do believe you said 'I still exist'. What did that mean, Antoine?"

"I don't know if I was dreaming about Darius…or about myself."

Antoine wandered to the back of the Chateau.

He sat in front of a glowing computer screen with a glass of red wine. The brilliant glow of his phone shined against his face, as he thought of Delia, sleeping in the next room. She was the only one, now, who could help him.

But there were thoughts that permeated his mind. As he sipped the wine, he stared at the computer screen, and put on his glasses. The monitor glowed on the lenses, as he shifted his face.

He opened the web browser and navigated to an internet search site. He sat downwards in his chair, slugged down, and cocked his head to the side. After a few moments of silence, he reached down towards the desk and brought the glass of wine to his lips. And then, he quickly placed the wine back on the desk as his eyes widened. He typed a bit on the keyboard, clicked the mouse to the side, and sat back in his chair.

Searches for *The Hooded Man* flooded his screen. He stared at the results for a few moments, and craned his neck towards the hall. He got up and opened the door completely.

Antoine stood in the doorway. He looked down the hallway – Ramiel, the Monsignor and Delia were all resting before they ventured to the cemetery. He then looked back at the same computer, where he had sat and searched for information about the 'Hooded Man', where he had sat and spoke with Delia about his existence, questioned…and did nothing.

"Damn!" He slammed his fist against the door. "Damn!"

Later in the night, the group rose and readied to venture out to *Les Enfants*. Delia was the last to rise, but she appeared once the others raised the activity level in the Chateau from walking back and forth, splashing water on their faces, clearing the puffiness from an early evening nap, and readying to venture out in the devil's hour.

They left the Chateau in silence, and walked into the woods to the rear in silence, their feet crunching through leaves against the silence of the night.

After a bit, Antoine and the Monsignor started talking about Antoine's business ventures in Miami.`

The call of the loon interrupted their conversation. Antoine held up his hand. "Quiet. Do you hear that? I think he may be coming."

"Who?" The Monsignor stopped and stood next to Antoine, as they both looked upwards towards the sky. The clouds had parted and the sky was filled with stars. A branch snapped off in the forest, and Antoine fell silent.

"Don't move," he said, as he slowly crept deeper into the woods. "The call of the loon is what indicates that he is coming. I am thinking that someone doesn't want us to exhume Darius."

"Well we must," the Monsignor said. "Let us go. I walk with God, Antoine. He will lead the way for me. I must not lose sight of that. He is far more powerful than any demon that is chasing you."

The Monsignor placed his arm around Antoine's shoulders. "Come, my son. Let us do what we are meant to do."

They proceeded. As they walked deeper into the woods, Antoine thought about the first night that he had traveled through the same trees, under the same stars, with different clouds rolling past above, and under the same blue moonlight. The night that he had exhumed Darius before; when the ritual of resurrection was performed, when his chest bled, when the corpses rose from their graves, and when the demons held flaming swords.

He remembered Asmodai.

The powerful, lumbering, muscular beast who ushered in roaring winds, who froze time and stood motionless, who stood above the grave that Antoine had hidden in. And there was a sobering thought to that whole memory. Antoine knew that he could not take things back; he could not relinquish his demons. For the past was always there, it would always follow him as long as he walked the earth.

They reached a clearing. The darkness held fast. Another, much larger branch snapped, this time much closer. Antoine closed his eyes, shook his head. "I cannot deal with him anymore, Monsignor. He has been coming for me for far too long. For years. He is teasing me. He is probably yards away. Maybe even feet. He probably can hear our conversation."

The Monsignor looked outwards, and squinted. "I don't see anything."

"Of course you wouldn't. He only appears when he wants to. And even then, I may only be able to see him when he does."

"Well, let's proceed then. We will run out of night soon. It is fleeting quickly." They approached the edge of the cemetery, and Antoine led the way, deeper through the stones, walking in various different directions through rising markers and monuments.

Giovanni did not join the others when they went to exhume the body. He waited in the Chateau. The night held fast; there was no moonlight, and the group walked close together through the forest; the leaves crunched under their feet, and the trees swayed with an occasional passing breeze. Antoine led the way, holding a flashlight, aiming it through the thick forest, as Ramiel walked beside him.

"You were close with Darius, were you not?" Ramiel looked back and forth at Antoine and the direction they were heading.

"Yes, we were."

"You two have a long history?"

"Yes, we do." Antoine stopped walking and looked over at Ramiel. "I miss him terribly. He is my maker. He appears to me sometimes."

Ramiel looked directly at Antoine. "He appears to you?"

Antoine nodded and started walking again. "As a ghost. He has visited me several times already."

Ramiel looked behind his shoulder. "Monsignor – could you come here for a minute? We may have just had a revelation."

Antoine and Ramiel both stopped walking again to let the Monsignor catch up. "What is it?" he asked.

"Darius has been visiting Antoine lately as a ghost," Ramiel said.

The Monsignor nodded and looked at Antoine. "It won't mean anything concerning what he drank. He won't know. But he might be able to help us find this 'Hooded Man'."

"So let's forage on," Antoine said. "The plan will proceed. Can you guys help me wrap up his body so we can take it back to Ned? He'll need to extract some blood to have it examined."

Delia sat on a grave marker and lit a cigarette.

Antoine shoved the shovel into the ground and winced at its hardness. "Soil is stony," he said.

Monsignor Harrison stepped forward and looked over the hole that Antoine had been starting to form. "The stones protect him. Keep digging. We must forage through them. There will always be obstacles. We must press on, Antoine."

Antoine looked at the Monsignor, who stared back at him through the darkness, and then he looked back down at the hole he was digging. He remembered, not so long ago, digging a similar hole in the earth, without any assistance, and back then, it had seemed so much easier. Like the soil gave way more easily, he felt he had been stronger. But now, the soil was stony, he was with several other immortals who governed his actions.

But there was no Asmodai.

At least not yet.

And then, when his shovel hit a large rock, sending a shower of sparks, he stopped, drew the shovel up towards the ground, and stopped, leaning on the pole. He looked over at the Monsignor, then to Ramiel, and back to the Monsignor. "Is he going to help?"

The Monsignor smiled and took a few steps closer to Antoine. "He cannot help, dear Antoine. Darius is your maker. This is all you. Ramiel is here, of course, for his support. He loves you. So very much. But he cannot help you. Nor can I. This is something that you alone must accomplish."

Antoine closed his eyes and turned back towards the grave. He pictured the coffin sitting below, probably caked with dirt, the wood rotted from groundwater. "He is rotting down there. I can tell."

Ramiel stepped forward and placed his hand on Antoine's shoulder. Antoine closed his eyes for a moment as Ramiel spoke. "Antoine, you don't know that for certain. It hasn't been that long since Darius passed. There still may be time."

Antoine continued digging, as Ramiel stood back with the Monsignor and Delia. They watched Antoine fight through the stones, tossing the small, egg shaped rocks off to the side, and listening as one or two would ricochet off a nearby grave marker. For hours it seemed, they waited. Waited as Antoine continued hoisting dark earth over his shoulder; as Delia sat on a nearby bench and smoked a cigarette, as the Monsignor paced up and down the path, and as Ramiel crouched next to Antoine as the coffin was revealed.

Antoine pulled at the top of the casket, as it crumbled into his hands. Ramiel reach down into the grave, tugging at Antoine's shoulder. "Let him go, Antoine."

As the lid of the coffin tore away, and the stench of rotting flesh permeated the air, Antoine hung his head down and closed his eyes. The warm tears streamed down his face, and he turned around, looking up at Ramiel and the Monsignor, and cried out. "Delia! Come here! He is truly gone!"

Delia appeared at the grave and looked downwards, to where Antoine crouched over the coffin. Antoine looked up at her. "Look at him." He sunk his head down and felt the warm tears slide down his face. "Just look, Delia. He is gone. Truly gone. His body is gone. Totally rotted out. Is there nothing left to save?"

Delia stooped down and extended one leg down into the grave onto the top of the liner. "We will look," she said. She eased herself into the grave and stood next to Antoine, over him, and placed her arm around his shoulders. "I am so sorry, Antoine. So very, very sorry."

And then Antoine stopped and looked towards the sky. Ramiel produced a syringe. "There is no need for that, Antoine." He bent down and took a small sample of blood. "Amazing that it hasn't dried up yet."

Antoine looked down and watched Ramiel's hands, mesmerized, as Ramiel leaned forward and plunged the needle into Darius' torso. Antoine spoke without breaking his gaze. "Darius only died a few days ago. And I was insistent on no embalming."

"That makes sense if you had wanted to resurrect him."

Antoine looked over at the Monsignor, who was checking his phone. The screen illuminated his face.

"So why can't we?" Antoine asked. "Why can't we bring him back?"

Monsignor Harrison put his phone away and took a few steps closer to Antoine and Ramiel. "It's the decomposition, Antoine. It's too far along. His body will be liquefying. We'll be lucky if we can even find out what this 'Hooded Man' is having us drink – given all the gases and chemicals produced when a human body decomposes."

Antoine dropped the pieces of the casket that he had been tearing away, and climbed out of the grave. He walked to the edge of the forest, as the Monsignor, Delia and Ramiel stood at the grave looking on at him.

But it was only Delia who looked over at him and understood. For the Monsignor and Ramiel were only governmental subjects; they did not really care, they only were there to protect the interests of *The Inspiriti*. But Delia, who was the leader of *The Inspiriti,* looked at Antoine directly as he leaned against a large Oak at the edge of the cemetery. It was done. Darius was truly dead. There was no body to resurrect this time around.

It didn't matter what type of incantation he was able to perform. Darius was gone. Off to the astral plane. And there was nothing that he or anyone else could do about it.

After the coffin was reburied, they headed back to the Chateau.

The group reached the clearing just beside the cemetery where some random graves were placed. The night was quiet, and the wind had died down. "Follow me and take every step that I do. There is no light and there are grave markers everywhere," Antoine said, looking back at Ramiel and Monsignor Harrison. He waved forward with the flashlight.

Antoine remembered the feel, and the crunching of the gravel beneath his feet. It wouldn't be much longer until there was a break in the path and they would have to turn right. If they kept proceeding forward, they would smack into a life sized statue of an angel. No time for first aid this evening.

"Keep with me," Antoine said as they reached the break and headed off to the right. "I can just imagine if Darius were here with us. He would have grabbed the flashlight from me and taken over."

Antoine stopped and held his arm out, stopping the other two men. "Wait a minute. I just heard something."

Antoine looked over towards the forest, and then back over at Ramiel, who was scanning the cemetery. Antoine took a few steps back. "I can sense his presence…"

The Monsignor placed his hand on Antoine's shoulder and brought his head close to Antoine's, and whispered. "Is this who I am thinking it is?"

Antoine nodded, and the group ducked down next to an oversized monument. Antoine turned off the flashlight and they listened. There was still an impenetrable silence. Antoine turned around and saw Ramiel make the *Sign of The Cross* and close his eyes. The Monsignor was fixated on the edge of the trees, just beyond the remaining rows of graves.

"Stay here," Antoine said. "I know this cemetery like the back of my hand. You three don't. I'm going to try to get a better feel of what's in that forest. If he is there, he is being mighty quiet."

The Monsignor nodded and huddled close to Ramiel. Antoine dashed off to the left and through several markers. He crept to another larger monument, considerably closer to the edge of the cemetery, and then stopped. He looked onwards, into the blackness, and ducked back behind the monument.

Some thunder rumbled in the distance, and Antoine felt a drop of rain on his cheek. The sky started to come alive, as the cloud parted and some moonlight shined through. He could see the stones, the blue hue on the blades of grass, and as he looked over towards the edge of the forest, he saw the mist coming.

Was Asmodai here to settle an old score?

Antoine remembered the first time that he faced him in the same cemetery under similar conditions. But here, Antoine was not resurrecting Darius, as he had in the past. There was no ritual to perform. He was simply acquiring the body to study the blood. Why was he coming this time?

The mist traveled down the stone path and swallowed the markers on either side. Antoine leaned against the monument, and looked over to where Monsignor Harrison and Ramiel were huddled. He could see them well now that the clouds had parted and the moonlight was shining through. And then he returned his attention to the approaching mist.

And Antoine thought that he remembered. He thought that the night he resurrected Darius was a face-off with Asmodai, and he knew, at any moment, the beast would make his appearance, approaching with thunderous footsteps, toppling trees and ripping branches and limbs to shreds, riding winds like that of a hurricane.

But what he saw, when the mist began to clear, was something completely different. For the beast was not there – it was not Asmodai who emerged from the trees; it was not the demon and his legion of the damned that filled the cemetery with flaming swords – it was hood that he recognized. It could be none other.

And the crystal caught the moonlight, and directed it back towards his face. The red hot potion was boiling inside, as he swung it back and forth, and the mist danced around him as the winds picked up –

Come with me and drink from the blood decanter…

They all froze, watching the hooded man approach on a cloud of white, swirling mist; the mist moved through the cemetery, wrapping around the stones, billowing upwards like low, blanketing clouds, covering the grass, the stones, and the everything in a cloud of white. The mist moved closer towards the men, like the rising tide covering a beach, moving closer with each passing minute.

"That is *him*!" Ramiel said. "That is the man with the glass vase of blood! Do not let him get any closer!"

Ramiel ran towards Antoine and tugged at his arm. "We have got to get back to the Chateau. We can't let him approach us. Or we'll be here where Darius is buried!" Ramiel turned to run, and then called back. Antoine and the Monsignor stood, side by side, watching the hooded man approach, step by step, a few feet at a time. They stared in unison and saw the decanter, as the man held it upwards towards the sky. Their heads moved in the direction of the decanter, their eyes transfixed on the swirling, crimson potion. The hooded man looked towards Antoine and Monsignor Harrison. He looked towards them with a faceless stare.

This potion will be your salvation. Come with me, drink.

Ramiel fell to his knees and crawled towards the open grave. He reached inside the bag and fumbled through the tools, and found a rag. He held it up to his eyes and covered them. He reached outwards with his arms, flapping away, reaching out towards his companions. "Antoine! Monsignor! We must go now!"

But they did not hear him.

The blood decanter was lowered to the ground, as it levitated and lowered in the cradle of the white mist. The mist cleared from around it as it set itself on the ground and swirled outwards. Antoine and the Monsignor both looked down at the decanter, as the potion glowed.

Ramiel got up on his feet, holding the rag over his eyes. He took an uncertain step forward, holding one arm out in front of him. He felt the solidity of Antoine's back, patted upwards with his open palm, and grabbed his shoulder, pulling him back. Antoine lost his footing and they both fell to the ground, toppling over each other, and down into the open grave. Dirt loosened and fell on top of them.

Antoine struggled and coughed. "What the – Ramiel!"

"Stay in here! The Monsignor is still up there." Ramiel looked upwards towards the opening. The mist was swirling over the top of the grave. He looked over at Antoine, who was looking down at the casket.

"Antoine…the Monsignor is still up there."

Antoine closed his eyes and sighed. "Is it too late for him?"

Ramiel looked upwards at the mist which still blanketed the opening. "I'm afraid if we climb out we will become enchanted also. I was surprised I was able to break his hold on you."

Antoine nodded and looked over at Ramiel. "Thank you, Ramiel. You must be my guardian angel or something…"

Ramiel shot Antoine a knowing glance and smiled –

There was a loud crash up above, shaking the ground. Dirt loosened and the sides of the grave and showered on the two as they crouched on the casket. The casket shook on its runners, the sound of steel against steel pierced their ears. Ramiel and Antoine looked upwards, and then back at each other. Ramiel stood and reached for the sides of the grave, grabbing a thick root. Antoine grabbed him arm. "No, Ramiel. Don't. I've talked to Darius. We have been down here too long. It's too late for the Monsignor."

Ramiel shook Antoine's arm off and climbed upwards, into the mist. At first, all he saw was the cloudy vapor. But that was only the beginning. The mist lightened, gradually at first, and then with an increased determination, towards a bright, white hot light, assaulting his eyes; he screamed, attempted to cover his eyes, but was thrown backwards against the opposite side of the grave. Antoine reached up and dragged Ramiel back down into the grave.

There was a crash of thunder directly above them, and they both looked upwards. The mist had cleared. As they gazed above they saw a cloudless sky of stars, and the same familiar blue moonlight.

It was stark and silent. The chill in the air returned. Antoine looked over at Ramiel. "We should go up there. See if he is okay."

Ramiel nodded and started to climb up the side. Antoine followed and peeked his head above the threshold of the earth. Monsignor Harrison was sitting on a top of a monument, but the mist was gone. The hooded man was gone. It was as if nothing had ever happened.

They both climbed out of the grave. Antoine called out to the Monsignor. The priest looked up, and and smiled. His teeth glistened against the moonlight. He looked over at Antoine and Ramiel. The Monsignor smiled, and his face quivered, his eyes widened. He threw his head back, and laughed, a deep belly laugh. Antoine and Ramiel looked at each other and shrugged, as the Monsignor stood on his feet and held his belly and bent forward, laughing deep from the pit of his soul.

Antoine walked a few steps closer to the Monsignor. Antoine cocked his head to the side and extended his arm outwards to the priest. "Monsignor Harrison…"

And the Monsignor stopped laughing just as abruptly as he had started, turned and faced Antoine directly. Antoine couldn't help but notice that the priest somehow looked…different. His eyes were still wide with life, but he stopped, and looked at them, hovering like a clown. And then he threw his head back and laughed again. "I am finally saved! I always thought that maybe…just maybe…that I would have had faith in something that was nothing. But now I know it's *something!*"

Ramiel's face shifted as he walked over to the Monsignor. He walked over close to the man, as he had calmed, and Ramiel put his arm around the priest. "You doubted your faith your greatness?"

"Oh please!" he said. "I have been questioning my faith for years. It was a long time running. I didn't have the courage to tell others – besides you."

Ramiel shook his head and looked over at Antoine. Antoine shrugged his shoulders. Ramiel grabbed the Monsignor's arm. "I need to speak to you more specifically about what you experienced tonight, Monsignor. Your doubts, they are very common. I would imagine even among the Clergy at times. But tonight…this 'Hooded Man'…he was not a harbinger of salvation."

The Monsignor pulled free from Ramiel and stood apart from the two men. He glared right at them. "Don't *either* of you question my *faith*!"

Antoine looked over at Ramiel, who placed his arm on the Monsignor's shoulder. "It's not your faith that we question. Its tonight's events. You do believe that there will be false prophets, right?"

The Monsignor scoffed and said nothing. Ramiel looked over at Antoine. "Let's go back and pick this up tomorrow?"

Antoine nodded, as they walked towards the edge of the forest and back to the Chateau. The Monsignor continued to tell his story of how he spoke with the hooded man, how he drank from the decanter, was saved, and would be immortal forever.

As he talked, Antoine looked over at Ramiel, and they exchanged worried looks.

Ramiel watched the Monsignor. "Then you certainly believe, as well, that tonight could have been a temptation of falsehood? A delusion?"

The Monsignor threw his head back again in laughter. "Let's go, boys! Stop being silly. The night is about to end, and I'm ready to retire. You guys can stay here and perform whatever incantations for Darius that you like, but I am going back to the Chateau!"

Once they arrived, Antoine closed the door behind them. They rushed towards the back of the Chateau. "Giovanni!" Antoine called. "We need help in the kitchen!" They ushered the Monsignor to the kitchen table and sat him at one of the chairs. He continued laughing, his deep belly laugh, as the group examined his eyes.

Antoine looked down at Monsignor Harrison. His eyes, completely stark white, were surrounded by black and bleeding lesions. Ramiel went to the kitchen sink and took a washcloth and ran it under some cool water. "Monsignor, your eyes are white!" Ramiel inhaled a deep breath as he touched the cool washcloth to his flaming wounds.

"*I saw God!*" He sat up, placing his hands on the table. "I can see nothing now…but I saw God!"

Ramiel held his hands up to the Monsignor's eyes and winced. "Your eyes must be burning. I know it. I can feel it."

"I saw God in that light! *I saw God!*"

Antoine shook his head and looked down. "You didn't see God, your Highness. God is not in that mist. He is not in that decanter. Or that potion. That is the blood of Satan! You didn't see God. You saw Lucifer. You drank from the Devil."

THE TOWER OF BABYLON:

BLOOD RAIN

They once thought she had been a witch.

And for those crimes, they sought to burn her at the stake. It was the same morning, early with a chill in the air, which she remembered – as she woke in her bed, the covers still pulled up towards her neck; she could still smell the soot and the smoke and ash.

There was a knock at the door.

Delia closed her eyes. "I'm still resting." And after, a few minutes of silence followed. She was taken back to that same morning; that morning when a similar knocking was heard. But on that particular day, her door had been made of wood; the small dwelling that she lived in was made of hardened clay – and it was hundreds of years earlier.

As she drifted back to sleep, she could see the door in front of her – the old wood, the musty odor, the tapestry hanging over the window which caught a light breeze.

The door banged with a thud.

She sat up in bed.

She could still feel the grit in her eyes, as she had only retired a few hours previously. She still wore her bedclothes; a white, plain dress, and her hair, dirty, mussed and caked together with twisted locks.

And the knock came again, and she woke.

I have come for you, Delia.

She paused and crossed her arms over her breasts. "Who are you?"

I am coming for you and I will give you the dark gift.

The door splintered open, as the wood crumbled and a piece of the door broke off and crashed to floor. Delia sat up, looked forwards, and saw the figure standing in the doorway. There was a certain statuesque presence; a dark figure against the brilliance of the sun, dust clouds billowing around, billowing into her room. But there was a certain feel to the visitor. For the shape of the silhouette was distinctly feminine; Delia could see the outline of something that looked like a veil. "My name is Claret Atarah. I come to you in peace."

She sat up in bed and watched the woman walk into her room, as the dust settled. Delia swung her legs around the bed and felt the cold, hard wood. She turned and looked at her visitor. "Your name…is so exceptional. Where do you come from?"

Claret sat next to Delia on the bed. She looked Delia directly in the eyes. "I come with a warning. There is great turmoil in your country. Talks of heresy. They are burning the accused at the stake."

Delia closed her eyes and nodded. "How do you know all of this?"

"I come from a different time," she said. "A different place. I have a special power – a gift, if you will – that was given to me by a man many, many years ago. I want to give you that gift as well."

"What gift is this?"

Claret stood and walked over to the window. "It's a gift that will let you live, dear Delia. It's a gift that I must give you, and it must only be me. And for this gift, you will become my child." She pulled the tapestry to the side and looked outside. "They are coming, dear Delia. They will be here today. If you do not accept my gift, you will burn and die. I travel through time, across dimensions, and I have found you. I know of the power you hold within. The gift will unlock that power."

"The power I hold within? What power is that?"

Claret turned around. Delia dropped her dress to the floor, standing nude in front of Claret, and walked over to the washbasin. She splashed some water on her face.

"Do you want the gift I speak of?"

Delia stood and washed herself. "Tell me more about it, Claret. I do not know you. Nor do I know of you. Why do they believe me to be a witch?"

Claret stepped forward and sat on the edge of the bed. "You have gotten fairly well known in your town, have you not?"

Delia nodded as she pulled on a clean dress. She joined Claret, and sat next to her on the bed. "No time for sitting," Claret said, grabbing her arm as they both stood. "Come with me," she said. "Let me take you away from here, and I will explain everything."

Delia watched Claret as the world changed around her. The blue skies grew dark, as the landscape shifted and turned, as if they were entering a tunnel without moving. She still held Claret's hand, although she was traveling behind her. As the tiny beams of light flew past them, and the darkness held steadfast, she closed her eyes.

She remembered visiting Domrémy-la-Pucelle, very close to her domicile. She saw the same soaring roof, the roof with one side reaching upwards towards the left as she faced the small, wooden door. The roof reached towards a point, and dominated her view. But now, the villa was gone, and they were traveling in darkness.

"I am taking you to a different time," Claret said. "And a different place. I am taking you on this journey with me to show you where the story truly begins."

Delia felt a cool wind against her face, as if they were moving a great speeds, covering vast distances, but when she looked down at her feet, it appeared as if they were standing still. As she looked around her, she saw wisps of brilliant white light flash past them, so it did appear that they were moving quite fast. She called out to Claret. "Where are we going?"

Claret turned and smiled. "Come with me and see…"

The darkness started to lift. And as the haziness cleared enough to gauge a sense of atmosphere, she saw desert sands. Small, clay square huts lining the streets, and as they walked forward, she could feel her feet in the hot, stony sand. A hot, dry wind blew against her face. The temperature was stifling. She looked up at the sky at the piercing sun.

"We are in Jerusalem, Delia. Come follow me. Through the market. Don't speak to anyone. Just follow me and I will lead you to a safe place."

"Is this not safe?"

She followed Claret, who did not answer. Delia watched her robe, her flowing red hair blow in the hot desert wind. And Delia looked around. All of the new images, those of which she had never seen before, except in books. She looked around the market, at the dusty tables, teeming with activity. She saw the tapestries hanging on the sides of the small, stone one-story buildings, attached to the walls with wooden sticks, reaching outwards over the windows. There were vendors sitting on small wooden tables, in front of fruit and fish; others led camels through the dusty passageways. And then they sought the shade and waited behind a merchant. Claret leaned against a small stone house, and Delia sat in the sand next to her. "We will wait until the shroud of darkness," she said.

Delia hung her head down and looked at the sand, and the small pebbles, when she felt her head getting heavier and her eyes closed.

When she opened her eyes, it felt like it was well into the evening; the sky was dark and starless, and when she looked up at the clouds, they were floating by, fingering their way across the sky, like dark, fluffy cotton against a pale blue light.

"How long have I been sleeping?" Delia asked, getting to her feet.

"Not as long as you think," she said, and walked out in to the center of the market. "It is safe now. Let us go."

"Where are you taking me, Claret?"

Claret stopped walking, turned around and took Delia's hand. "Follow me this way." She led Delia past the market, into an alleyway, and onwards down the alley to a small, wooden, windowless door. She opened it and stepped into a small room. There was a small, wooden table and three plain wooden side chairs.

"Sit," Claret said. "There is wine in the corner. I will get you some."

Delia looked around the room. It was plain. Claret was a pauper. There were no other rooms to the house. A small stone bed in the corner with a tattered blanket. Two windows through which the hot breeze would blow. And a small table and chairs. Nothing else.

Claret dragged a stone urn and tipped some red wine into a simple stone goblet. "No matter how the clouds part, nor the skies clear, I open my eyes to blood rain; wash the tears away, and weep again for a different purpose."

Claret pushed one of the goblets of wine in front of Delia. She looked up at her and nodded. "Drink."

Delia looked directly at the goblet, and then up at Claret.

Claret nodded. "Drink and you will live forever. You will not have to worry about those back in Lyon burning you at the stake. Drink this and you will always live. You will never die. And I will give you the gift of immortality. You will always live, you will always be young."

"But what if I don't drink?"

Claret stood and walked around the table. She knelt next to Delia, and pulled her chin up gently. Their eyes locked. "Because if you don't drink," Claret said, "then you will certainly have a great misfortune befall upon you."

Delia looked at the cup, and then shook her head. "I don't understand. Claret, I don't understand. Please make me understand. What is coming?"

Claret sat in the chair opposite Delia, reached across the table and took her hands. She looked into Delia's eyes. "Many years from now, Delia, you will be a great leader. You will be one of the founding members of an organization that advocates for our kind. But there will be a significant misfortune – a misguided warrior who will be a false prophet. He will convince all of our kind that he is the salvation. The light. But he not, Delia. He is not."

Delia looked down at their clasped hands. And then back over at the cup, and back into Claret's eyes. "And so you are warning me?"

Claret nodded and smiled. "I have been watching you Delia. Watching you from afar. In different times, different places. That is why I selected you. You are destined to be a mother figure, one who will lead and become a Matriarch of our kind." Claret stood and walked to the window. She pulled the tapestry aside and craned her head around the wall, looking outside. "My warning is simple. You drink from the cup, you will have no worry. I will give you the gift. But there will be someone, thousands of years from now, who will seek to destroy our kind. You will be my child because it is written. It is your destiny to be so. And so it will be. But this cup – this sacred cup – will be the key to your eternal salvation."

"How will it be that?"

Claret turned around and walked back to the table. She took the chair opposite Delia again. "Because this cup was used by Christ himself. This is the cup which He bled into. The cup which He shared His blood with his disciples. This is the cup. And you must drink from it. And you will live forever."

Delia looked down at the cup and her eyes widened. She looked back up at Claret. Her face shifted and she glared at

Claret with stony eyes. "You lie. This is not the cup. Where are we? What are we doing here? Take me back!"

Claret sat back and laughed. "You silly, stupid little bitch. You think I am lying to you? You *chose* to follow me. You made the choice. Free will. Have you read your Bible lately or do I need to take you back to Paris to go get it? Free will. We all have it. You chose to follow me. We are in the year 33 A.D. It was a pretty significant year, from what I recall. Do you remember?"

Delia stood and looked down at Claret. "Yes. I have read the Bible. I know that Christ was crucified in that year."

Claret nodded and stood. She looked into Delia's eyes. "Then you should also be aware that Christ is now gone. Went back to Heaven. He has left the earth. And now I am here. I have the cup. So if you've read your Bible, He rose from the dead."

Delia nodded, not taking her eyes off of Claret. "Yes, I have studied the Gospels."

Claret moved a few steps closer, and Delia took a step back. "So are you are refusing to drink from my cup? You will not take my wine?"

Delia scowled. "You are using it for blasphemy! I will not be a part of that evil!"

Claret took a deep breath and let it out slowly. She took a hand and smoothed her hair back. "Suit yourself," she said. She lunged forward and pinned Delia against the wall, opening her mouth wide, and then plunging long, pointed fangs into Delia's neck.

The piercing was a type of pain that she had not felt before; and as she felt the hot blood run down her neck, she closed her eyes as tears streamed down her face. *"My God, why have you abandoned me?"*

Delia waited in the vestibule for Antoine to return from speaking with Father Bauman. She touched her neck for a few moments, remembering the time that Claret had taken her back in time to Jerusalem when she was still a young woman. She walked over to the doors to the worshipping area, and looked through the slit between the doors. She could see Antoine sitting in the front pew. Father Bauman was next to him. She recognized his salt and pepper hair. She opened the door, feeling the fresh, cool air against her face. She called out. "I think I know who is responsible for this!"

Antoine and Father Bauman stopped talking and looked back at Claret. Antoine stood. "What are you talking about?" His voice echoed against the empty church and the high ceilings.

She rushed as fast as she could towards the front of the church, her cane creaking on the floor. "It's Claret, Antoine. It's her. I think maybe I had blocked this memory. I was so upset with her for so many years. I didn't want to accept that she was my mother. I just couldn't accept it. But she transformed me against my will." She looked at the priest. "I was once a good, Christian woman, Father."

Father Bauman got up and walked over to where Delia stood. He placed his arm around her as she told them how Claret had transformed her and tried to make her drink from the Christ cup. "Antoine. Father. I believe she is trying to dominate our kind. I believe she has convinced the 'Hooded Man' to sell his soul to evil and carry out this horrid task. Our kind is dying, Father. They are drinking from this decanter. This imposter."

Antoine shook his head. "That doesn't make any sense, Delia. Why would she want to wipe out her own kind?"

Delia raised her arms and then let them flop back down by her sides. She tossed her cane onto a pew with a bang. "Why wouldn't she? Antoine, she has been hell bent on dominating our kind for as long as I can remember. If she wipes us out, then she can start to repopulate the immortals with all of her own creation. They would all be her minions, loyal to her – and only her – for all of eternity. She is trying to be a goddess."

Father Bauman tugged at his chin and looked down at the floor. "Well, then the only way to save your kind is to drink from the true Christ cup. That is the true salvation. *The Blood of Christ.*"

365

Antoine and Delia looked at each other, both wide-eyed and bewildered. "Father," Antoine said. "How can we get immortals to drink? The 'Hooded Man' has been traveling through cities and the immortals are flocking to him. They are heading to their deaths!"

"What does he do?" Father Bauman asked.

Antoine picked up Delia's cane and handed it to her. "Rumor has it that he arrives on a cloud of white mist. It's always when his victim is alone. He is a faceless man in a hood, he carries the decanter – and inside it is a swirling red potion. He claims its blood that brings salvation. But it brings death."

"Imposters," Father Bauman said. "There will be many."

"Let's go, Delia," Antoine said. "It's time to go find the cup."

Father Bauman nodded. "I hope you both make the right decision," he said. "You both have been coming to me for guidance, like Darius did. I am always willing to help, both of you. You are not damned like you think you are. Just follow the right path. Make the right choices. The blood – the true blood – saves all."

Antoine looked back as they started to leave the worshipping area. "How will I know what the right path is?"

Father Bauman smiled. "You will know, Antoine. Open you mind, open your heart. And you will know."

Antoine opened the door to his small, silver Mercedes for Delia and she climbed in. He tossed her cane in the back seat and sat in the driver's seat, as the engine roared to life.

"So we need to figure out how to convince our kind that this man is an imposter, right?" Delia fidgeted with her bag as Antoine weaved in and out of traffic.

Antoine focused on the road. "Darius told me, a while back, that once he has a hold on you – this 'Hooded Man – that there is nothing else. It's like he controls your mind." He shook his head. "I don't know if there *is* a way to convince everyone that he is an imposter. How will we do that? Once he appears, he controls your mind…looks what happened to the Monsignor."

"How is he doing, Delia? Since we arrived back in Miami, I mean."

"From what I have heard, he has returned to Rome and Ramiel is nursing him back to health. The unfortunate thing is, he won't be around for much longer. At least if things progress the same way they did for Darius."

Delia looked out the window and shook her head. "I don't even know if this is something we can prevent."

As the Mercedes proceeded towards the Miracle Mile, the clouds covered and blocked the sun, and it looked like it was about to pour down rain. Antoine flipped the wipers on. And after a moment, a red smear fleshed across the windshield.

"What the?" Antoine instinctively pressed on the brakes.

Delia looked up from her lap, and watched the red smear increase in size.

"It's the blood rain," she said. "The decanter has overflowed."

Antoine looked over at Delia and shook his head.

Delia continued. "Claret told me about this when she took me back to her time. To Jerusalem. She said the blood would rain when the blood decanter spilled over."

"What does this all mean, Delia?"

She sighed as Antoine pulled into the parking lot of his rented condominium. "It means we need to get inside. We need to get *below*. I mean below the earth. It means the earth is about to be cleansed. And the dead will rise. We have to hurry, Antoine. We don't have much time."

There was a light rainfall over Jerusalem, a rarity in the midst of the brilliant afternoon sun. It had come rather suddenly, the cloud formed in a bright blue and cloudless sky, just over a certain sector of huts towards the east of the marketplace. "It's the blood rain, *I know it!* The blood rain is coming!" Claret said, walking over the window, pulling the tapestry aside, looking out at the activity a few blocks away, down the alley, as townsfolk carried rolled tapestries over their shoulders, carried small satchels of peppers, and led camels with long leads. Some looked upwards towards the sky after a deep, rolling thunder clapped above the tiny buildings.

Claret handed Delia a small, white cloth. She held it up to her pierced neck.

"Look outside the window," Claret said, ushering towards the opening.

"What is blood rain?"

Claret paused for a moment, and turned around, looking back at her and the bed that they had shared so recently. "Blood rain. It comes when the demons awaken. When the dead rise from their graves. It's when the decanter spills over, falls from the sky. The blood rains on the ground and awakens the dead."

Her visitor nodded.

Claret sighed and looked back out the window, watching the activity on the dusty streets. The market was closing up as the clouds blocked the sun. People were scurrying to cover their wares; some were close to an interior door and tossed fruit and fish in boxes, placing them inside doorways. Others simply ran. "It will come," she said. "No time soon. Not in this time. Thousands of years from now. But it will come."

"How do you know this?"

She turned around and faced Delia. "I know it because that is what I see. And the blood will rain in every city in the world. Every country. And in every *time*."

Delia's face shifted.

"Every time," Claret said. "I took you here to transform you. Show you my heritage. But when the blood rains from the sky – it will rain in Paris, it will rain on your Vaudeville stage; it will rain on my descendant Antoine in Miami in the early twenty-first century as well. Time will not be a protector."

When the group had been back in France, there was a knock on the door of the Chateau as the sun faded. Antoine, sitting on the sofa, sighed as he heard the knocking.

"Had you been expecting someone?" Ramiel asked.

"No," Antoine sighed. His weariness was evident on his face. "I was getting ready to relax." He got up and padded over to the door, peered through the side window, and gasped – "What the – "

He flicked the deadlock and swung the door open. The man standing on the front porch looked older, yet quite familiar. "*Ethan?*"

The small Hispanic man extended his hand. "Hector, actually. I am Hector now. I have not been Ethan for a long, long time."

Antoine's mouth fell open as he noticed the salt and pepper hair, the lines around his face. "You've grown old!"

Hector nodded. "Yes, I have aged significantly, Antoine. I was near death. Lying on Ponce de Leon. But a man saved me. The Astral took me in and saved me."

Hector stepped inside as Antoine stepped aside. He looked around and whistled. "Wow, I thought your Miami estate was something. This Chateau is otherworldly." And then he nodded and looked at Antoine.

Antoine questioned the man as he took his coat and laid it on the center table. "What are you doing here? We haven't seen you since Darius had passed."

Hector nodded as Antoine showed him into the living room. Giovanni gathered some snifters from the bar and brought a decanter of cognac to the coffee table on a small, silver tray.

Hector sat back in a large, upholstered armchair and crossed his legs as Giovanni offered him some cognac, which he refused with the wave of his hand. "I was compelled to see you, Antoine. I grew old because I too, like Darius, drank from the decanter. I have been researching the 'Hooded Man' for years now, and may have discovered a way to stop him."

Antoine and Ramiel both looked up and over at Hector at the same time. Antoine spoke as Ramiel reached for his bag. "You are not serious?"

"The theory is that he is the spirit of a man who lived once – a George Nathan Foley. Do you remember him Antoine? He lived in Miami."

"Name doesn't ring a bell."

Hector nodded fished a small spiral notepad from his bag. He flipped a few pages in and grabbed a pen from the coffee table. "Do you mind Antoine?"

Antoine nodded.

Hector sat back in the plush chair, crossed his legs, and rested the small notepad on his thigh. "Do you remember when you were speaking with Cristoph in Rome?"

"Yes."

"Okay then. You have to see – those at *The Inspiriti* used Cristoph to gather information about you, your sector and your closest followers. To protect you."

Antoine nodded and looked at Ramiel. "Are you saying they knew this was going to happen?"

Hector placed his notebook on the coffee table slowly, and looked back and forth at Antoine and Ramiel. "No...but I am saying that they have a member who has known for thousands of years."

"Who?" Antoine asked.

Hector sighed. "The one who had knowledge about this is the one who is directly tied to Claret."

Antoine downed his entire snifter of cognac. He shook his head and threw the glass against the wall. "Giovanni! Wake Delia up please! We need to speak to her right away." Antoine sat back in the sofa and closed his eyes. "So she has known." He shook his head.

"Yes, she has," Hector said. Ramiel rushed to Antoine's side and put his arm around Antoine. He leaned in close to Antoine's ear. "Don't, Antoine. Don't let your temper get the best of you. She is a well-respected member of our society. Let's calm down and listen to what she has to say."

Claret waited in darkness, sitting in the sand and staring at the stars. But it was also the night so many years later, that she sat, sitting cross legged in the sparse grass across the stone path, feeling the cool dirt under her skin, when she waited for Delia. Now Claret was in a different time, and waited for the Hooded Man to come out – the one who they said carried the decanter.

Giovanni opened the sliding doors between the front sitting room and the back hall and Delia stepped in. She looked at Antoine. He looked back at her, and the room was silent for a few minutes. "I know why you called for me," she said, sitting in a small side chair not far from the others. She looked up, as if searching for something to say, and then back at Antoine and Ramiel. They leaned forward on the sofa, looking back at Delia.

"It's true," she said. "Back when I was much younger, Claret visited me at Domrémy-la-Pucelle. So many years ago now, it seems. It was before the days when I had started in Vaudeville over in Paris. But these were the days when witches were hunted. Women burned at the stake for heresy, and one morning, I woke to Claret at my door. This was the first time in memory that I saw her."

"And what did she do?" Hector asked. "Tell them what she did."

Delia nodded, looked down at her fidgeting hands. "She took me back in time. I didn't know then that she could time travel. But she took me to Jerusalem – just after the Crucifixion of Christ. And she told me then about the 'Hooded Man'."

Antoine slammed his fist on the coffee table. "So you *have* known all along!" He got up and started to pace around the room.

Delia stood. Her face shifted and her eyes widened. "No Antoine! I had not remembered about this until just recently. The memory was blocked!"

Antoine stopped pacing and glared at Delia. "Then why would you suddenly remember it now?"

"I don't know, Antoine. I don't know."

Ramiel leaned back on the sofa and looked up at Antoine and then over at Delia. He then gestured for Antoine to sit. "I have seen this before," he said. "Did Darius ever tell you about Tramos?"

Antoine shook his head and sat down. Delia took her seat as well. "No, he didn't speak much of Tramos to me," Antoine said. "I know the guy exists, that's about the extent of it."

Ramiel continued. "Well, I think this could be a similar situation. Darius came to Rome as well, when he was mortal and dying. When he spoke to us, we had agreed to full confidentiality, but given the circumstances, I must divulge this." He took Antoine's hand and looked directly in his eyes. "Darius had a similar memory – where Tramos inserted himself into Darius' thoughts, on the night he was transformed, and told him about the 'Hooded Man'."

Delia's mouth dropped open. "So you are saying Claret did the same thing with me?"

Ramiel raised his eyebrows and looked at Delia. "It's *possible*. The older immortals have that power. They have for centuries. But both Tramos and Claret are even older. They may very well have the same power to change your memories like that."

Antoine looked at Delia. "What else did she tell you?"

"That was really all she said. She told me about the 'Hooded Man'. She wanted me to drink from a cup that she claimed held Christ's blood.

Ramiel stopped. "Wait a minute. She had the cup?"

Delia shrugged.

Antoine looked up. "She had the cup once. That goes deep into her genealogy."

There was a ray of sunlight that filtered through the trees. It was strong yet gentle, like a hand caressing his shoulders.

He could feel his muscles relax.

He looked down and saw the blades of grass reaching upwards from the earth, as the sun sank deeper into the sky.

He reached for the shovel. "Where does he lay now? Is there a certain depth?"

Giovanni sat, hunched over, his hands running over the grass, back and forth. He finally spoke. "I think he was placed at the normal level. Six feet, give or take. No need to bury him deeper, since he was human."

Hector nodded, stood, and drove the shovel into the grass. The dirt still felt stony. He shifted the shovel back and forth, as he felt the rocks start to loosen.

It was now much closer to dusk. The daylight was fading, as the sky transitioned and developed an auburn tint. Hector looked up towards the sky. "It won't be much longer now. Why do we always have to do these things at night?"

Giovanni stopped digging and looked over at Hector. "Do I need to explain this to you again?" And then Giovanni stopped speaking. "Did you hear that?"

The two men stopped and listened, as Giovanni scanned the cemetery. The daylight was almost gone, and a mist was rolling in like a blanket.

There was a faint squeaking, like a rusted gate being opened, coming from the other side of the cemetery. Then a scratching, like a nail being dragged over a piece of wood.

"I heard it that time," Hector said, as both men looked towards the direction. Giovanni took a step forward.

"I can't see anything," Hector said. "The mist is too thick." And it was. The rolling clouds, the light, white mist, which came every evening to Les Enfantes, was quite different that particular evening. It was no longer a layer covering the earth and stones, but it expanded, a giant cloud which crept closer to the tree, as the two men dropped their shovels.

Giovanni turned towards at Hector. "He's coming. I can sense it."

Hector craned his neck forward. "How can you be sure?"

The scratching continued.

"What is that noise?" Hector asked. "Like a scratching sound?"

Giovanni looked over at the trees as the wind picked up. The sky had darkened, but the clouds parted enough to let some moonlight in. It reflected against the mist, which appeared as a cloud, billowing and expanding, moving towards them, inch by inch, across the cemetery, swallowing gravestones, the path, foliage, and small benches.

"That mist is getting closer," Giovanni said. "I know about that mist. It's time to get back to the Chateau. Leave the shovels. We'll continue this tomorrow."

Giovanni grabbed Hector's arm and they turned in the direction of the Chateau, walking away from the mist, moving quickly, determined, and looking back at the ominous cloud, following them with continuity, reaching through the forest, billowing upwards over the tree tops. "The mist is what carries him here." His eyes widened. "We must go! He carries the decanter!"

And Giovanni was right.

Hector looked towards the forest, watched the mist roll its way towards them, like a blanket of snow against black darkness, and then turned around. Giovanni was tugging at his arm. "Hector please! We must leave now! Before his arrival. If he comes here while we are still here, he will convince us to drink. And that is what is happening now."

They ran back to the Chateau.

Hector slammed the door behind them as the mist swallowed the front of the chateau. Giovanni looked through the curtains and all he could see was the white, swirling vapor. "Antoine! Come over here!"

Antoine looked over at Hector. "I'm sorry for making you go back out there. I know we initially wanted to get a sample of his blood, but clearly, that mist is standing guard. And I just wanted to check again. To make sure."

Hector nodded. "I can understand your need to check again. But he was too far gone, I'm afraid. Nothing has changed, unfortunately."

Antoine's footsteps clacked against the woodwork as Hector removed his jacket and draped it over a side chair in the front living room. Antoine joined Hector at the window.

Antoine shook his head. "It's him. Darius told me he came in a white mist. He rides the clouds."

"He is coming for us," Delia said, after she looked up from her knitting and joined the others.

Giovanni locked the door. "Keep it locked."

As Giovanni went into the living room and sat at the desk at the wall, Antoine clicked on a small lamp, and returned his gaze to the window. The mist moved continuously, swirling just outside the window. Antoine moved his hand towards the window pane, as his finger-tips stopped just short of the glass. The mist swirled, rotating in a circle around his finger-tip, separated only by a thin layer of glass. Antoine sighed. "You found me, didn't you?"

Antoine heard the familiar footsteps against the hardwood in the foyer. He saw Giovanni, holding a stack of papers. Antoine tried to smile. "Locking the doors won't stop him. He's out there. In that mist. Look at the movement."

Antoine touched the windowpane with his fingers, and the mist swirled, in a clockwise motion, spinning around his finger, as the motion spread, so did the cloud, which had swallowed the house.

Thunder rumbled in the distance. Antoine looked upwards. "He's getting closer."

Hector joined the two. "Can we hide you in your coffin? Let you sleep? Will this pass?"

Antoine shook his head. "I cannot hide. He has found me." Antoine looked at Giovanni, and then Hector, and then back at the window. "The only way out is farther in."

A tree snapped outside as thunder crashed, a loud, deafening boom directly above the chateau. "To the basement," Antoine said. "I know where we can go."

Giovanni grabbed Antoine's arm and stopped him just as he was about to move. "You seriously aren't thinking about going there, are you?"

Antoine pulled free and looked at Giovanni directly. Giovanni instinctively adjusted his white cloth that was tied around his head. Antoine looked away. "We have no choice. Come on."

All of the immortals moved through the house, turning off all of the lights, and shutting all of the drapes. Hector went to each window and checked all of the locks, as Antoine poured a large basin of water over the fire. Smoke poured into the living room. Giovanni started coughing.

"Damper's already shut," Antoine said, and then looked over to Hector. "All locked?"

Hector nodded as Delia took a deep breath and looked at Antoine.

"Not that it will make much of a difference anyway," Antoine said. "But maybe it will hold him for a bit."

The crash was deafening; the windows shook, and all three of them could feel a rumbling in the floor. They each looked at each other.

The front door crashed inwards, as they made their way to the basement.

Antoine foraged through the darkness. He waved his free hand out in front of him, feeling nothing, seeing nothing. He looked behind him, and when he couldn't see Giovanni or Hector, he paused. "Guys, are you there?" His voice reverberated against the silence. For a few moments earlier, the three men had been walking down the creaky, wooden stairs, and Antoine had pulled the string to a dingy, incandescent lightbulb on the landing, and once it was lit, it revealed a dusty, earthy basement, with more dirt than cement.

But that was before the three of them walked into the dark corner. And then, when Antoine turned around, he was alone. "Giovanni? Where did you go?"

Looking towards the other side of the basement, expecting to see a set of wooden stairs, he saw only darkness. But Antoine had been alone before. Aside from Roberto, he had been able to forage through life by himself. But Giovanni. Where had he gone?

The silence was so profound. He called out several times, both for Giovanni and Hector, and there was no answer. Had he been abandoned?

Claret paused. Her red hair caught the wind, and she stood, feet spread apart, and looked onwards at the man. His hood was still drawn closed. He stood like a statue, holding the decanter in his right hand.

"You carry the blood decanter! You have been a murderous torture to our kind for years!"

The clouds parted.

He raised his arms towards the sky. "There is no decanter!"

She looked down at her feet. Some gravel fell down the side of the mountain, but she held her place. And, as she looked at him closely, standing on the other mountain peak, she remembered.

"It was you!" she said. "You were the one!"

And then she saw him.

Thousands of years before, she saw his hand draw the tapestry back, on the side of the door, as she slept, still just a child, under the night Jerusalem sky.

"It was always you!"

She remembered holding his hand through the streets, through the dusty markets, under the knitted tapestries. "Take down your hood! Show your face!"

But the man did not.

He raised the decanter towards the sky, as the clouds above him swirled and turned red, and droplets of blood rained from the sky. The decanter filled with blood, until it reached the crest. The man tipped the decanter downwards, as the blood rained to the ground below. Tiny droplets of crimson rained against the night sky, coating the cars in blood, the puddles in the streets and on the sidewalk corners were red and bright, hot and boiling.

No one really knows if everyone experienced the blood rain from the sky that particular night. It wasn't determined if the blood rained only for a select few; those who were open to the other worldy dimensions, the time and space that exist right alongside the time and space that we, as a human population, experience each and every day.

But it was the blood rain that opened everyone's eyes to the existence of the astral plane. No longer would it would be a myth; nevermore would the urban legend of the doorway to the netherworld at One Andelusia Avenue be merely an urban legend. For there were those, the ones who felt the blood raining from the sky, those who would feel a droplet on their cheek, wipe it away, and be startled when they saw it was a droplet of blood.

The ones who were awake, the observers, ran inside their shops and houses. Doors slammed, all along Ponce de Leon, as blinds were drawn and closed signs were displayed in shop windows. As the droplets of blood slowly fell from the sky, the clouds grew darker; the sun faded.

The storm was coming.

Antoine, Delia and Hector had found the portal beneath the Chateau in France, and were transported to The Astral in Miami, stood underneath the porte cochère outside the offices on Ponce de Leon. They huddled close together, watching the red rain fall from the sky, watching the pink puddles mix with water, run down the side of the street towards the storm drain, and funnel their way under the city.

Delia shook her head. "It has happened," she said. Antoine and Ethan looked at her. She continued. "We must get inside. I have heard the rumors around the blood rain. The dead shall rise. The resurrection is about to happen…"

Antoine knocked on the door, and there was no answer. The winds increased in intensity, to such a degree that an entire tree blew down the street.

Delia's faced shifted as she peered out from under the small awning. The clouds were swirling, black and angry; the sky had turned red. There was a moment, when she saw the drops raining from the sky, the drops of blood that looked like tiny red bulbs, falling down towards her, splattering on the street, bright cherry splatters against stark, grey concrete.

Antoine rapped on the door.

A light snapped on inside the offices, as the three turned towards the direction of the door. Delia stood directly in front of the door and straightened her posture as the lock clicked and the door swung open.

Antoine's eyes widened. "Anthony!"

"No time for pleasantries now, Antoine! We must get below. Follow me!"

Anthony led the three through the main offices to The Astral. The lobby was lined with several leather couches and small side chairs, a large coffee table with an assorted variety of periodicals, and a small water cooler off to the side. They walked past a large reception desk. The offices looked like they could be a hub of activity. But now, the offices were stark and empty.

Anthony led the way through the hallways to the interior offices. "Everyone's gone," he said. "They've either all gone down below, they've been transformed, or just…devoured."

They reached a tiny, windowless office. Anthony started picking up side chairs and clearing the furniture from the area in front of the desk. Antoine and Ethan immediately jumped in to help, carrying a coffee table and placing it off to the side, as Delia stood next to the desk. "Does this have anything to do with the hooded man?"

Anthony stopped rolling the Persian carpet, stood, and placed his hands on his hips. He paused for a moment to catch his breath. "You notice the setting sun?"

They all nodded.

"This has been happening for years now apparently." Anthony bent down and continued rolling the carpet away, revealing a large door in the floor. Antoine noticed the small, black handle – a square indentation with a small ring in the center of the square. The indentation of the edges of the door ran through the floor; a break in the flow of the woodwork indicated that the door was large, expansive, flush with the floor, and, when covered with the rug, completely hidden.

"When Sheldon was the Director here, you three would have never been welcome down below." Anthony looked over at Antoine. "When he was interviewing you, were you aware of his true intentions?"

Antoine's face shifted. "He had told me it was to write a book."

Anthony scoffed, and reached down for the small ring in the floor. "You should read his files. Lots of info in there."

Antoine paused for a moment. He certainly remembered Sheldon Wilkes. He could still see the portly man sitting in a chair, downing caviar and crackers, drinking whiskey on ice, and jotting notes on a large, yellow legal pad. But he thought the man was dead.

"Oh he is dead, you are correct," Anthony said. He pulled at the ring. Veins protruded from his neck and his face turned red. He grunted. Antoine kneeled down and helped Anthony with the door, as they hoisted the large door up and outwards. It leaned against the desk.

Anthony dusted his hands off and Hector, Delia and Antoine all stood above, looking downwards into an expansive, dark cavern. A set of steps, carved in stone, led downwards and around to darkness. "I've sat in this very office," Antoine said. "And I had no idea that this was here!" He knelt down and peered downwards. But he saw nothing.

Delia shuffled towards the edge, leaning on her cane. Still standing, she peered down the stairs. "Smells musty," she said, looking up and over at Anthony, who stood on the opposite side of the office. "It's completely underground," he said. "The fact that I am even showing you the existence of this place – with who you are and *your* organization – is unprecedented. But Monsignor Harrison visited here last week. He assured me that we would band together as one to combat this problem. This hooded figure affects us all. Not only because he is exterminating your kind, but because we at The Astral are required to document this event."

Delia nodded. "You have the complete support of *The Inspiriti*. That I can assure you."

"That is what Monsignor Harrison said. Now let's get down there, and I will explain everything to you. But this blood rain that is falling – things can only get worse. We have to band together now. It's the only hope for survival for either of our kinds."

The blood continued to fall from the sky as the night wore on.

In Ascension Cemetery, the blood droplets created a thin coat of crimson liquid on the grass; it clung to the blades of grass like tiny red dewdrops, and then, just as quickly as it had begun, the blood rain ceased falling. The thunder grew ever more distant, the lighting, while still occasional in brilliant striking, faded away.

But the blood remained.

And once the clouds parted, the sky remained red. The tiny droplets of blood started a methodical movement, and in a very strict, regimented fashion, moved down the blades of grass and reached the ground. The drops slithered across the ground, reaching towards a plot of land just in front of a tombstone, and pooled; banding together to form a tiny red sea. Slowly, the sea formed, until a puddle of blood soaked into the ground.

The earth rumbled and shook, as the winds increased. The leaves shuffled and branches swayed. A wolf called out in the distance.

And then it started.

On the sidewalks of Ponce de Leon, it started first, for the blood reached the bodies there first, before the white worms had a chance to devour them, for they were a new crop of bodies, that were there nightly.

As soon as the blood touched the bodies, eyes opened, stark white and sightless. Arms reached upwards towards the sky. And living corpses sat upwards, rose to their feet, and walked in search of blood.

And bodies clawed their way out of the earth in cemeteries. Rotted hands threw dirt aside as the rotted bodies experienced renewed life, rising out of their graves, and joining the earth above.

Antoine lunged forward and locked in an embrace with Anthony. He reached up and mussed Anthony's dirty blonde hair, and gave him a kiss on the cheek. "I haven't heard from you for years! I thought you were dead?"

Anthony smiled and nodded. Delia introduced herself as they walked in the front lobby. Antoine turned to face Delia and Ethan, and placed his arm around Anthony, hugging him close. "It's been years," Antoine said. "Delia…Anthony here was once a researcher for The Astral."

"Still am," he said.

"Anyway," Antoine said. "I was his subject. But when the green mist came…things got lost. I got lost."

Anthony beamed a bright, white smile. "I'm glad you're back." He then looked over at Hector. "And who is *this* fine specimen?"

"I'm Hector, I was once known as Ethan, and I am twenty-two. Although I may look far older to you."

Anthony nodded. "I have heard about the 'Hooded Man'. He got to you too?"

Hector shook his head. "No. Claret. When I was young, she convinced me to follow her on a journey through time, and I lost my immortality. Yes, I drank from the decanter. But in a different way."

"What do you mean?" Anthony asked.

"I mean, she told me what she was up to. She tried to get me to join her, but I refused. And she took my gift away."

Delia shook her head. "I knew it was her. I knew it was her all along. I just needed the proof. And Hector, thank you for giving it to me."

THE CRUCIFIXION

Claret stood on a stone pulpit overlooking the Catacomb Enclave. She looked downwards in front of the crowd as the Monsignor placed a heavy, purple robe around her as she closed her eyes. The pulpit was raised well above the square, surrounded by statues of significant Immortals. Claret opened her eyes and looked out at the crowd.

"She is not Christ!" Someone screamed from the crowd. "She must be put to death!"

Antoine stood in the crowd and looked up at Claret, as she was led to the edge. Her usually kempt red hair was dry and matted, dirty and untended. But she did not sway her presence. Her eyes scanned the crowds, and her face was locked and lips pursed.

The crowd silenced.

For a few minutes, she stood on the pulpit, as the crowd waited patiently. Antoine took a deep breath. He raised his voice above the clatter of the crowd. "Why have you done this?" His voice echoed across the large, stone walls, as the chatter immediately silenced. "Why are you murdering our kind?"

Claret shot a glance towards him, as Antoine took a cautious step back into the crowd.

"I still have a score to settle with you," she hissed and glared at him. "Don't think I haven't forgotten about your time in *Cairo*!"

Antoine folded his arms, raised his eyebrows, continued looking at her, but said nothing. And he thought of the time in Cairo. The hours after the excavation at Luxor, in the time with Darius and Azra, when he was walking through the dusty marketplace, as Claret trailed his every move. "I think that matters very little now, if at all."

Antoine pushed his way through the crowed, towards the front, and looked up at the pulpit. "All that matters now are your crimes against the immortals."

Claret looked down at him and hissed. "You will never rise to my spot, Antoine!"

The soldiers tightened the chain around her waist and Claret was silenced.

Monsignor Harrison stepped forward and raised his arms as Claret looked over at him. "To my fellow immortals, we have Claret here, Empress of the Immortals. You all know of her. Many of you descend from her. Others have been running from her. Now you are here to judge her."

Large, heavy red drapes were pulled apart behind the pulpit with golden cords, and Claret was ushered behind them, as the drapes fell shut, and the chatter from the crowd swelled.

Before the trial, Delia sat outside the holding chamber, on the floor and up against an earthen wall, and drew her knees up close to her bosom. She listened for any sound that might come from the chamber.

Claret was silent.

Delia closed her eyes and leaned her head back.

She remembered visiting Domrémy-la-Pucelle, very close to her domicile. She saw the same soaring roof, the roof with one side reaching upwards towards the left as she faced the small, wooden door. The roof reached towards a point, and dominated her view.

But there was the night that she sat, sitting cross legged in the sparse grass across the stone path, feeling the cool dirt under her skin, and she waited. She waited for her to come out – the one who they said would take her on a journey through time and space.

And then the door opened.

She was wearing a long, dark robe. Claret smiled, and walked to where Delia had been sitting. Claret sat down next to her. "Do you understand now? Why I took you there? Back to Jerusalem?"

Delia looked down at her knees. She sat in the grass, amongst green blades taller than her legs, she picked at some of the wildflowers. "I don't see why you brought me there, Claret. To prove a point? To make a statement?

Claret remembered the purple robe; the same velvety, heavy drape that was placed on the back of Jesus Christ after he was whipped and questioned. She knew exactly where it lay. Back beyond the trees, at the threshold of Golgotha, there was a small cave.

The chains were heavy on her back, much heavier than the robe had ever been. "Release me!" She hissed, her eyes wide. She lunged forward but her captors did not move.

There was a certain heaviness to the air; dampness penetrated the ground, as water ran across stones. Each time she moved her legs, the water splashed and echoed against the stone walls.

The sun started to set over the horizon on Golgotha.

Claret was in chains inside a dungeon that did not see the sun; she was shackled to the wall in the same fashion that Antoine had been years earlier, but this time, she was powerless and weak.

She needed to drink from the decanter.

She looked upwards towards the door, as the metal bar braced open.

Antoine and Darius walked in, and Delia followed shortly thereafter. She spoke immediately, and stopped just short of where Claret was lying. "You shall be crucified."

Claret looked up at Delia, who did not make eye contact with her.

Delia continued. "You shall be nailed to a cross and left to hang on Golgotha. You may stay there for all of eternity, for you will never lose your immortality. But you will not be given the gift of death."

Claret's mouth dropped open, but she was smiling. She laughed a bit, more to herself. "You think death is a gift?"

Delia paused, closed her eyes for a moment, and smoothed her hair. She opened her eyes and looked back at Claret, who was looking directly back at her and patiently waiting for an answer. Delia took a deep breath, and sighed, and looked downwards as she spoke. "Death would be a gift, for you, Claret. For you."

There were times when Delia had remembered the first time Claret came to visit her; those sunny, cold French mornings, when the breath was cold and stagnant. The air lifted her chest – its viscosity penetrated her lungs, opening them up; a cool vice which helped her breathe so much easier. But in those days, far gone, there was a moment, when standing on the front porch in the sunlight in France, she heard the clanking of chains. The shackles that she wore. That she remembered.

And then there was a moment, in the darkness, that she saw Claret, hanging on the wall in chains, her hair hanging long down her naked torso; the dirt that caked on her shoulders and back stood out in contrast to her pale skin. She opened her eyes, and looked up at Delia. "Do you know why I came to you? All those years ago? Do you know why I *chose* you?"

Delia shook her head and looked down. "I don't understand how you can be so powerless right now."

Claret laughed and threw her head back, and rested it on the stone that jutted from the wall. She laughed for some time; it reverberated against the walls, and Delia watched her as tears started to well in her eyes. Claret then snapped her head in Delia's direction. "You will realize that I am still your Mother. You will *respect* me."

Delia took a step towards Claret, raised her arm, and caressed Claret's chin with her finger, ever so lightly. "Yes. Oh my, dear. My sweet dear Claret. You are my mother. You may be. Yes. But you are still an ancient whore. Your travel through time has given you so much wisdom. But there is a time when one's reign must end."

Claret glared at Delia. "Do you remember what I said to you? Not when I met you in Domrémy-la-Pucelle but in Paris. Do you remember what I told you backstage?"

Delia could not forget.

She could still feel the sweat that had gathered in the small of her back from the heat of the lights. She could still smell that sawdust and taste the lipstick that had been so heavily applied. "Yes, I remember, Claret."

"Mother. I am your mother."

Delia's face fell. Her frown gave way to new lines running from the corner of her mouth to her chin. And she leaned forward, bringing her face right next to Claret's. "You are *not* my mother, Claret. You are simply Claret. My true mother died well before I met you. I watched her casket being buried. And I remember when you visited me in that cemetery. You are *not* my mother."

Claret smiled. The saliva on her teeth caught the light. "Don't you see though? How I am your mother now?" Her chains rattled as she reached her arms outwards. Her arms could not reach Delia, and although she looked down at Claret's bloodied wrists, she took a few steps back.

Delia looked down at Claret. "Where *were* you when I was in Paris?" The door swung open as rattling chains resounded against the stone walls. Claret's eyes widened. "Where was I? I was with you. Stupid ungrateful bitch! Such a fucking cunt."

Delia approached Claret, and knelt down in front of her. "You were not with me, Claret. You were never a mother to me. You tried to take me under your wing. But all you were trying to do was gain power over me." Claret opened her eyes, squinting against the light. "It's time, Claret," Delia said, reaching for her wrist. She held her arm up to the light. The gashes were bleeding again. She unlocked the cuffs and Claret fell back against the wall, wincing. Delia turned her attention to the soldiers and nodded.

The two men grabbed Claret from the floor and pulled her to her feet. She shivered, naked and dirty; her hair was caked to the sides of her face with blood and sweat. "Don't...I have done nothing to deserve this!"

Claret's tiny wrist was swallowed by the men's muscular hands, and they dragged her to the door. "Put these on!" She was handed a pair of shackle chains.

"Take her," Delia said.

Monsignor Harrison stood behind the pulpit, and looked down at the crowd in the Catacomb Enclave. The large, red drapes behind him were pulled together and shut tight. The immortals gathered for the trial were in the hundreds; all waiting. There was a murmur rolling through the enclave, as

Ramiel entered from behind the curtains. He approached the Monsignor, who nodded as Ramiel spoke into his ear.

Antoine stood in the crowd and watched Ramiel. There was a time when he thought the younger immortal was somewhat of a competitor, but now, as Antoine watched Ramiel unconsciously brush his long, brown hair off to the side and hook it around his ear as he was speaking with the Monsignor, he realized that Ramiel was a peer.

A definite peer.

Ramiel exited through the curtains and pulled them shut once again. The Monsignor looked out towards the crowd. He raised his arms and the talking silenced. Antoine focused his attention on the Monsignor.

"We still have Claret with us here. She is behind the curtains now. I will bring her to you and stand her before you. And it will be up to all of you what we shall do with her."

The crowd raised their fists into the air. "Crucify her! Let her die nailed to a cross!"

The Monsignor took a step to the side as the drapes were pulled open with giant golden cords. Claret stood in a purple robe and a crown of thorns. Blood streamed down the sides of her head and across her cheeks.

"Do you want her to die? For sins against the immortal race?"

The crowed swelled in chorus, raising their arms. "Crucify her! Crucify her!"

Monsignor Harrison leaned against the edge of the pulpit. He looked out at the crowd, as the cheers slowly died down, and after a few moments, there was silence. He looked at the crowd, scanning his head back and forth, and nodded slowly. "So you want this woman to die? This mother of our kind? You are cursing her to a similar fate of the Christian Jesus Christ. Do you think she is deserving of that kind of horrid punishment?"

An unseen male voice called out from the crowd against the silence. "She is murdering our kind! Crucify her!"

Antoine paused for a moment.

He had studied Christ in recent years, as part of his involvement with theology, and in particular with Sheldon, after speaking with him at length when Sheldon was interviewing him for his book.

Sheldon had said other things then, and spoke about Christ on that same stormy night, now years ago, when Antoine was still questioning what direction his life might take. The silence in the room after Sheldon offered his background research was stifling. Until Antoine spoke.

"Do you think that the Christ Blood is truly saving? I mean, what do you truly believe?"

Sheldon set his notebook down and looked at Antoine. "It's what *you* believe, Antoine. What is it that you believe? You come from an area which has a completely different belief. Is this what you believe? That the Christ Blood is the salvation?"

Antoine shook his head. "I don't know. But when we were in Luxor, when we found the cup, it sent Claret into such a frenzy. I just couldn't understand it."

"Understood," Sheldon said. "That's understandable. You found the Cup there. The true Cup. That's power, my friend. Power beyond this realm. And to that, I must say I have run dry. May I have another whiskey?"

Antoine got up and went to the bar on the other side of the parlor. He plucked a few ice cubes from the waiting bucket, and plopped them into the glass slowly. They each clinked as he spoke. "So what are your thoughts, Sheldon? From your studies, I mean. Certainly your background in Theology has helped you a great deal in these matters."

Sheldon sat back and sighed, as Antoine handed him his glass of Whiskey. "You would be surprised," he said, as he took a sip. He placed the glass on the side table and looked back up at Antoine. "There are many who believe that the Blood of Christ is salvation. Others believe that drinking from the cup itself is a cleansing process. Redemption. In the Catholic Mass, it is believed that the symbolic wine transforms into the Blood of Christ."

"But what do *you* believe, Sheldon? I understand all of the textbook jargon you are giving me, but what does Sheldon Wilkes believe?"

Sheldon sat back for a moment, cocked his head to the side. "I believe that there is definitely something out there, Antoine. I believe there is life after death. And yes, I believe the cup brings salvation, and Claret keeps it as spiritual currency. She holds so much power just by having it in her possession."

Ramiel peeked his head through the curtains, and was handed a rolled golden parchment paper, tied with a red ribbon. He handed it to the Monsignor as the crowd looked on. Claret stood on the other side of the pulpit, her head hung low.

Monsignor Harrison adjusted his glasses and unrolled the parchment. He studied it for a minute, handed it back to Ramiel, nodded and removed his glasses. He sighed, looked at the crowed, and then looked over at Claret. She was hunched over, bloodied and battered, held up by several soldiers.

"Claret, look at me."

The soldiers dragged her over close to the Monsignor.

"Claret," he said. "You have deceived our kind. We still do not fully understand your motive for this, other than your eternal hunger for power amongst your own kind. You have behaved as an imposter – claiming that your decanter was an avenue of salvation for our kind, while it brought death. As you stand before me, and as you stand before your descendants, I ask you one last time: why did you do it?"

Claret opened her eyes and looked at the crowd as the Monsignor looked on. The crowd was silent.

Claret opened her mouth, preparing to speak, and then closed it. Finally, she spoke, looking out at the crowd.

"I am your Empress. You all descend from me! Without me, you would not even exist! My 'Hooded Man' is a faithful servant. And I gave him direct orders – to cleanse our kind. There were those who were chosen to drink from the decanter to cleanse our society of immortals that were not living up to the standards that I decreed thousands of years ago!"

The crowd murmured as Claret looked over at the Monsignor. "And he will continue, Monsignor. The 'Hooded man' will not stop. You will never stop him. Because he is death. And I have selected those in our population to…revert back to their original human state. The decanter serves as a catalyst for that."

The Monsignor glared at Claret. "You chose them for extermination."

Claret smiled and shook her head. "I am keeping our ranks where they should be. Dispose of the problems. That's what a leader does."

The Monsignor was handed an additional rolled parchment paper decree. He unrolled it and held it at arm's length, and cleared his throat. "Claret Atarah," he said, looking over at her, then at the crowd, which had hushed to silence, and back at Claret. He then continued. "For crimes against immortals, and for extermination other immortal members, we find you guilty as charged. You will hang from a cross on

Golgatha until you burn and dry from hunger. You will then be exterminated and will cease to exist."

Conversations in the crowd swelled as Claret struggled to break free from the soldiers' grip. "You will not exterminate me! I am your ruler! You bow down to me! I cannot be killed!" She stopped struggling and threw her head back in laughter. "I cannot be killed," she said, as Monsignor Harrison signaled to the soldiers. They dragged her through the curtains as the crowd cheered.

Antoine stood next to Delia in the crowd at the base of Golgatha. Delia leaned against Antoine's shoulder, as Claret was led to the wooden cross, as the soldiers placed her arms at either side, and her feet were tied at the base. She fought with the soldiers as Monsignor Harrison held up a long nail.

"You all will perish!" She hissed as nails were driven into her feet and arms. She squirmed as the nails tore into her skin, spurting blood into the air, and onto her arms and legs. She looked up at the Monsignor.

"These nails signify the pain you have brought your immortal community. For those sins, you will be stripped of your immortality. Your body will age and rejoin your soul in this time, leading to a final and eternal death. Damnation forever."

The cross was raised in front of the crowd. Antoine's mouth fell open.

The Monsignor looked over at Antoine and Delia. "She will hang here until her body catches up to her soul. And then we will remove her and burn her."

Antoine nodded and shook his head. "What a horrible way to die."

Delia squeezed his arm. "Christ died this way, Antoine. Yes, it's horrendous. And Christ did nothing to deserve it. Claret tried to exterminate her own kind."

"So why didn't the Monsignor choose to dispose of Claret another way? Why crucifixion?"

Delia looked up at Claret hanging on the cross as the crowd started to disperse. "It sends a message to all of the immortals. That the crime of exterminating one's own kind garners serious punishment."

"We're never getting into Heaven, Delia. We are damned. It's about time you opened your eyes."

Delia shook her head. "No. The cross has always been a symbol of hope. There is hope for our kind as well."

Antoine shook his head. "What about us? Immortals. We are the damned. There certainly is no Heaven for us."

"I have had a lot of discussions with Father Bauman, Antoine. And I have come to the conclusion that the damned are never truly damned. We just *believe* that we are."

Antoine stood at the base of the hill and watched Claret after the crowd had dispersed. Delia and Ramiel sat on some nearby stones. He looked up as Claret squirmed on the cross, and when he looked at her closely, he saw that she was not the same Claret. The blood that dripped from the wounds on her ankles and wrists had begun to dry up. The sun started to set as Claret hung her head down.

Antoine turned around and Delia raised her head. Antoine looked Delia in the eyes. "Do you think she's gone?" Delia craned her neck around Antoine to see Claret hanging on the cross, and shook her head. "It would not be this subtle."

Antoine watched out towards the horizon as the sky turned purple, and the last moments of sun were slipping from the horizon. He paused for a moment as he saw movement.

He pointed out towards the desert. "Delia! Ramiel! Look!"

The both got up and joined Antoine at the base of the cross, looking out towards the edge of the sky.

There was movement.

Like a billowing cloud, forming and expanding on the terrain.

Come with me.

They all froze.

Ramiel stepped forward and placed his hand on Antoine's shoulder. "Is that who I think it is?"

Antoine nodded. "I think so."

The white cloud expanded and moved closer towards Golgatha.

Drink from me…

Antoine froze and pushed Ramiel and Delia aside. "It's him!"

Delia shook her head. "No. Don't. Stop Antoine. Stay here!"

Antoine stood behind Delia and Ramiel as the Hooded Man, in his flowing red cloak, with his faceless darkness, levitated towards Golgatha. They looked up at him, his enormous presence, as Claret hung on her cross in the foreground.

Delia looked up at the Hooded Man as the winds increased in intensity. Claret awoke and squirmed on the cross.

Delia took several steps towards the Hooded Man and looked up at him. "Remove your hood! Show us who you are!"

Claret craned her neck to the right. "Don't you do that! You keep your identity as I instructed you!"

Drink and you will live forever.

"No!" Delia said. She raised her arms up, towards a sky that was getting increasingly angry, as the clouds swirled above them. "*Remove your hood!* You can be saved!"

And the Hooded Man brought his arms up towards the side of the hood.

I do not carry the decanter. I no longer carry the symbol of death.

Ramiel shouted over the increasing winds. "Then what do you carry?"

Thunder rumbled as Claret stopped struggling.

The 'Hooded Man' paused for a few moments, and removed his hood. The darkness permeated the air, just for a moment, a flash of black which flew away in an instant. Antoine, Delia and Ramiel looked up, as the darkness dissipated, and the sky calmed.

Antoine's eyes widened. "You're a man!" A person. A human, with balding hair, glasses and a warm smile. "You have been doing this all this time?"

He looked down, as he levitated down towards the group of immortals. "My name is George Stanley."

Antoine, Ramiel and Delia all looked at George, dumbfounded.

George looked down at the group of Immortals gathered at the base of the cross. "I had my problems when I was living…"

Claret hissed and writhed on the cross just as George joined the others.

"Let me handle this," George said, approaching the base of the cross. He reached under his robe and pulled out a small, plain cup. He held it up so Claret could see it. She looked down.

"Is this what you are looking for?"

Ramiel nudged Antoine. "Is that what I think it is?"

She screeched and foamed at the mouth. "Give it to me! I need it now! Listen to my commands!"

George shook his head and looked down. He held the cup and walked over towards Delia, placing it in her hands.

"I give this to you," he said.

Antoine shook his head as Ramiel looked on, grinning.

"I don't understand," Antoine said.

George turned around and looked at Antoine directly. "I drank from this cup, Antoine, and the spell was broken. The decanter is an imposter. It brings death. This cup brings life. It's no wonder Claret wants it so much."

"How did you get it?" Delia asked.

"Claret had been coming to me when my wife was dying from cancer. She appeared to me, she came to me in voices.

And I will be the first to say it. I was a troubled human. I was not a model or an individual with morals."

"That's probably why she chose you," Antoine said.

George nodded. "Yes. Most likely. I had my weaknesses. I opened myself up. And then she started speaking to me. This voice. That told me to acquire four young men. And I kept them in cages in my basement."

"They became the Four Hoodsmen," Delia said. "I remember that."

"Yes," George said. "I killed myself shortly after questioning. If you remember the morning of the 'Four Funerals', that was when I was apprehended."

"And then what happened to you?" Ramiel asked.

"After I hung myself, I was in my cell, and my vision gradually faded to black. The next thing I remember, I came to on a beach of stones, underneath an angry, red sky, and I was thirsty. So very, very thirsty. I think I may have gone to Hell."

"You didn't go to Hell," Delia said. "You were in purgatory. I know a lot of these matters."

George nodded and Antoine and Ramiel looked on. He handed the cup to Delia. "You take this. I no longer need it. You are aware of its power. So am I. I know you will use the power correctly. It has removed this curse. I am no longer cursed to carry a decanter of death."

Delia handed the cup to Ramiel. "Go bring this to the Monsignor. Have him drink from it."

AGNUS DEI

Oh my angel.

You have carried me through the rivers of blood and the forests of hatred. You have protected me. My sunken eyes. I close them so I cannot see the turmoil. I plug my ears with my fingers so I cannot hear the screaming.

But you protect me, without fail.

My war angel.

When the evil beast dies, the ground will open up and angels will emerge from the burning timbers and ashes; she will protect; he will serve and never deny. For the angel is without sex, without reservation and will always place the safety in the arms of the protector.

For the hills of Golgatha are always underneath the shadow of the clouds, and where she hung, nailed to a cross, her arms spread wide, reaching outwards over the world, her face seeking Heaven; bright red blood dripped down her arms, spreading a virulent red patchwork.

"You drain me of my life force but you will not end me!"

But in a fleeting moment, she was gone. Claret's body had shriveled and decomposed and slithered right off the cross in a putrid mess.

But there was one still there, standing off to the side; one who watched the crucifixion, who watched the 'Hooded Man'

remove his hood and redeem himself, and watched Claret die and slither off the cross.

She had stood with the others, but went unnoticed. She listened to and observed all of the conversations, but did not say a word.

And when everyone cleared away, she mounted her steed against a backdrop of fire and the sound of hooves approaching her as she ignited the ground around the cross. She raised her sword and pulled on the mane. "Raise your swords and follow me!" Her horse galloped forward, through the smoke, and orange lights, through the unknown and throughout the unknown.

And then, when she vanished into the smoke and clouds, there was a feeling of loss. Several of the soldiers who had hung back, paused for a moment, watching the flames. "She sacrificed herself for us."

Things seemed to quiet for the moment.

There was no longer the sound of explosions. The fire that was burning was starting to die down. The embers were still hot; they were still bright red, a brilliant orange, but there were no flames.

"And what of her? Where did she go? To save Claret?"

One of the ancient immortals, an old man with a stark white beard down to his knees, looked onward. The old man shook his head. "No, no. To where she went, Claret will never be. Claret will forever be gone and never will return. Forever damned for her sinful curses."

"So where is she then?"

The old man sat back and stared ahead at the horizon. The smoke was starting to clear, revealing the meadow ahead, the flames gone. "My son, you will understand soon. In time. But for now, what you see is a meadow. Once with a cloud of smoke and flames, and those flames were burning for so much time. And causing so much torment. But the meadow will bloom once again. For that, I am certain."

"So she is gone forever?"

He smiled, as he looked towards the clearing horizon. The daylight was just starting to finger its way through the parting smoke and dust, as when the smoke rose towards the sky, the first beams of sunlight fingered their way to the dirt below.

"No, my son. She is just starting her mission."

For Mehki

2004-2015

The Story Continues in War Angel

The War Angel

A NOVEL BY A.L. MENGEL

"I am the last of my kind."

"My ancestors have all died and gone from this world, and now, alone, I stand in the center of the hilltop and look upwards towards the sky. It is still dark, angry, burning with crimson red. The painted wisps, the black clouds race across the heavens above me. But as I look down, over towards the barren earth, I see the result of her crucifixion."

And then there was silence.

Then the sound of stones rolling down a hill as the sun beat down above with ferocious intent. "Take her," he said. His hair, I remember, was stone white. But that's all I remember about him, I was so weak with dehydration. "Take her to the bowels. To the dungeon. Chain her up. And give her water. She is near death. We must keep her for the trial. No food. Only water. Go now!"

I laid against rough stone, my eyes watching the door. It remained closed.

~~*

She sat back and closed her eyes.

There was a fire in a pit in the center of the holding cell that reflected a warm, orange glow on her cheeks. Such a contrast to the stark contrast of chilling "Many years ago, there was a man who wore a hood, and he rose from the bowels of the earth. A personification of evil. He wiped out my race. Everyone who I had ever known. And relied upon. Everyone…gone."

"How did he do it?"

She shifted and reached for her wine. "He carried a decanter. And he cast a spell."

The fire crackled against the silence of the room. She opened her eyes, and saw him writing in a brown, leather bound notebook. "So have you heard me?"

He looked up without a word and nodded.

She waited a few moments, then continued. "I'm the last. I can be assured of that. We were wiped out. Clean. And then, I was forced to embrace a life of solitude."

"So were you…" He set the book down and looked over at her. "Do you realize that this city – this metro area – this huge area, has no need for you?"

She looked down at her drink. She nodded back and forth. "I have considered that, yes."

~~*

Emaleth cried for three days and three nights.

The sun set on the fourth day, and there was an insurmountable feeling of dread that overcame her; she parted the curtains and looked out the window. The same threes rose from the yard, the same garden reached out towards the mountains on the eastern side of the house.

But she had been gone for too long now.

Emaleth paced across the floor, as the cold stone made the soles of her feet dusty. "Where are you? What are you in my life?" She looked up the ceiling. "Are you my tutor?"

There was a scuffle outside the door, and it interrupted her trance. The clapping of hooves across the dirt outside, running from her right, to the center and left and then off into the distance.

Something different occurred outside of the Ponce de Leon. Anthony and Doug walked silently into the lobby and stopped at the door. Anthony looked over at Douglas, with worry awash in the lines across his face. "I don't think it happened," he said. "I think we are okay for now. But I can assure you – we will need to investigate outside."

~~*

The chair creaked as she craned her head back towards the screen door behind her. She turned around in her chair, staying seated. "Need me in there, Henry?" she called in her deep southern drawl.

But there was no answer. She returned to her washing, took a few more strokes, and stopped again.

She turned again in the creaky old wooden chair. "Henry?!" she called, louder and more insistent this time.

No answer again.

Laying the wet clothes down on a towel, she dropped the washboard in the basin and wiped her hands on her apron. It was time to go inside and see what Henry was up to.

The screen door creaked as she opened it slowly, giving way to a silent house. Even as she bent her head inside the door and strained to listen, she did not hear anything but the ticking clock nearby in the kitchen.

She peered inside and waited for the blackness to clear and her eyes to adjust to the darkness of the foyer.

"Henry, I'm gonna come up and see what she is doin'."

She called up through the winding stairs, which rounded the foyer and the spokes in the railing, like fingers of dark wood posed as bars in front of expansive oil paintings of the owners of the mansion that reached upwards towards the darker cranberry colored walls of the second floor.

A door handle from the second floor clicked open, a door creaked open for a moment, and then silence.

"Henry?" she called again. "Do you hear me?"

The squeaky door slammed. Heavy footsteps followed, moving towards the edge of the dark wooden railing, as

Mary looked up at the clear crystal chandelier as it shook from the rumbling of the footsteps.

Henry dashed down the stairs, his bight white eyes contrasting his very dark skin, his eyes open as wide as saucers, his light brown button shirt covered in bright red blood.

"I'm leavin'!" he yelled, taking steps two at a time and jumping down to the foyer, shaking the chandelier as he did so. Mary grabbed his arm and stopped him just as he placed his hand on the knob of the front door. He turned his head to face her. He paused for a moment, breathing heavy, his mouth partly open and salivating, eyes still wide and the look of fear on his face.

"What is goin' on up there?" she asked, determined for an answer.

Henry grabbed her hand, ripping it off his arm. "I am not staying in this house!" And he stormed through the door, and ran out to the backyard into the coming sunlight. Mary stood and watched him run past the dead garden, farther off to the edge of the garden towards a path that led towards the mountains.

Mary shook her head, let out a deep breath, closed the door, and turned her attention to the upstairs. She wondered why Henry might act like this, but she was concerned about Emile.

"Emile?" she called once she got to the foot of the stairs. "You alright up there?"

There was no answer.

She ascended the stairs, each one creaking under the weight of her foot as she did so; her determined methodical course of taking each step, one by one, ate at her sanity. What was Henry so upset about? The calm, quiet, normally reserved man had just stormed past her down the stairs, running for the door in a desperate attempt to leave the house and the woman upstairs who he loved and served so loyally, the woman who he was so close with that he agreed to deliver her child.

Mary reached the top of the stairs and looked down the hallway, past the numerous photographs and paintings to the last white door at the end of the cranberry colored walls, shut tight with no sound coming from it.

"Emile?" she called one more time, craning her head to see past the edge of the wall.

Still no answer.

The floorboards creaked as she moved towards the door in the silence of the early morning; the new and infant light permeated the hall from a nearby window, but that light did not deter Mary's rising fear any more than the silence added to it. So many days before, she had walked the distance from the top of the stairs to the door of the master bedroom so many times in so little time. The distance on other days seemed so insignificant. Today, it seemed almost insurmountable.

But she made it.

After a series of methodical creaking steps and racing heartbeats, she stood in front of the door, and she held her breath for a moment, moving the side of her head close to the door, listing in an effort to hear anything that might give a clue.

Silence.

"Emile, I'm comin' in," she said quietly and carefully, as she turned the squeaky doorknob, the concern showing on her face. "I hope you're ok cause I'm comin' in right now."

~~*

The sun rose silently on the eastern side of New Orleans. And in the city, on the blocks of lowered steel shudders, and the street sweepers cleaning the streets of the French Quarter, as the yellow warmth of the early morning sun approached, there was a certain tranquility over the city. It could have been the usual post weekend party stupor, or it could have been the time of day when those consumed in deep thought were active. But to Natale, there was a certain liking to that time of day. And then, when he grew tired of the New Orleans mornings, he chose to move to Miami.

But before that, he traveled by steamship, across the Atlantic, to Cherbourg, and then, by train, to Lyon.

There was one in Lyon – a Darius Sauvage – who had been living there, who was the perfect specimen. The select choice. And there, in Lyon, he would stay, until the deed was done, and until prophecy was fulfilled.

I thought that I would be watched over. Someone would come with me. Walk the path, protect me, lead me through the torment. But that isn't what happened. I foraged the path alone. I was not afraid. For I knew that you were with me. You were always near. My War Angel.

"There was a certain day. A morning filled with brilliant sunshine. I remember it so well. When I first saw you."

The light shined toward the bedroom. Delia shielded her eyes. "Are you here for me? To take me away? Drag me to Hell?"

There was a silhouette of a man against the brilliant white light. "No," he said. He moved closer to the bed, but did not come into focus. "Do you know what is your destiny? Do you realize what you have been chosen for?"

Delia paused for a moment, and looked down at the covers. She focused on her hands, noticed the bulging veins, the dark age spots, and the spiny fingers. "I cannot do this task you ask of me," she said. "I may be immortal but look at my age. I cannot do what you think I am destined to do."

The man moved closer to the bed, and sat down, still a dark silhouette against the shining sun. "You have been selected," he said. "Do you not think that you can overcome the physical limitations?"

Delia thought of Paris. Of the days past, in the Vaudeville days. She saw the same hot, bright lights shining in her face, she could still see her feet dancing across the same dusty, wooden stage. "It was many years ago that I was so energetic."

The man stood and turned towards her. She looked up at him. He was surrounded by the brilliance of the sunrise. "Don't you see what you are meant for? Don't you understand your calling? You spent years – centuries – protecting evil. Now it is time for you to forage for the better good."

COMING SOON FROM PARCHMAN'S PRESS

Mengel, A.L.